Praise for *Breakfast with Buddha*

"A laugh-out-loud novel that's both comical and wise . . . Merullo is a practiced hand at publishing witty, pointed prose . . . It is Merullo's comic bent and his mastery of the language that causes his road trip novel to sideswipe clichés by balancing irreverence with insight."   —*The Louisville Courier-Journal*

"Merullo writes with grace and intelligence and knows that even in a novel of ideas it's not the religion that matters, it's the relationship; it's not the concepts, but the people, and here are two intriguing men, one with his eye on the destination and his foot on the pedal, the other who knows that we travel farthest when we are still. You'll enjoy sitting in the back seat of the car as Otto drives on deep into the luminous heart of his childhood."
—*The Boston Globe*

"A wonderful, heartfelt novel that frequently surprises as we're lulled by the sights and sounds of the open road."
—*The Providence Sunday Journal*

"Insightful, amusing, loving . . . There are lovely moments of enlightenment that are not accompanied by angels with flaming swords; rather, there is that peaceful blue sphere that is available to all of us."   —*The Seattle Times*

"[A] pleasant, engaging novel . . . Roland Merullo would be a great guy to take a road trip with."   —*The Washington Post*

"Merullo is a pleasing writer . . . His gift is slipping gentle spiritual lessons into easy-reading narratives . . . with such effortless charm."   —*The Christian Science Monitor*

"We can now add Roland Merullo's voice to the large chorus of the road in *Breakfast with Buddha*. It's a worthy trip . . . Merullo is a graceful writer whose style and perception of place have been honed by his previous novels."   —*The Ft. Lauderdale Sun*

"Undeniably appealing . . . Seductive." —*The Hartford Courant*

"Enlightenment meets *On the Road* in this witty, insightful novel." —*The Boston Sunday Globe*

"Full of fun . . . A joyous book with a very happy ending." —*The Greenfield (MA) Recorder*

"Visionary . . . Captures the spiritual struggle for true belief and inner peace with wit, clarity, and subtle reality." —*Library Journal,* starred review

"A sincere and thoughtful book that will not only entertain you but will stay in your mind for a long time." —*The Hilton Head (SC) Island Packet*

"In this merry but poignant novel, Merullo uses just the right recipe of humor and insight to characterize the spiritual curmudgeon and the spiritual savant." —*Shambhala Sun*

"Merullo's skill with the pen enchants the reader with a fresh awareness of how man confronts his spiritual side in a chaotic world. The monk's character is rich with humor, silence, and understanding. It matters not that his audience shares a religious conviction with this man but that change can occur in a skeptical soul." —Bookreporter.com

"A comic but winningly spiritual road-trip novel . . . Breezy and affecting." —*Publishers Weekly*

"The skillful Merullo, using the lightest of touches, slowly turns this low-key comedy into a moving story of spiritual awakening." —*Booklist*

"[Merullo] provides a realistic framework that plays to his strengths as an astute observer of society and sympathetic analyst of individual psyches . . . Merullo has grown so persuasive over the course of two luminous little novels that readers might well follow him even if he turned next to, say, Mornings with Mohammed." —*Kirkus Reviews*

Praise for Roland Merullo's Previous Novel,
Golfing with God

"Amid the laughs and playful banter, *Golfing with God* is a serious story of self-examination and growth, the hardest games of all."
—*The Washington Post Book World*

"Merullo weaves humor and humane theology into his engaging plot."
—*The Boston Globe*

"Merullo writes such a graceful, compassionate and fluid prose that you cannot resist the characters' very real struggles and concerns. His prose is as wonderfully down-to-earth as his tale is heaven-sent."
—*The Providence Sunday Journal*

"[A] delightful little book."
—*The Cleveland Plain Dealer*

"*Golfing with God* salts its serious story of growth and self-examination with humor and telling insight . . . Amid the lightness of this tale is the deeper story of a man, much like the rest of us, looking to shed his pride and dampen his urges."
—*The Orlando Sentinel*

"A tender story and a clean slice of life, full of smart, clean prose."
—*Milwaukee Journal Sentinel*

"Merullo's patient good humor makes the journey with Hank a surprisingly universal undertaking."
—*The Sunday Seattle Post & Seattle Post-Intelligencer*

"Will appeal to fans of Alice Sebold and Mitch Albom . . . Highly recommended."
—*Library Journal,* starred review

"An uplifting and humorous look at life and faith, a philosophical view of our role in this world and the next."
—*The Southern Pines (NC) Pilot*

Breakfast with Buddha

Also by Roland Merullo

FICTION

Leaving Losapas
A Russian Requiem
Revere Beach Boulevard
In Revere, in Those Days
A Little Love Story
Golfing with God
American Savior

NONFICTION

Passion for Golf:
In Pursuit of the Innermost Game

Revere Beach Elegy:
A Memoir of Home and Beyond

Breakfast
with
Buddha

A NOVEL

by

Roland Merullo

ALGONQUIN BOOKS OF CHAPEL HILL

2008

Published by
Algonquin Books of Chapel Hill
Post Office Box 2225
Chapel Hill, North Carolina 27515-2225

a division of
Workman Publishing
225 Varick Street
New York, New York 10014

First paperback edition, Algonquin Books of Chapel Hill, August 2008.
Originally published by Algonquin Books of Chapel Hill in 2007.
Printed in the United States of America.
Published simultaneously in Canada by Thomas Allen & Son Limited.
Design by Anne Winslow.

This is a work of fiction. While, as in all fiction, the literary perceptions and insights are based on experience, all names, characters, places, and incidents either are products of the author's imagination or are used fictitiously.

Library of Congress Cataloging-in-Publication Data
Merullo, Roland.
        Breakfast with Buddha : a novel / by Roland Merullo.—1st ed.
        p. cm.
        ISBN-13: 978-1-56512-552-0 (HC)
        1. Self-actualization (Psychology)—Fiction.   2. Inheritance and
succession—Fiction.   3. Buddhists—Fiction.   4. North Dakota—
Fiction.   I. Title.
PS3563.E748D75 2007
813'.54—dc22   2007007978

ISBN-13: 978-1-56512-616-9 (PB)

18 17

For

Arlo Kahn

and

For

Michael Miller

Humor is a prelude to faith and
Laughter is the beginning of prayer.

— REINHOLD NIEBUHR

Like the lark that soars in the air, first singing, then
silent, content with the last sweetness that satiates it,
such seemed to me that image, the imprint of the
Eternal Pleasure.

— DANTE, "Paradiso"

Genuine belief seems to have left us.

— WALT WHITMAN, "Democratic Vistas"

I hear America singing, the varied carols I hear.

— WALT WHITMAN, "I Hear America Singing"

Acknowledgments

I would like to thank my excellent travel companions, Amanda, Alexandra, and Juliana; and everyone at Algonquin for their work on this book, especially Chuck Adams, Ina Stern, Courtney Denney, Brunson Hoole, Janet Patterson, Kelly Clark, Craig Popelars, Michael Taeckens, and Aimee Rodriguez, who all went the extra mile. I am also grateful to several North Dakotans, especially Kay Solberg Link for her hospitality and Gaylon Baker for his wide-ranging knowledge of the state.

ONE

My name is Otto Ringling (no circus jokes, please) and I have a strange story to tell. At first look it may appear to be the story of a road trip I made, at the suggestion of my wonderful wife, from our home in the suburbs of New York City to the territory of my youth—Stark County, North Dakota. In fact, it is the account of an interior voyage, the kind of excursion that's hard to talk about without sounding foolish or annoyingly serene, or like someone who thinks the Great Spirit has singled him out to be the mouthpiece of ultimate truth. If you knew me you'd know that I am none of the above. I think of myself as Mr. Ordinary—good husband, good father, average looking, average height, middle-of-the-road politics, upper part of the American middle class. Friends think I'm funny, sometimes a little on the wiseass side, a decent, thoughtful, forty-something man who has never been particularly religious in the usual sense of that word. My story here will strike them as out of character, but there's nothing I can do about that. I promised myself I would just tell the truth about my road trip, and let those who hear the story embrace it or mock it according to their own convictions.

So, in the spirit of full disclosure let me say this: Before the drive to North Dakota, like a lot of people I know, I suffered now and again from a nagging puzzlement about the deeper meaning of things. I functioned well, as the saying goes. My wife and children and I had a comfortable life, really a superbly satisfying life: nice house, two cars, restaurant meals, love, peace, mutual support. And yet, from time to time a gust of uneasiness would blow through the back rooms of my mind, as if a window had been left open there and a storm had come through and my neatly stacked pages of notes on being human had blown off the desk.

By the time I returned to New York, that wind had gone quiet. Outwardly, nothing had changed. I did not start practicing levitation. I did not shave my head and undertake radical dietary adventures. I did not quit my job and move the family to a restored monastery in the Sicilian countryside or leave Jeannie and the kids and shack up with a twenty-two-year-old editorial assistant from the office. Inwardly, however, in those back rooms, in the deeper recesses of thought and mood, something felt entirely different. And so, even though I am a private man, I made the decision—again, at Jeannie's suggestion—to write down what had happened during my days on the American road. If nothing else, I thought, the story might drop a few laughs into someone's life, which is not a bad thing these days.

So let me begin here: I am an ordinary, sane, American man. Forty-four years young. Senior editor at a respected Manhattan publishing house—Stanley and Byrnes—that specializes in books on food. I've been married to the same woman for almost half my life. We have two teenage children—Natasha is sixteen and a half, Anthony four-teen—an affectionate mixed-breed dog named Jasper, and a house in one of the pricier New York suburbs. Jeannie works, very part-time as a freelance museum photographer and very full-time as an attentive mother. It's not a perfect life, needless to say. We've had our share of worry and dis-appointment, illness and hurt, and, with two teenagers in the house, we sometimes experience a degree of domestic turbulence that sounds, to my ear, like a boiling teakettle filled with hormones shrieking on a stove. But it is a life Jeannie and I made from scratch, without a lot of money at first, or a lot of help, and we are proud of it, and grateful.

Six months before my trip, a sour new ingredient was dropped into the stew of that good life, into the swirl of dinner parties, arguments over homework, and two-week rentals at the shore in August. My parents, Ronald and Matilda, seventy-two and seventy, were killed in a car crash on a two-lane North Dakota highway called State Route 22. In full possession of their mental faculties, in excellent health, they were familiar voices on the end of the phone line one day and unavailable the next. Gone. Silent. Un-touchable. Hardy farm people with forceful and distinct personalities who were turned to ash and memories by a drunk just my age in a careening blue pickup.

We all went out to North Dakota for the memorial ser-vice. (My sister, Cecelia, who lives in New Jersey, took the train; she inherited my mother's fear of air travel.) Tears were shed. There was talk of the old times, good and not so good. There was anger at the man—soon to be impris-oned—who had killed them. I expected all that. What I did not expect was the enormous feeling of emptiness that surrounded me in the weeks following my parents' burial.

It was more than bereavement. It was a kind of sawing dissatisfaction that cut back and forth against the fibers of who I believed myself to be. Sometimes even in the sunniest moods I'd be aware of it. Turn your eyes away from the good life for just a second and there it was: not depression as much as an ugly little doubt about everything you had ever done; not confusion, exactly, but a kind of lingering question.

What's the point of all this? would be putting the question too crudely, but it was something along those lines. All this striving and aggravation, all these joys and miseries, all this busyness, all this stuff—a thousand headlines, a hundred thousand conversations, e-mails, meetings, tax returns, warranties, bills, privacy notices, ads for Viagra, calls for donations, election cycles, war in the news every day, trips to the dump with empty wine bottles, fillings and physicals, braces and recitals, Jeannie's moods, my moods, the kids' moods, soccer tournaments, plumbers' bills, sitcom characters, oil changes, wakes, weddings, watering the flowerbeds—all of this, I started to ask myself, leads exactly where? To a smashed-up Buick on a country highway? And then what? Paradise?

All right, I'm a fan of the old idea that if you live a decent life you rise up to heaven afterward. I'm not opposed. But sometimes, riding the commuter train home past the tenements of Harlem, or calling Natasha and Anthony away from their IMing long enough for the frenzied modern ritual of a family meal, or just standing around at a friend's fiftieth birthday party with a glass of Pinot Noir in one hand, I'd feel this sudden ache cutting along my skin, as if I were suffering from a kind of existential flu. Just a moment, just a flash, but it would pierce the shiny shell of my life like a sword through a seam of armor.

I'd had similar moments even before my parents' deaths. But after that day—February 7, a frigid North Dakota Tuesday—it was as if a curtain had been lifted and the ordinary chores and pleasures of life were now set against a backdrop of wondering. The purpose, the plan, the deeper meaning—who could I trust to tell me? A therapist? The local minister? A tennis partner who'd lived ten years longer and seen more of the world? I found myself thinking about it at night before I went to sleep, and while standing on the train platform on my way to work, or watching TV, or talking with my kids, and even, sometimes, just after Jeannie and I had finished making love.

And so, I suppose, such a state of mind left me perfectly primed for my extraordinary adventure. If I can risk a sweeping observation, it seems to me that life often works that way: You ask a certain question again and again, in a sincere fashion, and the answer appears. But, in my experience, at least, that answer arrives according to its own mysterious celestial timing, and often in disguise. And it comes in a way you're not prepared for, or don't want, or can't, at first, accept.

TWO

When they retired from farming, my parents remained in the house where my sister and I had been raised, and they leased the two thousand fertile acres surrounding it, land that was planted in sunflowers, soybeans, and durum wheat. After their deaths, the duty of selling off the old farmstead fell upon my shoulders, as I am the older and—I have to say this—only responsible child. It was not a job I wanted, God knows. There was more than enough on my plate without that helping of high-plains beef. But there are duties you don't turn your back on: your child is hungry, you make dinner; your spouse is ill, you take care of her; your parents die, you settle the estate.

Two things made this duty more complicated than it might otherwise have been. The first was my younger sister, Cecelia, a nice enough woman who is as flaky as a good spanakopita crust, and who, as I mentioned, does not tolerate air travel well. And the second was the fact that, though I had zero interest in keeping the house and land, I did, for sentimental reasons, want to salvage a few pieces of my parents' sturdy antique furniture. So, how best to sell the house and move the furniture—given my sister's unpredictability and the long distances involved—became, in my mind, the North Dakota Question.

Over the course of our marriage, Jeannie and I have developed a nice ritual. On Thursday evenings, no matter what else is going on, we sit together for an hour over a glass of wine and we talk. These conversations range from Natasha's taste in boyfriends (outrageous hairstyles, enormous vocabularies) to the excesses of the president of Belarus. We laugh, we tease, we debate, and we sip good wine—out on our fieldstone patio in warm weather, and at the kitchen table in cold.

One of these conversations—it was April, the maple trees were in bud, we sat indoors—was devoted to the North Dakota Question.

"You're procrastinating on this," Jeannie said, in her typically straightforward fashion.

"Thanks."

"You've always had North Dakota issues. You've always avoided them."

"It's not issues. It's a house. Land. It's five or six old oak tables and chairs and so on. . . . *Issues.* You sound like my sister."

"Which is another issue."

"Your siblings are more or less normal—you can't relate. You grew up in central Connecticut. No one has issues about central Connecticut."

Jeannie laughed. She has beautiful chestnut hair, just touched with a streak of gray now, and she has so far resisted the temptation to cut it short. We were in the kitchen and were drinking, I remember, a cold, fruity Vernaccia;

I reached across and refilled her glass. Above our heads, something that might have been called music thumped in Anthony's room. I glanced at my wife and saw that, around the edges of the North Dakota Question, a familiar kind of empathy and understanding floated. Aged love, time-tested, what could beat that?

Jeannie twirled her glass. My parents' marriage had been solid but tumultuous, their relationship composed of weeks of tender mercies and a stoic, high-plains peace, interrupted by volcanic arguments over something as simple as the way my father put his toothbrush in the holder, or how Mom cooked the oatmeal. I wondered if they'd been having one of these famous fights when the front bumper of the pickup smashed through Pop's door at seventy miles an hour.

"You're going to have to drive out, you know that," Jeannie said at last. "Cecelia has to be there and she'll never fly. And you'll need to rent a trailer to cart the stuff back."

"Movers could do it."

"Movers can't sell the house."

"Real estate agents can."

"You should go and make your peace with the place. You know you should, Otto. And you need some time away from us and away from work. It's been years since you've had a real break."

"I could fly and meet her there."

A frown. Then a shriek and door-slamming somewhere above us. We waited a few beats to see if it was anything serious. No.

"And leave Cecelia to drive there and back?" Jeannie said. "Alone? In her fourteen-year-old Chevrolet, with her twenty-year-old maps? She'd end up in Honduras."

"She could intuit her way. Consult the spirit guides."

The frown again. So much contained there in the flex of a few muscles. All of history, it sometimes seemed to me. All of ours, at least.

"She made it out for the service okay," I said.

"Okay? Getting off the train in Fargo instead of Minot and having to hire a car and driver with her last hundred dollars? You and I at the Amtrak station watching passengers get off, the train pull away, no Aunt Seese? That's your idea of okay?"

"Reasonably okay," I said. And then, "What about this? What about we make a family trip out of it? Two weeks in August. Just the four of us in the minivan. Aunt Seese takes the train."

It was one of those offerings you know are dust before the last syllables are out. At work, on a fairly regular basis, I was on the receiving end of similarly frail proposals. The author of a book that sold three hundred copies saying she had an idea for a new project, an exhaustive treatment of the Bulgarian sour pickle. She could make it work, she knew she could.

Jeannie set down her glass and began to count on her fingers: "One, we trade Cape Cod for greater Bismarck, which means sea breezes and seventies for tornado warnings and ninety-six in the shade. Two, our dog and our two beautiful offspring sit in the back of the same car for three thousand miles, round-trip. Three—"

I held up my hand. "You had me at two. Look, let me at least run it by the kids. I have the vacation time. I could take three weeks instead of two, one on the Cape, the rest for the Ringlings on the Road. We could visit some chefs I know, historical sites, have some first-class meals, make an adventure out of it."

Jeannie looked at me for a three-count, a touch of amusement at the corners of her mouth. She said, "I have two words for you, my love."

"And which two might they be?"

"Not . . . likely."

And on that note our sixty minutes of alone time ended.

THREE

During dinner I decided not to go anywhere near the North Dakota Question. Jeannie cooks, the kids set and clear the table and sweep the floor, I like to wash the dishes. Though we are fairly relaxed in our parenting style, we have two rules: show basic respect for the others at the table; and no books, magazines, schoolwork, or electronic devices while food is being consumed. Natasha and Anthony had apparently been arguing about something upstairs, and they passed the meal buried in slightly different versions of adolescent sulking, Natasha picking at her food, Anthony wolfing it. During cleanup they muttered and snarled, then pounded off to their separate door-slammings and various algebras.

When the sink was clean, dishes stacked, I made my way up the stairs carrying my hopelessly optimistic family vacation plan in both hands like a pot of dying geraniums to a sick aunt.

I knocked on Natasha's door and found our scholarly daughter at her computer, headphones on, the walls around her papered with soccer players from the U.S. women's team and posters of teen boy rock stars with flat stomachs and pouty lips. Still sour-faced from the argument with her brother, she took off the headphones and, somewhat reluctantly, turned to me. I pulled up a chair. I noticed for the thousandth time how much she resembles my mother through the eyes. A high-plains, gray-green, pioneer directness, as if, beneath the freckles and long lashes, lay windswept stone. At moments, I worried that, like my mother, she would make a steady, dependable, but not particularly warm wife. Then again, I'd come home two hours early one afternoon that winter and discovered her and her genius boyfriend, Jared, making out on the living room couch, and there had been plenty of warmth there. An abundance of warmth.

I said, "Tasha, you know I have to go to North Dakota to settle Gram and Gramps's property."

"I know, Dad." A glance at the computer screen. Maybe Stacey was writing to say that Neal's new hairstyle wasn't as cute as his old one, or that Ilene's choice in skirts that day had been off the wall. It was important to answer such things without delay.

"Well, I thought it might be fun if we made a road trip out of it. The four of us. Jasper, too. We could try camping, or stay in nice hotels, or a combination. Swim, eat, see the big sights. A family adventure. What do you think?"

She looked at me for what seemed the span of her childhood, then said: "Camping, Dad? With, like, my brother the disgusting beast?"

"Okay, so minus the camping out of the equation. What do you think of the idea?"

The look in her eyes was suddenly the look of a thirty-year-old. It is a law of the universe that your words come back to you—and in exactly the same tone of voice. "Dad," she said, "be sensible."

I AM AN UPBEAT sort of person, in general. It's a valuable temperament in the book publishing world, where there are eighteen failures for every success and where the tidal sweeps of fashion knock even the most sure-footed soul into the hard surf at least once or twice a year. It's a valuable temperament in the rough waters of raising teenagers, too. And so, though I'd gotten exactly nowhere with Natasha, I stepped down the hall and knocked on Anthony's door, thinking that, if I could convince him to come out in favor of the family road trip, then he and Jeannie and I could gradually work Tasha free of her resistance.

That spring, Anthony was going through the ordeal known as puberty. His nose and ears were growing too fast for the rest of his face. His skin was breaking out. Dark hairs were showing themselves above his top lip. His sister, of course, never tired of reminding him of these troubles, and Jeannie and I were often having to act as referee. When I went into his room, I found him lying on his bed tossing a baseball into the air and catching it, over and over again, in a sullen hypnosis.

"I remember doing that," I said, sitting sideways on the bed and squeezing his lower leg once. Anthony was at the age where he did not particularly like to be touched. "Some nights I'd try to get to a thousand catches."

"On those boring North Dakota nights, huh, Dad?" He stopped tossing the ball and looked at me.

"They could be pretty bad. But it's a cool place in other ways. You've never seen the real countryside there. Wild buffalo. The Badlands. Native American stuff."

"Yeah?"

"It's like a different world," I went on, encouraged. "Gram and Gramps liked it there." I saw a familiar shadow come over his pimpled face; he and my father had been close. "Still sad about them, huh?"

"Yeah."

"I have to go out there, you know, to settle the estate, sell the house."

"When?"

"August. I should drive, and August is the only time I can get away from work for that long. Want to go?"

"Where?"

"North Dakota?"

"Driving?"

"Sure. I thought we'd make a family adventure out of it. All of us."

"Nah."

"What about just me and you, then?"

"Nah. I was thinking of going out for football. I was gonna ask if I could stay at Jonah's house when you guys go to the Cape."

You're 135 pounds, I wanted to say, but I didn't. I had been a 135-pound football player myself, seen a total of about fourteen minutes playing time, and had a lot of good memories from those days, and one shaky knee.

"What if we made the trip before football?"

"It starts August 3, Dad."

"All right. But in principle you'd like to go, right?"

"Not that much, to tell you the truth. I'm into, like, my

own private space these days. You know, all that time in the car together, motel rooms. Not my thing."

THERE IS A PATIO at the back of our house. It's the usual setup—outdoor furniture, potted plants. Standing or sitting there you can look down toward a stream that cuts its weak flow into a brush-filled ravine. It's all we have in the way of wildness, and some evenings, sitting in a patio chair facing those trees as darkness fell, I'd feel a fleeting sense of some other way of life, less domesticated, less safe. Not free of family obligations, exactly—I loved being part of a family—but with fewer of the responsibilities of modern American middle-class suburban life. Fewer of the particular concerns and duties that are payment for the safest, richest, easiest lifestyle in human history.

That night, after the visits with Natasha and Anthony, I went out and stood on the patio and stared off into the trees. Our faithful dog, Jasper, came and leaned against my leg, a silent pal. Though Jasper was more affectionate these days than either of our two kids, I knew they loved me. I knew they'd swing out away from Jeannie and me over the next years, then come circling back. When they were in their twenties and thirties, we'd all be close. . . . But by then they'd have their own lists of concerns and duties, their own oil changes, doctors' appointments, and business meetings, maybe their own kids. Very possibly their careers would pull them a thousand or two thousand miles away, leaving Jeannie and me to grow old the way my parents had, buoyed by a phone call once or twice a week, flowers on Mother's Day, hectic visits. Why were we all so proud of a style of living that splintered the family like so much dried-out firewood?

I heard the screen door close and recognized the scrape and tap of Jeannie's shoes on stone. She came up beside me in the dark. Jasper moved over and leaned against her knee.

"No go on Dakota?" she said.

"No go. I've been out here pondering the meaning of life."

"That bad, huh?"

"Not so bad. They're good kids. Just drifting out into their own orbits already. It's natural, it's right. Though I guess I have this image . . . I don't know. . . ."

"Of some perfect, endless family life?" she said. "All happiness and McDonald's commercials?"

"No McDonald's, but, yeah, I guess so. Something that doesn't just dissolve in a burst of cell phones and grumpiness, then whoosh away into biannual visits."

"You're an idealist by nature, my love. I just go along, taking what comes."

"What comes is pretty good."

"More than pretty good," she said, and then, "I've always thought work solved the idealist part for you. I mean, a beautiful photograph of a glistening lamb chop with purple new potatoes and asparagus. There's some imagined eternal perfection represented there, something lasting. Your books are . . . unmottled. Is that a word?"

"It's the eternal part I'm thinking about, I guess."

"Nothing we can do about that, honey."

"I know, sure. But does that mean we have to just go along with everything, live like everybody else lives, by the same assumptions? Is that the best we can do?"

"It's your parents' dying. You lost them, and now you're worried about losing the children, which won't happen."

"I just don't want to look back with regret, that's all. If there's any chance to look back."

"What do you have in mind? Go and live on a Greek isle?"

"I don't know. At least the family would stay together longer if we lived on a Greek isle. Do things as a unit instead of flying off into iPods and e-mails and jobs on the other edge of the continent."

"You took a job 1,800 miles away from your parents."

"I know it. And I love our life, I do. I just . . . question it sometimes lately, on some level. I can't describe it. I've been feeling this way for a while now, even before my parents died. Midlife, maybe. I don't know."

For a few minutes we were quiet. Jasper trotted away on the scent of a porcupine or squirrel, or because he didn't like the conversation, didn't like hearing about death and abandonment, couldn't imagine a life without Tasha or Anthony there to scratch him behind the ears as they lay on the couch in the TV room. Aside from the occasional skunk, there was no danger lurking for him in the darkness, nothing to fear. He hadn't known his parents, or siblings, didn't have children, probably didn't worry about what would happen to his loved ones and to his soul after he died. Off in the distance, beyond our little stream, we could hear traffic on the Hutchinson River Parkway, a steady drone of tires and engines, even at this hour. Everyone going, I thought, always going, always hurrying, but headed where?

"You know what you need?" Jeannie asked, after a while.

"What? To drive my loony sister to North Dakota and back?"

"Yes, but before that. You need to retire early and go upstairs with your extremely affectionate wife."

FOUR

Sometimes, after making love with Jeannie, I'd lie there beside her and feel as though the multifarious complexities that surrounded our life had been whisked away like particles of fog on a warm wind. Mind would be clear, body at peace. A fresh optimism would bloom along the windowsills of the bedroom, laying its frail, scented wreath across the sheets and pillows, and I would be clear-minded and capable, and what had to be done would be obvious, and my ability to do it beyond doubt.

That, or something like it, is what happened on the night I've been describing here. Before the lovemaking there was the sour taste of obligation postponed, there were the stunted conversations with the kids, two of the three people I love most on this earth, and there was the patio sadness yawning off toward a meaningless eternity.

After the lovemaking there was the calm understanding that the trip to North Dakota would be only ten days, two weeks at most, that my odd sister was a good-hearted soul. Jeannie and the children would survive perfectly well without me. Little chance I'd enjoy the trip—even postcoital calm doesn't turn a tree root into a truffle—but it seemed at least possible that, by getting so far away from the ordinary routine, I might gain a new perspective on things.

It was a wonderful feeling, really, that sleepy, sure state. I think sometimes that our national obsession with sex (and if you don't think there is a national obsession with sex, just browse the magazine racks in the local chain bookstore) is really nothing more than a profound spiritual longing in disguise: the desire to exhaust all other desires and feel loved and sated, at peace with our fragmented modern selves, linked to those around us. At peace, at rest.

I wonder, sometimes, if the same deep desire lies at the heart of addiction to drugs, to drink, to eating, to work: are we all just desperately looking for some strategy that will get us past the shoals of modern existence and safely into that imagined, calm port? But those strategies—injecting heroin, say, or spending eighty hours a week at the office—work for a time and then stop working. Eventually the bill comes due. It occurred to me, as I faded toward sleep, that, while I wasn't addicted to anything (well, good food, perhaps), I had devised a strategy of my own, a weaving together of favorite pleasures—food, family time, sex, work I enjoyed, tennis, vacations, TV, reading. They made a harmless enough tapestry, a pretty landscape of pleasure speckled with moments of selflessness, annoyance, worry, fear. But it was a strategy all the same, and it had started to wear thin, and then my parents' dying had punched a hole in the worn section. That night, I had the feeling there might be something on the other side, waiting to show itself to me.

All through spring and half the summer I thought about

that "something," wondered, pondered, let the episodes of doubt wash over me and leave me slightly less steady on my feet. I knew I'd have to go to North Dakota, but all through May, June, and part of July I was somehow able to pretend to myself that it would be a quick, easy, painless errand, just a tiny glitch in the predictable pattern that was my life.

FIVE

In New York, over the course of the month of August, you go from the feeling that summer will never end, to the feeling that it has. But before it ends, the publishing world slips into a kind of hibernation: the more successful editors, agents, and authors flee Manhattan for the Hamptons, the Vineyard, the Cape, the Berkshires, Upstate. Skinny sons go out for football and come home starving, scratched up, elated. Daughters work the mall job and the babysitting job and are lulled to sleep at night by visions of their very own car. Suburban wives garden and chauffeur, shop and cook, and lie in the sun at the tennis club pool. And suburban husbands, of course, naturally, it goes without saying, pack up one of the family cars with a suitcase, maps, a couple of sport coats, and head off, where else? To the prairies of western North Dakota.

It was an uneventful leave-taking. Just after breakfast I knocked on Anthony's door and stepped into his "own private space" to say good-bye, only to find my son all but unconscious on the bed, face down on the sheets in nothing but a pair of blue Bronxville Broncos gym shorts. Natasha was away on a lucrative four-day babysitting junket for friends of neighbors who had a house on Block Island and tow-headed boys who could shout "GIVE IT TO ME! NOW!" in three languages. And Jeannie was off making breakfast for a friend who'd had some kind of stomach surgery and could not yet cook or drive. We'd had a nice meal the night before (shiitake risotto and chocolate pudding), and said our good-byes then, so I was set for the road. Still, I procrastinated just a bit, waved at my son's backbone and said a silent farewell, took my time going downstairs.

The refrigerator hummed. A lemony morning light fell across the tablecloth, touching a vase of homegrown flowers there and the scattered pages of the *Times*. So thoroughly had the domestic life enveloped me over the past, what, twenty years, that I felt, once I'd at last closed the back door behind me and was striding toward the driveway, that I was peeling away several layers of skin and setting off into America's dusty center in my bare raw flesh.

But I went. Out the driveway. Right on Palmer, through the center of town, and then down Highway 87, past the Hall of Fame for Great Americans, along the Harlem River, and over the George Washington Bridge. I was headed toward the city of Paterson, New Jersey, where Spanakopita Cecelia lived. My sister, the odd duck.

There was the excitement of the road, there was the sadness at leaving Jeannie and the kids and Jasper behind. There were the miles of crowded expressway. And then, as I took the Main Street exit (PATERSON: MAKING EVERYONE WELCOME, the billboard said) and turned into a Latin stew of discount shops and grand old buildings and went past the Greater Faith Church of the Abundance, a creeping dread worked its way up from the soles of my running shoes. Out of embarrassment, I've so far refrained from saying how my sister makes her living. Here's a hint: After working my way through downtown Paterson, I turned onto her street, and there, jutting out toward the road like a garish fingernail, was a lavender and cream sign.

CECELIA RINGLING

TAROT AND PALM READINGS

PAST-LIFE REGRESSIONS

SPIRITUAL JOURNEYINGS

Journeyings, I thought. *Journeyings* was perfect.

This lifestyle of hers had been a stone in my parents' sensible work shoes from the day Cecelia moved east and had business cards printed up. Their idea of "journeyings" was to drive to Minot in August for the ox pull at the state fair. Their idea of "spiritual" was a trip to the Lutheran church in Dickinson on Sunday mornings, where they would hum along with the hymns and endure the sermon, have a buffet lunch afterward at Jack's Café, then drive back to the farm and the real business of life. "You mean," my father said to my sister once, when we were both visiting, "you mean to say you make a living telling people what they used to be a thousand years ago?"

I pulled in just beyond the sign and drove all the way to the end of the driveway so that the car would not be visible from the street. Foolish, of course, because the chances of anyone in Paterson recognizing my car or me were one in a hundred thousand. Still, around the office I have a certain reputation for being the no-nonsense midwestern type, and it wouldn't do to be seen going in for a past-life regression on my first day of vacation.

Before getting out of the car I sat still and took a few slow breaths. I told myself what I had been telling myself all spring and most of the summer, ever since I'd picked up the phone and given my sister the big news that we would be driving to North Dakota together: I would be kind. I would be patient. I would rein in the side of me that wanted to mock and ridicule. I would indulge, to a fair degree, Cecelia's odd culinary habits. I would remember that she adored my children and that my children had adored her since the days when they could not yet properly pronounce her name.

Ten days. Separate motel rooms. I would be kind.

But when I got out of the car and turned toward the house, I saw that she was sitting on the edge of her shabby deck, barefoot, and that she was not alone. I felt myself flinch.

Cecelia and her companion were not touching, but they were sitting in what seemed to me an intimate posture. I immediately girded myself, tried to keep a pleasant, open-minded expression on my face. My sister got the good looks in our family; I got the good sense. She has beautiful, wheat-colored hair, a large, happy mouth, and eyes—brown like Pop's—that give off a kind of shine you usually see only in the eyes of young children. There is a kind of structural perfection to her features, if that's the right way to put it, and it has always made me think of Michelangelo working with marble, and always made other men think of ways they might convince her to take off her clothes.

For better or worse, the number of men (and perhaps a few women, who knew?) favored by that good fortune is not a small number. Which is not a problem for me—I am the farthest thing from prudish, and, in any case, not one to throw such stones. Before I met and started dating Jeannie I had my wild times, let's leave it at that. The issue was not quantity, but quality. In high school, when she could have had a date with any boy in the sophomore, junior, or senior classes, her preference was the window-smashing, car-crashing, drug-loving son of the mayor. In college, it was a boyfriend old enough to have personal memories of the Civil War. After college, a motorcyclist with crossbones tattooed on his neck. Then, in this order: a yoga master who bilked the ashram and was chased back to Delhi in disgrace; a dreadlocked bicycle repairman/poet with pet piranhas; a septuagenarian orchestra leader participating in the first studies of male-enhancement medications and not shy about introducing that topic into dinnertime conversation at the Ringling home. It was, I often said to Jeannie, a serial menagerie of masculine misfits.

And we met them all. They came for visits and stayed a night or two, or five. They came for Thanksgiving and Christmas and Fourth of July and Buddha's birthday. Jeannie cooked for them. The kids loved them (especially Jack or Jacques, the bicycle fixer, who gave them free tune-ups on their ten-speeds, riding crazily around the block in high-speed test runs, hands clasped behind his matted curls, legs pumping furiously as he sang Bob Marley's "No Woman, No Cry"). To each of them I was unfailingly pleasant and welcoming.

I should pause here for just a moment and say this: I enjoy the variety of humanity. I am not one of these people who wants everyone to live the way I live. What causes more trouble on our troubled earth than people like that? The Homogenists, I call them. *Look at me!* they say. *I'm happy! I'm right! I'm law-abiding, productive, and pleasing to God! All you have to do is live like I do and we'll have world peace!*

And if you don't live like them they'll slaughter you.

I am the farthest thing from a Homogenist. I love my life but I'm not foolish enough to believe that everyone else would love it. Certainly not Cecelia. I just wanted some stable, long-term companion for her, someone the kids could call "uncle," someone who wouldn't disappear one day, leaving behind his greasy wheel sprockets, list of methamphetamine customers, or broken viola strings. My parents had wanted the same thing for her, and it made me sad that they'd died without ever seeing it.

As I walked toward Cecelia and her new beau, I began to think that this time she'd outdone herself, eclipsed her personal record for the most unusual lover. Because, as my sister stood up, and then the man beside her stood up, I saw that he was wearing a dress. Or what appeared to be a dress. A gown perhaps. A robe. The robe was deep maroon with gold or saffron trim and wrapped around him in a mysterious way so that it seemed to hold itself up by magic.

My God, I thought, Aunt Seese is dating the Dalai Lama!

But not really. The robe was messier, and there was something in this fellow's bearing that reminded me more of a long-haul truck driver than a peaceful monk. True, his head was shaved, but he wasn't smiling. He was two or three inches shorter than my sister and built like a middle linebacker, with a wide rough face that could have belonged to a man of thirty-five or a man of sixty. It was almost as if he were a combination of all his predecessors: part yoga master, part biker, with a glint in his eyes like that slimy orchestra guy.

Cecelia swished toward me in her long hippie skirt and hugged me warmly but too long, throwing a little back massage into the bargain. When we finally parted, she hooked me by one arm and half-turned toward the World Wrestling Federation cross-dresser. "Otto," she sang, "this is my guru, Volya Rinpoche. Rinpoche, this is my darling brother."

Rinpoche bowed slowly, then brought a thick calloused paw out from beneath his skirts and gave me a crushing handshake.

Cecelia turned to me, cheeks aglow, and pronounced this memorable sentence: "Otto, sweetheart . . . Rinpoche is going on the trip to North Dakota."

And I, of course, pretended not to hear.

SIX

I decided, as I sometimes do (I suppose I've learned this in business, I'm not particularly proud of the tactic), to delay. Though I had figured on losing only ten days, round-trip, to the North Dakota errand, and though—with the packed car, full tank of gas, and a driving schedule all worked out in my mind—I had an itch to get on the road and put some miles behind us, I decided it couldn't hurt to linger for an hour or so at Cecelia's and see if she'd let logic prevail. This was a tactic I often used with her. She would come for a visit all excited about teaching Anthony to knit (because such activities should not be, she said, "gender specific"), or instructing me and Jeannie in the fine art of Wanna-Panna meditation (because she'd just taken it up and it had deepened all her relationships), or training our half-Doberman, Jasper, to eat vegetarian (because it would speed up the "transit-time" of his digestion and help him live longer), and, over the years, Jeannie and I had learned not to confront these initiatives head on. Instead of getting into an argument, we'd slip Jasper a quarter pound of bacon just before his tofu treat mix, and so on. It was all harmless enough, and I'd figured out that while my sister was consistently wacky, her wackiness was inconsistent, her interests as fleeting as a bumblebee buzzing around your ears. Swat at the bee and you risked a sting; ignore it and let it do its buzzing, and soon it would be off to other pastures.

So, though I'd heard perfectly clearly when she said Volya Rinpoche would ride with me, I was pretty certain it was just another of the well-intentioned but odd ideas that twirled inside Cecelia's gray matter for a few seconds or a few days at a time then dissolved into the ether.

"Show me your garden," I said, because that was always a safe subject and a sure distraction. With the bare-armed, maroon-robed Rinpoche floating along somewhere behind us, we strolled down to the sunniest section of my sister's pleasantly cluttered back yard and inspected her plot of vegetables. Cecelia is a world-class gardener, has been since my parents gave her dominion over a twenty-foot-square piece of tilled back yard when she was six. Until the wildest of her teenage years set in, she'd practically wallpapered her room with ribbons from the Stark County 4-H competition. Tomatoes, potatoes, onions, lettuce, four kinds of squash—she seemed almost to will bushel baskets of vegetables from our black soil, undeterred by the scorching summer sun and brief growing season.

"Magnificent," I said, as we stepped single-file along the rows of yellow peppers and cherry tomatoes, Swiss chard and baby eggplant. "This reminds me of when you were a girl. You always had a magic touch with gardens, Seese. You still do."

I turned and saw how happy and proud she was, her beautiful face giving off a summery glow. She plucked two cherry tomatoes and handed one each to Rinpoche and me.

"You don't have to wash them," she said. "They're completely organic."

"I expected nothing less." The tomato was like a grenade of flavor bursting against the teeth.

"It's almost lunchtime. I could make us a nice salad. I have some good bread. Okay?"

"Fine, sure," I said. The bread would taste like compressed sawdust, but I consoled myself with the idea that we could stop for something soon after we got on the road. I love to eat, love everything about food—the growing, the preparation, food photography, restaurant design, the history of the menu in various parts of the planet—and, despite a regular exercise regimen, I have the modest bubble of a belly that testifies to my passion. One of the promises I'd made to myself about the trip was that I would indulge Cecelia's culinary quirks but not at the expense of my own. There are lines one does not cross.

She picked a handful of vegetables, lifted her skirt into a kind of bowl in front of her, and carried them into the house that way. For a moment the man I thought of then as Volvo Rinpoche and I were face to face in a faint gust of patchouli. He was giving me a direct look from out of his rough face. "Nice tomato, eh?" I remarked, and he lifted his eyebrows and smiled widely, as if I'd said something very clever. It occurred to me—perhaps because he hadn't yet spoken a word—that his English might be weak.

The house was messy but in a welcoming way, mismatched vintage furniture, some kind of Nepali or Indian tapestries on the walls, statues of deities from various traditions, crystals, candles, bird feathers, potted aloe plants. It felt more like our North Dakota farmhouse than my own suburban home ever did, and I experienced a twinge of memory about Mom and Pop. It occurred to me then—just the most fleeting of thoughts—that my return to North Dakota on this particular errand might not be such a simple matter after all.

We sat in Cecelia's kitchen at her wonderful old white metal table with its chipped porcelain top. She served Rinpoche first, and generally looked at and spoke to him as if she were the county chairwoman of the Catholic Daughters and he was the Pope. But we all had equal portions of an exquisitely fresh salad, mismatched mugs of iced green tea, and two slices of pressed sawdust . . . and to my great relief there were no prayers said over the food, no hand-holding, no chants, no blessings of any kind. Rinpoche nodded and smiled a great deal but said nothing. Cecelia asked about Anthony, Natasha, and Jeannie with so much genuine affection in her voice that I forgave her three-quarters of her oddities in the time it took to chew and swallow a bite of bread.

"They wanted to come," I told her. "The kids wanted to see their Aunt Seese. For a minute there I thought I could convince them to just load up the minivan and all of us make the trip together."

As she listened to this small lie, a flicker of something not-so-good touched Cecelia's features. It was quick as a hummingbird kiss, just a momentary dimming of the smile, but of course I noticed. We were, after all, brother and sister. I had noticed, too, walking from back door to kitchen, that she did not have any suitcases stacked up on a chair, ready to go into the trunk of my car. They could be in the bedroom, I told myself, but, as we finished the meal, as Cecelia turned her back and took our empty salad bowls to the sink, I began to have a sense that an unwelcome surprise was floating in the air above the kitchen table.

My own psychic abilities, heretofore undiscovered, were soon confirmed. Cecelia paused for a moment with her hands gripping the front edge of the sink, then turned and marched resolutely back to the table, maintaining eye contact with me the whole way. She sat down very deliberately. She said, "Otto, we have to have a conversation."

I said, "I noticed you haven't packed."

She said, "I'm not going."

"Not going? Since when? You have to go."

"I don't *have to* anything."

"Right. Good. I just took off two extra weeks from work, lost half my time at the Cape with my wife and kids, packed up, planned the whole trip, and why? Because you said you wanted to be there to 'say good-bye to the land' and because you are . . . uncomfortable . . . flying. And you wait until I get to your house to tell me you're not going!"

I could feel the Rinpoche next to me. In my peripheral vision he seemed to be smiling. I had an urge to punch him, and this was a big deal because I had not punched anyone since a fine day, twenty-two years earlier, when Michael Redgewick put a hand on Jeannie's ass at a UND graduate-student dance to which I had brought her.

"Something has changed," my sister said mysteriously.

"Right. Good. I appreciate it."

"Otto," she reached out and put her hand on my arm. "I know you think I'm a nutcake. You're nice, you try to hide it, but I know you think that."

"Nutcake is as nutcake does," I said stupidly. It had been

one of Mom's sayings when we were kids, and eventually turned into a family joke. "You couldn't have called me, at least, before I left home?"

"You wouldn't have come."

"You're damn right, I—"

"You wouldn't have met Rinpoche."

"I realize that. And I'm pleased to meet . . . does he speak English?"

They both nodded.

I turned to face the man. "I'm pleased to meet you, really. You seem like a very pleasant man, but," I looked at my sister, "Cecelia, what means more to me than meeting Rinpoche, nice as he is, is—"

"You never would have come. You never in a million years would have agreed to go to Dakota with Rinpoche."

"I'm not. I haven't agreed. I'm not doing it."

"It's important that you do, Otto."

"I won't."

"I'm giving him my half of the land, and the house, too, if you'll let me. Or you can take more of the land to make up for it. The land is worth some money, isn't it?"

I looked at her. I looked at Rinpoche. Every story I'd ever heard about softhearted single women preyed upon by con artists came honking around me like a gaggle of geese. I said, "Rinpoche, would you mind leaving us to fight in private for a few minutes?"

Rinpoche smiled and nodded—a bit too vigorously, it seemed, almost as if he were somehow making fun of me, but he stood and went out the back door without complaint.

When I heard the latch click I said, "Are you . . . is he . . . are you sleeping together?"

"Otto!"

"Is he trying to con you?"

"Con me? You are so off base that—"

"Mom and Pop's property, our property now, is two thousand acres of prime North Dakota wheat land. Do you have any idea what that is worth?"

She shook her head.

"Five hundred dollars an acre."

She reached up and put the fingers of her left hand to her throat, a gesture straight out of her earliest years. "You're kidding. A million dollars! Our little farm in the middle of nowhere?"

"Plus the house."

"I had no idea."

"Plus the mineral rights, which we'll retain, just in case. Still want to give it away?"

"Of course. Even more so. If you take, I don't know, say, fifteen hundred acres and leave Rinpoche five hundred plus the house, that would be fair, wouldn't it?"

"To whom?"

"To you. You have children getting ready to go to college. That's $750,000 for you! That would be enough, wouldn't it? Even after the taxes and the commission and everything?"

This stopped me, I have to say. She was squeezing my arm excitedly, and I felt a quick rainshower of shame on my face. "Seese," I said, "I make . . . I make a fair amount of money. Jeannie makes some, too, and she had a tidy inheritance when her mother passed on. You . . . you get by on what?"

She waved this question away as if it didn't matter any more than a cutworm in a row of carrots when, in fact, I knew that she had a sizeable mortgage on her ramshackle

"Look," I said at last, "you're a grown woman. If you want to throw away your half of the inheritance, I can't stop you. But spare me, could you? I came here to take *you* to see the house and the land before we sell it, not some monk, some guru, some . . . oddball."

"You don't see who he is, do you."

"No, I do not. But now it's you who isn't listening: I came here to take *you* to North Dakota, not some guy I've never—"

"I can't go, I have a regression going on with this old client and we're at a very key juncture and if I left her now it would be just horrible."

"Fine, regress her all you want, then. . . . How about this? How about I give Rinpoche airfare and he can meet me out there and we can get a signed document from you as to what you wish to do with your half of the property, and we'll sort out the details that way? I'll race out there—it'll only take me two or three days. I'm kind of excited about seeing the countryside, on my own, you know?"

"Can't," she said.

"Why not?"

"Rinpoche doesn't fly. He says it's unnatural. A stress on the spirit."

"How did he get here from Europe, then?"

"Boat."

"Fine. I'll pay his train fare."

"He'd get lost, Otto. The way I did. He doesn't know America at all. You have to take him, show him the ropes."

"I don't *have to* anything," I said, and when she smiled somewhat sadly I realized she'd spoken the same words only a few minutes earlier.

"Otto, my dear brother, please! I know you don't believe in what I do, but everything in your aura says you could be liberated in this life. Do you realize what a blessing that is? I had a dream about you with Rinpoche, just two nights ago. That's why I arranged it this way."

"Arranged, nothing, Seese. You tricked me. The word is *tricked,* not *arranged.* The correct term is *died,* not *moved on.* I can tolerate a lot of things but I really won't sit by and let the language be corrupted. I—"

"Otto, please. I've never asked you one favor in our whole adult lives, and now I'm asking. Once. Just please take Rinpoche out there with you and show him America, get him used to America. The country needs help, spiritual help."

"You've got that part right."

"And Rinpoche has been chosen to provide it. That's all I can tell you right now. He'll change your life, too, if you just let him."

"Why would I want to change my life, Seese? Think about it?"

"Your *interior* life. Your soul's arc through the various—"

I held up a hand, traffic cop on the spiritual highway. "I am a Christian, Cecelia. Not a particularly good one, not a particularly avid practitioner, but a Christian all the same. Good, sensible, Protestant stock, same as you. We don't shave our heads and walk around in bathrobes, and we don't seek spiritual counsel from those who do."

She tucked her hair behind one ear; it immediately fell back down. She said, "He's not into converting people. He doesn't label, don't you see? Ask him what religion he is and he'll say he doesn't care. But he has *peace of mind,* Otto, a deep, deep peace that nothing can shake. Can you say the same thing? Since Mom and Pop died, especially, can you? You said yourself it will only be a few days. And he has his own money and is very easy to be with. So could you do this for me? Just this one small thing? Please?"

WHICH IS BASICALLY the story of how, after another half hour of pleading, on my sister's part, and attempting to resist, on mine, I ended up agreeing to drive Volvo Rinpoche from NJ to ND. When we went outside to give him the news, the Rinpoche seemed interested, mildly curious, amused, but not in any discernable way grateful. His luggage consisted of one cloth bag that looked like an oversized, well-worn pocketbook with leather handles. He accepted a minute-long embrace from my sister, bowed to her in a tender way, and settled himself in the front seat as calmly as if he'd been making the insurance payments for the past six months. My sister hugged me double-long, a double-long spinal massage included.

I was behind the wheel, seatbelt on, without knowing quite how it had happened. I lowered the window. "You said you had a dream about Rinpoche and me," I said to Cecelia. "What were we doing?"

A gorgeous smile lit my sister's face. She leaned toward me, happy as a child, and said, "Bowling!"

SEVEN

Between Cecelia's house and the interstate on-ramp, some-where among the tattered wood-frame triple-deckers and boarded-up topless joints (Doctor's Cave Lounge, Go Go Girls!) of Paterson's vibrant downtown, Rinpoche and I got lost. Probably I should take sole credit and say "*I* got lost," but it is true that the presence of a Rinpoche there in the car's front seat acted as a significant distraction. Or, as Anthony used to say when he was in grade school, "a major annoyment." Getting lost did nothing to brighten my mood, which had been somewhat sour to begin with, and which turned bitter around the edges when I realized, driving away from my sister's house, that she had manipulated me expertly.

I knew it was only a matter of a few minutes until we found the road we were looking for, but it was an annoy-ment all the same. I thought I'd been retracing my steps from the interstate to Seese's house: We went past the same park I had seen on the way in—metal wastebaskets chained to the benches; we looped around behind a familiar line of

rehabilitated factory buildings. As I knew we would from
memories of other visits, we soon saw the sign for Interstate
80 East, but, for some reason, there was no corresponding
sign for Interstate 80 West, and all this, on top of the fact
that I always felt a twinge of guilt there, seeing people living in such a rough, poor, dangerous, noisy place, while
my family and I lived in safe comfort, had me banging the
bottom of my fist against the steering wheel.

And then, in front of another red brick factory building,
I came upon a thirty- or thirty-five-year-old man with very
black skin, white sneakers, and a neat pair of blue jeans.
He was sweeping the sidewalk with an attentiveness and
care that caught my eye as we passed. I must have caught
his eye as well, because he looked up and smiled, as if I
were a regular traveler on that route, a cousin or neighbor
or friend. I made a U-turn in a bank parking lot, pulled up
alongside him, and asked directions, talking to him across
the front of Rinpoche's berobed body.

"You were goin' the wrong way, man!" the fellow said,
and he was so sunny, so unabashedly helpful, and so precise
with the directions, that my mood sank a little further. This
happens to me on occasion in the presence of especially
friendly and well-meaning souls. I do not know why. I am
a friendly and well-meaning soul myself, optimistic, engaging, affable, and less cynical, by a factor of three, than most
of my Manhattan colleagues. But Cecelia's syrupy condescension, and Rinpoche's lippy grin, and this good man
with the broom and dustpan sweeping grit from the front
of an old textile mill as though he were dusting a sacred
icon—the combination made me feel like a curmudgeon.

In any case, thanks to the joyful sweeper, we found
the entrance to 80 West without any further trouble and

were soon humming along the interstate with the bridges and bricks of greater New York already giving way to the greenery of western New Jersey. My plan was simple: maximize time on the fast highways, maximize hours behind the wheel, get to North Dakota in three days or less, drop off the Volvo Rinpoche, do my business, and then enjoy a leisurely ride home, complete with fine meals and maybe a modest adventure that I could take back as material for office conversations. People would ask about my time away, my big trip. I wouldn't have to mention the guru, could talk about wading in the upper reaches of the Delaware, or a phenomenal little trattoria I'd stumbled upon in the wilds of western Indiana.

At the same time, though, I was determined to be civil and decent to my traveling companion. Here is a lesson I learned long ago, and which my kids remind me of whenever I need reminding: When you are a crank, you put yourself on the top of the list of people you make miserable. So I would be decent, I'd be perfectly polite. I'd give Mr. Rinpoche a taste of solid old midwestern American hail-fellow-well-met.

"So," I said, with the car already on cruise control and sailing past lumbering eighteen-wheelers, "tell me something about what it's like to be a Rinpoche. Am I pronouncing it right?"

He swiveled his shaved head so that the muscles of his longshoreman's neck flexed, and he fixed me with a gaze that might have come from Natasha surveying the clumsy eyebrow piercing of a new sophomore girl. As if to make up for the look, he smiled. Then he turned his eyes forward out the windshield and chuckled, and it was a low, mucusy, raspy chuckle, which floated across the seat and went on for longer than would have been polite in most circles. In fact, it went on to the point where I started to believe that he was laughing at me. Just at that moment he stopped, sighed somewhat sadly, and said, "Boring life," though it sounded almost like *wife* in his pronunciation. "Most very boring, boring life." And then he chuckled for another few seconds.

I was undecided at that point as to whether I liked or disliked the man. But I pressed on in a friendly tone: "Oh, come on. Seese says you're a big shot. You have centers all over the world. That doesn't sound boring to me."

"Boring, boring," he repeated, and coughed up some phlegm.

"No, really. Tell me what you do. I want to know."

"Want to know? Really?"

"Absolutely."

Again the swiveled head, the look, a last gurgle or two of the mucusy chuckle. "I sit," he said, and he lifted his coarse hands helplessly off his thighs and let them fall back again, two little slaps.

"Not good for the shape," I said. "You know, you sit all day you can get . . . wide. At our age, especially. My age, anyway."

Rinpoche seemed to hear none of this ridiculous patter. The hills to either side of the road were growing steeper now as we moved closer to the Pennsylvania border. He seemed taken with them. Wherever it was that he came from, they didn't have hills like this, apparently.

"How old are you, anyway?"

He shrugged.

"No, come on. If we're going to spend a few days together on the road we ought to be able to talk about such things."

"You should get off the fast road," he said.

"What? What fast road?" I thought he was making a comment about my hectic but satisfying career. I heard this remark as a preliminary foray into the terrain of spiritual advice, and I was having none of it. I'd made up my mind about that. I'd be his chauffeur. To please my sister, as a favor to a stranger. But the second he started trying to convert me, to advise me, to bring my aura into focus or lift me up into a higher chakra—I'd shut that channel down.

"This road," he said. "You should get off it now."

It was my turn to chuckle, but I was leaning toward dislike. We were on what was called the Christopher Columbus Highway, as if there might be something out where we were going that had not yet been discovered, or had been discovered only by people who didn't count. As if, when the road was named, all the population of New Jersey had insisted that the state was actually flat, and if you went too far you'd fall off, and Rinpoche and I were courageous enough to disagree and risk our lives, heading off into the uncharted seas west of Paterson. The scenery here, while nice enough, wasn't anything to get excited about—woods to either side, a few steep inclines, the occasional sorrowful driver slumped guiltily behind the wheel in the breakdown lane, with a circus of red and blue lights on the roof of the car behind him and the straight-spined trooper standing at his door in a pose of little sympathy. "This is the best road to where we're going," I said, with just the smallest edge. "If you have to go to the bathroom or something, there's probably going to be a rest area up ahead pretty soon."

Again, he did not seem to hear. Or, more likely, he heard and was ignoring me. Which was not something I appreciated. Just then we came across a sign saying there was a scenic overlook a mile ahead. He could relieve himself in the trees there if he really needed to.

For the next minute or so Rinpoche did not speak. I pulled into the scenic area, which was just a parking lot on a hillside with a few men loitering near their cars, trying to make a kind of eye contact that was at the same time shy and aggressive. The expression on their faces reminded me of the look on the face of a former colleague of mine, whom I'll call Fred, a man I'd twice bumped into at lunchtime as he was coming out of a GIRLS! GIRLS! GIRLS! club on Eighth Avenue, when we'd had our offices on Seventh. I suppose lust, whatever form it takes, has its own peculiar shadow. Its own aura.

We got out, me in my slacks and jersey and Rinpoche in his billowing maroon robe, and discovered that the trees in the valley in front of us had grown to a height where they obscured whatever view had once been so appealing. Apparently, this information had yet to reach the particular state bureaucracy in charge of roadside rest areas. So we just stood there side by side and looked out at the tops of trees. There seemed to be nothing to say. I thought of suggesting he go pee in the woods, then decided against it. Not the place to be seen walking down a trail into the shrubbery with a dress on.

We stood there staring dumbly out at the scene, and then, when a sprinkling of raindrops washed over us, we got back in the car and pulled onto the road. Seventy-two miles per hour seemed a safe speed—fast enough to get us where we were going in good time, slow enough to keep from attracting the attention of the troopers' radar. As we approached an exit, Rinpoche coughed in a meaningful way; I ignored him, tried to forget about his fast-road remark. Seventy-two miles per hour. Say, seven or eight or nine good hours per day. We'd be in Dakota by the weekend.

Those were my calculations as we crested a hill and saw two long lines of unmoving cars just a little ways in front of us. I uttered a mild epithet—nothing that wasn't heard a hundred times a day in the finest public high schools in the land—and bounced my fist once against the steering wheel. Rinpoche did not speak.

EIGHT

The vehicles in front of us were stopped dead. A hundred
yards from where we took our place in line, I saw someone get out of his car and walk along the median until he
reached the top of the next rise. The man stood on the hill
there like a scout, for a long few minutes, and then, shaking
his head, walked slowly back. He stopped to lean in near
the driver's-side window of one of his stalled neighbors
and give the bad news. Around me, people were turning
off their engines. We could hear urgent sirens, then see an
ambulance, two ambulances, a police car, and then a tow
truck going past in the breakdown lane.

"Fast road not so fast here," the wise Rinpoche observed.

I uttered the epithet again. Rinpoche glanced over, and I
thought, for a moment, that he was going to ask the definition of the word I'd used, twice now.

But no, he sat there quietly, doing what Rinpoches do,
and I could feel, in my depths, the stirring of a part of me

that I try to hide from the world. I should confess at this
point that I am prone to small fits of anger. Not anger at
other people; I don't usually blow up at my assistant at
work, at Jeannie, or the kids. But if I'm in the wrong mood
and something frustrating comes into my life—a new
computer on which I can't figure out how to arrange my
e-mails; a screen door with directions written badly in six
languages (put screw "A" insite hole "B" after titening bolt
"a" with wrench "g" but before placing latch "E" on *insite*
of the door handel), with a missing screw besides; a serious
printer's error on a book already late; a knotted shoelace on
a young child, out in the rain in front of the church where
his cousin is about to be baptized; a lawn mower that stalls
and won't start again, with the lawn half-cut—something
as petty as that, if I'm in the wrong mood, will set me off on
five or ten minutes of muttering, slamming cupboard doors,
or stomping around our small yard kicking tufts of dirt,
and so on. It is a pitiful display. I'm embarrassed about it,
ashamed. Jeannie and the kids have seen enough of it so it
no longer intimidates or even annoys them. "Dad is steaming off," Natasha will say, and they'll let me open and close
the new medicine cabinet door twenty times, saying, "See!
Look how cheaply this is made! Why is everything made so
cheap now, even expensive goddamned medicine cabinets?
Look at this, look at this Cheap Piece of Garbage! Would
somebody look at this!"

Nobody looks at it. The kids smirk. Jeannie washes a
dish. If it happens at work, my assistant, Salahnda, takes a
coffee break. Ten minutes and it's over, and I'm left chas-
tened and humbled. But for those ten minutes, I am as ugly
as a parent yelling at his child in the park.

It's interesting to me how these things get passed on,

how the sins of the father, or the mother, survive through the years and seep down into the lives of their children and grandchildren. I am occasionally haunted by this, in regards to my own children, haunted by a worry that I might, without knowing it, be passing something on to them, some unattractive tendency, quirk, or failing. Sometimes, after one of my small tantrums, I revive memories of my own dad, an otherwise steady Germanic soul, gone spitting and red-faced over a transmission on a tractor or some such thing. I'd get off the bus and walk up the long driveway, schoolbag banging shoulder blades, and there he'd be in the door of the bigger barn, wrench in his powerful hands, the belly of the tractor opened as if in an operating theater, the dark grease, the gears, the covering piece lying neatly on its back with the bolts held in it for safekeeping. Meticulous, he was. Exceptionally good with his hands, even by the standards of a Dakota farmer. Taciturn most of the time, but not unkind. And then there would be these little tantrums where he'd stomp and bellow and then mutter, again and again, the terribly sacrilegious phrase, "Jameson Crow! Jameson durn Crow!" and whack at the dirt with his wrench or his boot heel, his face the color of a McIntosh apple.

It wasn't a question of fearing him, exactly. He never took out his frustrations on me or Cecelia or Mom. But it was as if you were accustomed to coming home to gently rolling prairie—which I was, in fact—and then on this day you came home and from beneath the prairie soil there came a spouting gusher of fury and frustration, a dark brew. Ten minutes the gusher would go, half an hour at most. My mother, who had a radar for these moods, would bring him out a cup of tea and a hard German biscuit and at first he would ignore her, ignore the tray, and continue with his Jameson Crowing. Eventually he'd soften enough to go over and take a sip of the tea, a nibble from the biscuit, and that would signal the beginning of the end of it. He'd be on the road to recovery, the family would let out a collective held breath, and for a week or a few weeks or sometimes as long as a couple of months we would not see that side of him again.

So this trait had been passed down to me. That's the way it works, isn't it? Part of the ugliness in you is purely your own. But a portion of it is learned, or inherited. And, strangely enough, it seems immune to the scrutiny of your own conscience. Somehow, it's all right—your tantrums or whatever else it might be: shortness with the children, meanness to a spouse, eating too much, cheating a little bit at work or on the tennis court, watching pornographic videos when the family is in bed or stealing away during every other lunch hour for a drink at GIRLS! GIRLS! GIRLS! It's all right. We find excuses for our small and not-so-small addictions and transgressions. We rationalize. They are part and parcel of the judging mind, and so the judging mind excuses them.

All you can do, I suppose, is decide which of your demons are harmless and which are really trouble, and then find the courage to wrestle with the latter group. If, over thirty or forty years, you can put up a dam in the DNA and block such things from being passed down, or even pass them down in diluted form, then, in my opinion at least, you can die in peace.

But I was not at peace there with Volvo Rinpoche on Christopher Columbus Highway in the world-class traffic tie-up. After a few minutes of steaming off and trying to hold it in and realizing I couldn't, I got out of the car and had one of my tantrums by the side of the road, a little drum-dance of what Anthony used to call "flustration." I muttered and spun, kicking at tufts of grass on the median, looking up at the top of the hill and saying things like, "Great. Perfect. We go all of an hour and then we sit and sit. Perfect. Beautiful. Great way to start off the damned trip."

Because my sister's guru sat there as still as a fender and didn't agree, challenge, commiserate, or even seem to mind, I carried on a few minutes longer than I otherwise would have. Even the shrieking ambulances did not humble me.

At last, there was a small stirring ahead of us, drivers tossing their cigarettes down and climbing in behind their wheels. I muttered and cursed my lousy luck for another few seconds and then got back in the seat and did not look at Rinpoche at all. We moved forward slowly, single file, merging, inching, until we passed the cause of the delay—a car with its front third mashed in, glass sprinkled on the pavement, the driver's door ajar as if it had been ripped open, a star of broken windshield over the steering wheel. A medium-sized truck was also smashed up, facing the wrong way. And a third vehicle was lying on its side in a ditch off the right-hand shoulder. I felt then, besides the foolishness and shame, a whisper of that haunting emptiness I had been feeling of late. Just a whisper.

Rinpoche was fingering a loop of wooden beads at his belt. He said, "You don't need to go away from the fast road now, anymore."

But I did.

NINE

Having shown one of the uglier sides of myself to a perfect stranger, and to this particular perfect stranger, I felt embarrassed, of course, but also a sense of relief. I no longer had to pretend to be better than I was. At the next opportunity I left the interstate and wound down the exit ramp onto Pennsylvania 611. While I was doing this, I was pondering Rinpoche's comment about getting off the fast road, wondering if he'd had a premonition. It was the kind of thing Cecelia would have pounced upon as evidence that the future is known to us, that crystals heal and high-tension wires sicken, that when we suffer it must be in payment for the sins of previous lives. My wondering caused me to take 611 South, when I should have taken 611 North.

Not a big problem, I thought, when, two miles down the road I realized my mistake: 611 South would no doubt lead us to an east-west highway soon enough. And it was a pretty road, gliding near the upper reaches of the Delaware River, then down through small villages of hundred-year-old, peeling-paint homes with columned front porches. I could have turned around, but 611 South was narrow, a lumber truck was riding my bumper, and, frankly, I did not want to admit my mistake in front of my companion.

The landscape on this side road was gentler, and, gradually, it worked a soothing effect on my mood. Instead of the high, jagged, stony hills that marked the New Jersey–Pennsylvania border, we were now cruising through sloping farmland planted in corn and presided over by neat white barns. The "Slatebelt" it seemed this stretch of terrain was called, judging at least by signs we passed. Slatebelt Auto Repair. Slatebelt Sewing. I found myself thinking of my parents again, my father's fits of temper, his work ethic, my mother's understanding and stoicism, the way, as a pair, they had roughed up and smoothed over the edges of each other's personalities. Was it mere chance that had brought those two personalities together for fifty years, blended their genes to make my sister and me, then sent the blue pickup crashing into them on that cold February morning? Was everything just a random coagulation of cells, of lives? What about Anthony and Natasha, then: Could those souls just as easily have been born in the Slatebelt? On the banks of the Nile? In an Argentine village? Or had they somehow been destined for a life with Jeannie and me, as part of a greater plan?

At some point, mind still spinning with such things, I stopped in at a roadside store called Ahearn's Country Café, where I bought a bottle of green tea—in memory of my dad, perhaps, though he'd never drunk green tea in his life—and checked the glass cases in vain for German biscuits. Rinpoche seemed to require nothing in the way of nourishment. I asked him, twice, if I might treat him to a cup of coffee or a pastry, but he only shook his head and wandered contemplatively around the store, casting his calm eye upon a predictable Americana of slushies, an out-of-order ATM machine, and the refrigerated glass cases that held plastic bottles of juice and chocolate milk.

Not long after leaving Ahearn's, as I'd hoped we would, we came upon a major highway heading west. Route 22. Same number as the route on which my parents had been killed. Rinpoche's premonition—if that's what it was—about leaving the interstate, now this odd coincidence. It seemed to me for a few seconds that there might, after all, be some hidden design to the world's complex workings, some merit to the types of things my sister was always talking about: synchronicity, psychic wavelengths, auras, healing energies, all the frizz-frazz of people who couldn't deal with solid reality. A few seconds, however, and the notion passed. I took Route 22, which soon led us into I-78, which was choked with construction sites and one-lane work zones and spotted with billboards advertising homemade Dutch food at the upcoming exit. In my experience, this tasty cuisine consisted of meat with a side order of meat—pork, smoked beef sausage, scrapple—all the delicious fat left in, everything smothered in gravy. The billboards should have come with a Surgeon General's warning, or announced the availability of angioplasty at the next exit.

There were, on occasion, dead deer or possums by the side of the road. Rinpoche nodded his head once, solemnly, at each carcass. By then I'd almost forgotten my sorry outburst and my own questioning, and I'd fallen back into a place where I studied and then dismissed him within the whirl and tilt of my own thoughts. He was easy to be with,

I could tell that already, a nice relaxed presence. And yet, it felt to me, surrounded as I was by the roar of American commerce, that his world must be a world of artificial calm, a world of nodding at roadkill and fingering beads. He didn't know the strains of a regular life, of children's demands, their tantrums, their occasional whining and perpetual neediness. He didn't know the stress caused by irritating coworkers, or stupid bosses, or just ordinary chores and pressures—bills, home repairs, family emergencies. He wore his robe. He "sat." He had his centers, whatever they were—ashrams of some kind, I supposed. With a life like that, why wouldn't he be calm and pleasant?

"You know," I said to him, after we'd passed through yet another work zone and a long stretch of silence and were making good time again on the open highway, "all this Zen stuff, the sound of one hand clapping and so forth, it's fine, but I'd like to have an actual conversation with you. We're going to be in this car together for, I don't know, thirty hours or so, and if all your answers are going to be cryptic . . . well, that's not much fun."

He had turned his face to me and was smiling without showing his teeth. His skin was the color of the fine filament you find between the peanut and its shell, that silvery red-brown. His forehead and chin were strong, the latter cut by a shallow cleft. His eyes—I glanced back and forth between them and the road—were a sandy brown and speckled with flecks of gold. It was a wide face, open as a child's, and yet hardened as if he'd worked outdoors for many years.

"What is *cliptic*?" he asked.

"Cryptic. It means secret. Or not secret, exactly, but a kind of shorthand, a code. You know—cryptography is the study of codes. I ask you what you do, what Rinpoches do, and you say, 'I sit.' That's cryptic. That's not what we call in this country an open conversational style."

"Ah." He turned his face forward and made several small nods, as if digesting this lesson in American social behavior. "What do you work?"

"I'm an editor. I help publish books, on food. Big coffee-table books with pictures of beautifully prepared meals in them, or books with recipes . . . or, sometimes, smaller books about a particular kind of food, or a particular way of preparing food, or the history of food, or a biography of a famous chef. For example, one of our recent projects was a book about the history of the preparation and consumption of game meat. Elk, buffalo, venison, and so on. But that wouldn't interest you. You're a vegetarian, no doubt."

He shook his head.

"Not a vegetarian?"

"Not any -*arian*."

"But you're some kind of Zen master, a Buddhist at least."

"Not any -*ist*."

"Not Buddhist? Not a follower of his teachings?"

"He doesn't want the followers for his teaching."

"All right. But surely you're not a Christian."

"Of course. Christian."

"What kind of Christian then? Protestant? You're not Catholic, are you?"

"Protestant," he said, with his small smile. And then, a second later, "Catholic. All the -*ists*. All the -*arians*. Hindu, too. All the Hindus. Muslim. Sufi. I'm Sufi."

"You're playing again. Look at the straight answer I gave you, and you give me riddles. Nonsense."

"Cliptic," he said with a big smile.

"Worse than cliptic."

The gas gauge had fallen close to the red zone. In place of billboards offering Pennsylvania Dutch cuisine there was now a spate of advertisements for fast food restaurants in a place called, oddly enough, Hamburg. If the ads offered health warnings I couldn't see them as we sped past. At the next exit I pulled off and headed for the nearest gas station.

"Where do you originally come from, at least?"

"Siberia," he said, though he pronounced it *Sigh-berry-ya.*

"You're Russian?"

"South Sigh-berry-ya. Skovorodino."

"Never heard of it."

"Very far," he said. "Near to China. Near to Mongolia. Near to Tuva."

"And you started a center there?"

"I run away from there."

"When?"

"Twenty years. I was born there, taught there. My father was a great master there. I went to prison there. Run away."

"You escaped from the Gulag?"

"No," he said, in an unengaged tone that implied we were speaking of someone else, an uncle or neighbor, long-ago deceased. "Russia."

On that note I got out and filled the tank. Gas prices were breaking records that summer; filling the tank cost me forty-seven dollars. I wiped the windshield clean with the rubber-edged tool, trimming the water off in neat rows as the Rinpoche watched, intrigued. He seemed to be studying everything—the landscape, the design of the gas station's logo, the displays in the front window and the numbers on the pumps. Forty-seven dollars! If you made six dollars an hour, it took a day's work to fill the tank.

I went in to use the facilities, and on the way out I noticed an old man in overalls sitting on a folding chair just outside the front door. Rotund in cheeks and belly, balding, past seventy, he seemed to be one of these local people the chains sometimes hire for minimum wage, a fossil-fuel Buddha doing odd jobs. He sent a shining smile up at me. I stopped and asked him where we might find a place to spend the night. "Not a chain motel," I added. "Someplace real. I have a friend along, visiting from another country, and I want to show him the real America. An old inn. A B&B, something like that. Would you know of anyplace like that in these parts?"

"Lititz," he said.

I thought for a moment that he was being vulgar. Uncle of the owner, down on his brain cells, he was offering commentary on the body parts of female customers.

"Say again?"

"Lititz," he repeated, and waved his cane to the south, past the east-west highway we had just been on. "Little old town. Nice inn there. Feed you good, too, if you can afford it, and from the looks of things, you can. Go to 501, head south, and keep going. You'll feel like you missed it. Go on and on, an hour from this spot right here. Inn is right on the road. Feed you real good."

"But we're heading northwest," I said.

"Nothing that way. Go to Lititz, I'm telling you."

I thanked him and had turned and started to walk away when he rapped me on the calf with his cane. I turned back.

"Listen to me," he said, rather fiercely. "Go south. Lititz.

And don't eat too much there. Cut your life short. Chops the sex urge in half, too, you know."

"We wouldn't want that."

"No, we wouldn't."

I smiled politely, patted my belly, and hurried away, erasing his advice from my mind almost immediately. I got back in the car and was clicking my seatbelt on and there he was again, hobbling toward us, then pushing his face practically through the window. He gave Rinpoche a big smile and a wink and said to me, "You don't take advice good, do you, son?"

Rinpoche laughed. I mumbled something about being as open to advice as the next person, but that we had a schedule to keep.

The old man pushed two fingers into my left shoulder. "I'm telling you, Lititz is special, a special place for you. Look at my eyes."

I looked. Cloudy, silvery, intense. I felt the stubbornness rising up in me. *Back off,* I was tempted to say. *Go harass somebody else.* But then his face softened, his fingers tapped my shoulder lightly, and his voice turned into a kindly grandfather's voice. "Listen," he said, "I wouldn't send you down there for nothin'. You like your food, am I right?"

"Absolutely."

"This place has the best food within fifty miles of here. You're talking just a little ways off your route. Here." He reached into his overalls and produced a folded up scrap of glossy paper. "Coupon. Ten percent off. You trust me now, okay. Show your friend here the very best of Pennsylvania." He looked across at Rinpoche and winked again.

"Yes, I want to see this place," Rinpoche said, and that sealed the matter.

I FOUND ROUTE 501 without any trouble, and headed south along it, relieved to be away from the interstate noise, the hurtling semis, and the insistent advice of old men in gas stations. This was an even prettier road, lined with sedate, perfectly manicured farms and neat white barns, some of them made with a pale stone or surrounded by walls of that stone. There were small ponds in these yards, straight rows of corn, smooth carpets of alfalfa and beans in the fields, and I supposed that the old guy had been right: It was worth it, after all, to lose a bit of time going south if the territory was prettier and the food better. I could always make up ground the next day. Along the side of the pavement an Amish family clop-clopped in their black buggy. Another calm, artificial life, I thought, another little world within a world, separate from reality. But then it occurred to me to wonder if these lives were in many ways harder than my own, not less but more real. Rinpoche had been in prison, after all, if he was telling the truth. There was nothing artificially nice about that.

"If you don't want to talk about it, I understand," I said. "But, at some point, I'd like to know what that was like, the prison. I'd like to hear the story of your escape."

He nodded. Nodded, then uttered this memorable line, as if he'd been pondering it while I navigated Pennsylvania's country highways and took advice from its old men: "You are a good person, good soul."

"What? For asking to hear about your escape from a Soviet prison?"

He reached across and patted me on the forearm, two firm slaps. There were two or three syllables of the famous chuckle, and then: "You are a clean soul."

"I try to—"

"You are close to a major step."

And you haven't even looked at my palm, I thought.

"You don't see," he went on, "but you are now very close to a major step. You have the dreams about escaping, yes?"

Here it came then, the dreaded spiritual nonsense. "Listen," I answered, as kindly as I could manage. "I'm not such a clean soul, as you put it. I try. I'm a good dad, good husband. I try to treat people decently. But I have to tell you that I am a Christian—not in the judgmental, hateful sense in which that word is lately thrown about, but an old-fashioned Christian. A Protestant, in fact. That's my faith. That's what I live by. I don't go to church often, it's true. Those rituals don't do much for me anymore. But the basic principles—"

"You don't see," he said.

"No, I don't." And then, in another small fit of anger, I pulled the car over into a gravel driveway that led to some kind of metal storage building. I killed the engine, turned and gave the Rinpoche all my attention, then took a breath to calm down. "Look, I'm not fond of proselytizers."

He raised his eyebrows and kept them raised, then dropped them.

"I'm not a big fan of the touchy-feely, the past lives, the chakras, the important steps someone who doesn't know me tells me I am about to make. I'm an ordinary American man, with a wonderful wife and family, nice job. I try to be good. You'll excuse me for being blunt, but, really, I don't need anything—any words of encouragement from you or from any other spiritual teacher."

He watched me. There was the tiniest smile at the corners of his mouth. "Why angry?" he asked.

"Why? Because my sister is forever trying to convince me to do this or that—meditate, stop eating meat, start washing my hands with organic soap, and so on. It annoys me, frankly. I have a very nice life, thank you, and a faith of my own."

"Why angry?" he repeated.

"Because you frustrate me, you people. The evangelical so-called Christians telling everyone else how to live, when they can't even stay away from prostitutes. The New Agers telling everyone else what to do and not do when they can barely manage their own mortgage payment. What right have you to tell me about my important step, my dreams? You hardly know me."

But he was smiling at me as if he did know me. The smile was an odd combination of innocent goodwill and sureness, as if he were at once happy to see me standing up for myself, but also laughing at me, kindly, the way a father laughs at his two-year-old when she mispronounces a word. No, that's not right; that implies a condescension that wasn't there. It was more like a seasoned affection. Strong, even, yellowish teeth, lips stretched wide, longshoreman's face still and solid—the Rinpoche was looking at me as if he knew me through and through and liked me in spite of it.

"I'm sorry," I said. "I'm blaming you for things other people do. I'll buy you dinner to make up for it. It's just a sore subject with me, that's all. A sore subject with a long history. Family stuff."

"Okay," he said, and the smile broadened. He reached across and poked me in the arm, hard, with one thick finger, and chuckled. "Okay. Sorry, too."

I started the car and continued down 501. At just this point—this is the absolute truth—we passed a stone church in front of which stood a small sign carrying this message: IT'S NOT ABOUT RELIGION. IT'S ABOUT RELATIONSHIP.

"Sorry again," I said.

He said, "Open American conversation." And I felt a twist of something—anger, shame—in my guts. Or a combination of the two. Or maybe just hunger.

Another sign by the side of the road: GO IN PEACE. SERVE THE LORD.

Then a diner called Kumm Esse, and a sign there saying, TRY OUR STRAWBERRY PIE. I very nearly pulled in.

And just beyond Kumm Esse, another church, with another message, DISCOVER YOUR PURPOSE. SUNDAY 10:15.

It was the message center for the proselytizers of the world, all of them confident in their knowing, eager to make others like them, sure of what would spread happiness. I decided I'd go home and make a sign for my front yard that said LEAVE THE REST OF US ALONE, DAMN IT! but then, beneath all this, something was nagging at me. Why so angry?

Soon we drove up a gentle slope and into the village of Lititz. We found the inn just where the fellow with the cane had said it would be, right on 501. All I could think about then was the consolation of food. A good dinner, the best dinner Lititz could offer. Glass of wine, cut of meat, vegetables. Slice of strawberry pie, if strawberry pie happened to be the specialty hereabouts. That would calm me down. Two more days with Rinpoche and I'd be done. We'd leave early in the morning to make up for our little detour. We'd play music on the CD player, listen to the hot winds from the right and left, Rush Limbaugh or Rachel Maddow, a sports show, Dr. Joyce Brothers, Joyce Meyers, the Reverend Armando Fillipo Buck. We'd get through this and go back to our normal lives. I felt suddenly strong and sure of myself . . . and ready to eat.

Except that, as I found a parking spot on the street near the inn, and did a neat parallel parking job, I happened to remember—in the way you remember such things—a flash of recurring dream I'd been having over the past few months. Half a dozen times. Always there was some flood coming, or some animal, or, once, a churning yellow bulldozer. And always yours truly was sprinting for his life.

Escape.

TEN

The General Sutter Inn, located in the quaint village of Lititz, Pennsylvania, turned out to be the absolutely perfect antidote to a long day on the road. From his carpetbag, Rinpoche pulled a wad of bills, and he asked for the least expensive room, which turned out to be sixty-two dollars plus tax. He counted out the money slowly and carefully and smiled at the young woman behind the desk. I handed over a credit card, asked for something larger, and was given a key to a hundred-dollar room, also on the second floor, 212 in fact, my office area code. "What about dinner?" I asked Rinpoche. "My treat. I promised. Make up for any bad moments on the drive."

He lifted his eyebrows and flexed his cheeks—his face had an amazing elasticity, as if he'd spent years in a specialized gym developing the muscles over his cheekbones—and shook his head, no. "Just sitting now. Just sleep," he said. "Tomorrow we eat, Rinpoche and you."

"Fine. Good night then."

"Good night, you-are-a-good-man."

Rinpoche and I took the carpeted stairs together, then went along separate hallways without another word.

The inn was 250 years old, and seemed it. In the best sense. Creaking wooden floors, wainscoting, lace curtains, sitting rooms with three armchairs and a shelf of books. Room 212 faced onto the street that intersected with 501, and it was a little noisy but otherwise perfectly fine: a king-sized bed, an old-fashioned tiled bath, heavy mahogany dresser and desk in the style of the pieces I was driving all the way to North Dakota to fetch. A television the size of two half-gallons of ice cream stacked one on top of the other. There were exposed pipes, and the ceiling had suffered from a leak at some point, but I liked all that, liked it a thousand times more than the sanitized chain hotels with three hundred rooms, the kind of place I was used to from my business travel. I liked having an actual key instead of a plastic card, liked the old porcelain handles on the shower, liked the fact that you could actually open the windows, liked the absence of disinfectant smell, generic wall prints, an "entertainment center," and the "bar" with its four-dollar bottles of spring water and nine-dollar bags of nuts.

I stretched, sat on the bed, took off my shoes and socks, and called home.

"Is this the Prince of the Road?" Jeannie asked when she answered.

"It is. The prince is tired. He misses his wife. He is traveling with a man who wears a gold-trimmed red robe."

There was a rather long pause. And then, "Otto? Really?"

"The Prince of the Road never lies."

"Is it some kind of midlife trouble, honey? Is there something I should know?"

A two-second delay and then I lay sideways across the bed and burst out laughing. The laugh was like something from my childhood, and it seemed to wring the whole day's weariness out of me. When it died, it died slowly, in a fading out of smaller riffs. "Nothing except the fact that my wonderful sister tricked me into taking her spiritual master instead of her. I am traveling with the guru Volya Rinpoche, newly arrived in these United States by way of Siberia."

"You're making some kind of a joke."

"Dead serious."

"Seese didn't come? After all that?"

"Seese is back in Paterson regressing a good friend."

"And who is with you, really?"

"Volvo Rinpoche or Volya Rinpoche, something like that. Shaved head, nice smile, slight trouble with English, and mysterious as the day is long. I like him, I think."

"You think?"

"He's hard to get to know. Though Seese seems to have gotten to know him quickly enough. She wants to give him her half of the property. To start an ashram or something. About that, I am not pleased."

There was an audible sigh on the other end.

"Kids okay?"

"Tasha's fine. Anthony hurt his elbow at the football try-outs and is up in his room with a bag of ice. Jasper keeps going upstairs to see where you are, then out into the garage, then into the bushes near the stream."

"Give him some of my old T-shirts to sniff."

"Can't. I'm sniffing them."

"You're all right?"

"Fine. I'm a little concerned about this idea of Seese's. That's a hefty sum to be giving away."

"I told her the same thing. We'll see. Maybe something will change. There was a bad accident on the interstate. Two cars and a truck. Someone died, I think. The length of Seese's farewell hug might have saved my foolish ass."

"You have a nice ass, actually."

"We were held up forty minutes. Anyway, I had one of my little fits."

"In front of the guru?"

"Yeah. He handled it well. He's been in jail, in Russia."

"My God, Otto, it sounds like you should be keeping notes."

"Seese wanted me to show him America. This quadrant of America, at least."

"The kids miss you already. They'd never say it, but I can tell because they're not fighting. Want me to call them to the phone?"

"Don't bother them now. I've decided to write them. An actual letter. The old-fashioned way. Prepare them, would you?"

"They'll be shocked. They won't know how to open it. They won't know what it is. They miss you. I miss you."

"I'll sneak into bed with you as you dream."

"I wish."

We said our good-byes and I hung up and stretched a little more, musing on the notion that I had, by pure chance, found a woman like Jeannie. Or was it chance, after all? Seese had referred to it once as an "arranged marriage" in keeping with her idea that all relationships are part of the general plan, people brought to the same bed by the Supreme Intelligence who runs the universe. Arranged or not, part of the plan or not, after a few years of mutual adjustment it had worked out remarkably well. Jeannie and I had known nothing of life when we met and starting dating. We had been tremendously different in background, temperament, even hair color. I was a farm kid, she was a Connecticut sophisticate who chose grad school in Dakota to get away from an abusive mother and to pursue a short-lived interest in soil chemistry. Somehow, our physical infatuation and intellectual kinship had evolved into real love, her strengths filling in for my weaknesses, and possibly vice versa. We had our tiffs and bad moments, of course, but I rarely forgot to be grateful for her.

I stretched a bit more—the human vertebral column was not designed for office work, or for hours in the car—then washed up, put on my sport coat, and went downstairs for dinner.

In the 250-year-old dining room I was given a table looking out on a courtyard where a fountain splashed and bubbled and where a ten-foot-tall wooden sculpture stood, looking out of place. General Sutter himself, I imagined. At the check-in desk there had been a brochure giving the general's story—he had, apparently, "discovered" California, or some such thing—but I have to admit that, with a few exceptions, I am strangely uninterested in American history. All slaughter and deprivation, all courage and will, it left me cold, though I like old houses and places where you can see the mark of the past. I told this to my sister once and she said it was because I'd had no other lifetimes on this continent.

As I was musing on the idea of past lives (I'd heard once, perhaps from her, that reincarnation had been part and parcel of Christian doctrine until the sixth or seventh century after Christ's death, at which point some potentate in the Church had decreed it heretical), the waitress set before me a menu I can only describe as astounding. Here we were, deep in the green heart of Pennsylvania, and they were offering elk, buffalo, and seafood coquille. The wine list was just as complete, and after the waitperson (Aliana was her name, studying philosophy and the history of religion at Penn State) had stopped by three times to inquire, I at last settled on fresh Pennsylvania trout, a salad, and half a bottle of Pinot Grigio.

Buffalo on the menu—and we weren't within a thousand miles of North Dakota.

The wine arrived with a basket of warm rolls and what appeared to be about a pint of butter. I sipped, watched the water splash in the fountain. I thought about Natasha and Anthony and it was as if I could feel them in my chest, each of them there, all their past and all their future, right there.

In the midst of this affectionate musing the salad was served. As I started in on it, I was visited again by a wave of loneliness, and by the feeling that had been bothering me over the past few months. Not loss, not mourning, just a sort of quiet knocking at the door of my contentment. I ate and drank and pondered it. With the children, with me—was something missing? Were Jeannie and I simply looking around us and judging things against the standards of our neighbors, and the kids' schoolmates, and letting ourselves be satisfied with that? Friends of ours had taken their children and gone to live in India for a school year and had come back convinced that they had too much of everything, that America was largely lacking in any real spiritual dimension. But wasn't that merely a kind of guilt talking?

Would their having less make for the poor Calcuttans having more? And weren't there different styles of spiritual living, each suited to its own cultural particularities?

Aliana brought the trout, and as she set it before me, I
asked about her studies and her plans, just the usual small
talk that middle-aged people make with young adults. She
turned a frank gaze on me and said, "I saw how my parents lived, you know, just getting money, spending money,
worrying all the time. I wanted to figure things out a little
before I started in on that kind of a life. I wanted, you
know, to get the big picture in focus. My grandfather retired after thirty-five years of investment banking, left my
grandmother, and sailed around the world for two years,
trying to pick up younger women. It was kind of sad, you
know? I didn't want to follow somebody else's idea of success and end up that way."

"And the course work is doing that for you? I mean, giving you the perspective you want?"

She shook her head and smiled ruefully. "My boyfriend
is doing that for me. He's a yoga teacher. The course work
is just, you know, blah blah."

"I know," I said. "I remember it from my own blah blah
days. Sometimes there's something useful in there, though."

"Not yet."

She went to check on her other tables, leaving me with my
uneasiness and the plates of food. It was a nice meal—trout
dusted with almonds, mashed potatoes with some skin left on
(the way I liked them), grilled asparagus—sufficient even for
a picky New York food person, and, in almost every corner
of the globe, luxurious. I sent a quiet thank you toward the
plump fellow at the gas station, and pulled out his coupon,
which proved to be past its date.

I decided not to have dessert, left Aliana a fifteen-dollar tip on a fifty-dollar meal—because I liked her, was rooting for her, and because I have more money than I really need and remember what it felt like to have less—and went out and walked in the balmy air, up and down the commercial street in front of the hotel. Another Amish carriage clopped by with two beautiful children staring out the back window.

And then, back up in room 212, I flicked through fifty channels looking for I didn't know what. It was the usual messy stew: news, drama, stupidity, sports. I kept flipping. At home I would have been on the computer, or talking with Jeannie or the kids, or replacing a lightbulb, or lying on the sofa scratching Jasper's belly and watching the Yankees. But the Yankees weren't on, and I had decided not to bring my computer (Jeannie's idea, actually—*Get all the way away from work,* she'd said), so there was a small emptiness where those things would have been. And television was designed with just such an emptiness in mind. I flipped and flipped for almost half an hour without settling on anything, then drank half a glass of water, went to the desk, and wrote my elder child this letter—which she has saved—on General Sutter's stationery:

Dear Tash,

How are you? This is your old dad writing. I'm thinking of you and Anthony and missing you. If you two are on speaking terms, tell him I'll write to him tomorrow.

Being away from the family has given me time to think. I've been thinking about how, sometimes, because we all see each other every day, there is a tendency to take each other for granted, to get caught up in all the routine details of clothes, food, money, rules. You're at an age now when you are forming what will be your own future life, and your mother and I know that, and we only want that life to be the best that it can be. If sometimes it seems like we put you in a cage and move the bars in closer every day, well, we don't mean to—we mean to move them closer every *other* day!

I'm goofy, all right, sorry. It's been a long day. I'll tell you about it when I get home, but I'm riding to North Dakota with some kind of spiritual master your aunt hooked me up with. Nice enough guy.

I just wanted to write to say that I love you, that you and your brother mean everything to me and Mom, that your happiness means everything to us. When I get home, I'll take you out to breakfast at Mitch's if you can spare the time. Saturday. Any time you want to wake up. Breakfast at Mitch's at one p.m. if you want. A date. Jared will be sick with jealousy.

All my love,
Dad

I read the note over twice, folded it into an envelope, sealed it. I brushed my teeth and splashed water on my face then took off my clothes and got into the bed. It felt huge, as hotel beds always feel without Jeannie in them. I lay awake for awhile, hearing another horse-drawn carriage go by beneath the windows and thinking about how impossible it was to convey to your children the depth of your love. My own parents, it seemed to me, had just abandoned any idea of doing that. Or maybe their parents had never given them a decent example of how to even try. Or maybe they just assumed their love was so obvious it didn't need to be talked about. Or maybe the hard grind of farming life had knocked all the energy out of them. I remembered, once, on one of the rare times that we were out together as a family having a meal, seeing another family of four in the booth across the way. The kids were about the same age as Seese and I, which must have been preteen somewhere. But the mother and father were always touching them: arm around the shoulder, hand on the wrist. I remember that it made me sad, and that the sadness seemed unmanly somehow, and so I never mentioned it to anyone. It was part and parcel of the prairie life to keep your hurts well covered. I went to sleep thinking about that.

ELEVEN

Breakfast at the General Sutter Inn is served in a street-side café that sits just off the main lobby. The morning meal is free for guests, if they choose from a limited menu; or they also have the option to order from the more extensive regular menu and take a five-dollar credit.

I sat at a table looking out on the street. Still partially full from the night before, I eschewed the cornmeal pancakes and crab and shrimp quiche and asked for something simple: coffee, apple juice, and oatmeal with honey. Rinpoche was nowhere to be seen and I realized we hadn't set a time for breakfast. The food arrived quickly. I picked up my copy of *USA Today* and was reading about Israel's bombing of Lebanon's infrastructure and speculation about Cuba after Fidel and the big heat wave we were driving through. I looked up from this mix of news, glanced through the window, and caught sight of my traveling companion. He was out on the sidewalk, bending down, collecting something, putting stones or plants into a pocket buried in his robe.

After a few minutes of this, the good Rinpoche came in and sat down opposite me. A wide grin animated his rugged face, as if, given a chance to select from the entire population of North America, he would make me the breakfast companion first on his list. It was a nice feeling.

"How did you pass the night, sir?" I asked him.

He put his hands together at the side of his cheek and tilted his head onto them, eyes closed, tiny smile playing.

"That good, eh?"

The waitress swung by our table. Rinpoche ordered tea with one poached egg on wheat toast and she took his order while making a deliberate but only half-successful effort not to let her eyes wander across his outfit. It was not, apparently, the season for maroon in central Pennsylvania.

"Glad to see that you eat," I said, when she'd left us.

"You," he pointed to me, "you ate last night. Big!" He spread his hands out from his sides as if encompassing a three-foot-wide beach ball of a belly.

I was, in fact, suffering just a bit from a case of morning regret, and going very slow on the oatmeal. "How did you know that?"

He laughed as if I had made a joke. "Your face shows."

"My aura?"

"Yes, yes. Anyone could see." He pondered a moment, turned serious. "You can ask me now, any question. I will give you a wesson."

Just as he was saying this, the waitress brought his tea, and now, on her second visit, she could not at all keep herself from giving him, and then me, the famous once-over. I imagined her providing a detailed report to the cook and busboy. *Two true weirdoes out there this morning, Eddie. You have to take a look.*

"A lesson?" I said, when we were alone.

Rinpoche nodded.

"What are you talking about?"

"Ask," he said. "Anything. I teach you."

"Teach me? A bit presumptuous of you, isn't it?"

"What word?"

"Presumptuous. Uppity. You know, you're the teacher, I'm the student?"

"Thank you for teaching me that word," he said, smiling. "Say again please?"

"Pre-sump-tu-ous."

He laughed his high, trilling laugh—the complement to his guttural chuckle—and now the two businessmen at the table on the other side of the room were looking us over.

"You are editor," Rinpoche said. "You know books. You know language. Very good, thank you." He nodded twice, then pointed to himself with one hand and attacked his egg with the other, happily, joyously, apparently unaware that I had taken offense. He sliced off a piece of the egg so that the yolk dripped onto his toast. He observed the little yellow flood. He sliced the toast with his knife and fork, put the piece into his mouth, and chewed happily, thoroughly, contentedly. A sip of tea, and then, "I am guru. I know other things than you. You should ask. Every morning at breakfast I let you ask one question."

"Generous of you," I said.

Another pair of nods from the good Rinpoche.

I ate a few spoonfuls of oatmeal, sipped my apple juice, tried to calm down. I could feel, again, in my depths, a particular species of hot, swirling anger, well out of proportion to the event. Twice now in two days I had surprised myself, and not in a way I liked. No tantrums this morning, I told

myself. No nasty remarks. "Fine," I said at last. "What is
the meaning of life?"

He looked at his egg, chuckling happily, tilting his big
head sideways so that the chin and nose were not in a verti-
cal line. He nodded again that way, sideways, chuckling,
looking at his egg.

He then reached into his robe, flipped the folds a couple
of times, came out with his fingers clutched, leaned across
the table, and dropped a handful of dirt into my water glass.
At that moment the waitress was circling back toward us
with a pot of coffee, and the odd little drama at our table
stopped her dead in her tracks. She hesitated there for a
two-count, then spun on her heel and made for the kitchen
with an update for the cook. My glass was now cloudy,
filthy, a few crumbs of brown dirt on the table beside it.
Perhaps even a grain or two of sidewalk dust had fallen into
the oatmeal. Rinpoche took his spoon, reached over, and
vigorously stirred the mixture he had made, then sat back
and looked at me with his beaming kid's smile. After a moment he pointed to the glass and said, "Meaning of wife."

"What is? Rudeness? Oddness?"

"Why so angry?"

"Not angry," I lied. "Amused. Thank you for the lesson."

"You're welcome."

The dirt was beginning to settle so he took up his spoon
a second time, reached across, and stirred it.

"What is this, some kind of Zen trick?"

He laughed, of course. He ate a bit more of his soupy
egg, sipped his tea, smacked his lips loudly. "Meaning of
life," he repeated, now pronouncing the *l* perfectly. "Protestant trick." A huge smile now. "Catholic. A Hindu trick."

"Dirt in a glass?"

He held up his own water glass, dirt-free, and peered at me through it, then set it down. "The mind," he said, pointing at the clear glass. I was glad, at least, that he hadn't pointed at the glass of what was now becoming mud and said "*your* mind." By then the dirt was settling, the top part of the glass was somewhat clear again. "Watch," he instructed. And as we watched, the dirt in my glass settled slowly to the bottom so that the top two-thirds of the water grew translucent, then transparent. "Your mind," he said, pointing at the glass in front of me. He picked up his spoon. "When you—when some person—does things he shouldn't do. Watch." He put the spoon in the glass and stirred energetically again, took the spoon out, sat back with a look of complete satisfaction on his face. "Then you can't see."

"When someone does what bad things?"

"Kill person. Kill animal for no reason. Drugs. Anger. Eat too much . . . like that."

"Kill someone and eat too much in the same category?"

He laughed as if at himself and pointed at me. "Smart." Everything I said on that morning seemed to greatly amuse him. "Killing someone means more dirt. Glass filled with dirt for killing someone. Little bit of dirt for eating too much."

"I see. That's today's lesson."

"Yes. It is good lesson. If you want to see the life as it is in a true way, then you have to make the water very pure, very clean. This is not easy in this world but it is what you have to. You cannot upset the mind."

"Very good. Thank you for the lesson."

"You're welcome."

The waitress found the courage to make her approach at

last. Pouring the coffee, she could not keep her eyes from the muddy glass. "Scientific experiment," I told her. "My friend here is an expert in Burmese herbal medicine."

She smirked and left us.

Rinpoche was finishing his egg, lovingly mopping up the last of the yolk with an entire slice of toast. I took another bite of oatmeal, cool by now, gritty.

"Now you get to ask me one question," I said.

He laughed. "Very good, very good. Thank you." He ate the piece of toast in four big chomps, took another sip of tea to wash it all down, looked at the back of his strong hands as if pondering their design, then said, "My question is this: What did you do last night in the room?"

"Talked to my wife. Wrote a letter to my daughter."

"Your daughter is very nice. I saw her picture in your sister's house."

"Wonderful. Smart. And we have a wonderful son, too."

"Very good," he said. "Very good practice. The best practice."

"Practice? Practice for what?"

"Dying," he said, as if it were obvious. "Family love is the best practice for dying. For understanding that you are part of something big, not just your one separate body. This is why you are such a good man."

"My children are something more than mere practice for my own dying," I said, just as the waitress made another pass.

"Yes, yes," Rinpoche said. "You love them very much. That is why you are ready now, because of that and other things."

I nodded, curtly, and looked away.

"Love makes the water in the glass clean," he went on.

"I suppose it does."

"Jesus said so."

"Did he? Interesting."

"I am finding, in this life, the places where all the religions are the same. What Jesus said. What Buddha said. The way the Jewish people live and the way Hindu people believe. Maybe now I will make a new religion that holds all of them and people will not kill each other so much because of what they believe God is."

"Excellent," I said, but it was just too much for me on that morning, I'm sorry to say. I felt that we'd made a scene, and was embarrassed by that, and I was not at peace with Rinpoche's lesson, his interest in my sister and our land, his theories about my kids, his plans for world peace. Most of the warm feeling I'd started the meal with had drained away. I could not meet Rinpoche's eyes. He fell silent, watching me, and for a time we sat there like that, as if we spoke utterly different languages and there was no longer any hope of translation. I put some bills on the table, stood up, and led my companion, the religion-maker, outside into the heat.

TWELVE

I drove away from the General Sutter Inn enveloped in a mood that might be compared to that of a teenager who is being forced, by her well-meaning parents, to clean her room, or to study, or to tutor her brother with his Spanish, when all she wants is to be driven to the mall and to walk the gleaming corridors with her coterie of friends, staring through windows at the latest style of jeans and talking about boys. A righteous frustration, it might be called. A bit of anger sprinkled on top. And yet, inside the frustration and anger lies the reluctant sense that there might be something healthy involved in the parental militancy, something unfair about her pouting.

But, of course, it was not quite like that. I am an adult, and so, in my case, it was simply that I have a particular dislike of arrogance in all its forms, and Rinpoche's presumed superiority nagged at me like the e-mail of an obnoxious author, presuming the world would always sit in waiting at his door because he'd published one good book. At the same time, I have to say that there was some quality to Rinpoche that made him almost impossible to dislike. Just at the point where you thought he was locked up in his own little world of "wife wessons" (his mispronunciations followed no regular pattern), he'd talk about your children as if they were his nieces and nephews. Just at the point where you thought he was challenging your way of living, he'd call you a good man. Just at the point where you knew he was taking himself too seriously, he'd break out in joyous laughter at something he had said or done.

Still, as we put my bag in the trunk of the car, and his at his feet (an old prison reflex, I thought, because he never let the bag out of his sight), I felt knocked slightly off my ordinary balance. It did not help matters that a yellow ticket had been slipped beneath the wiper, and that Rinpoche wanted a detailed explanation of what it signified and why I was upset. Ten dollars to the town of Lititz. Cecelia would have called it a bad omen.

Following directions we'd gotten from the kind clerk at the General Sutter, we headed north for a few miles on 501 then turned off onto State 322. More farms here. A small orchard stretched out in front of one of them, maybe thirty trees in all, and I saw what I assumed to be a husband and wife there, picking fruit on ladders in the sun. They were working on the same tree, and the woman was wearing, on that hot August morning, a long plain dress and a plain light blue bonnet to match, and it spawned in me a whole line of thought about the Amish and the Mennonites. The line of thought was affected, in part, by the fact that the farms we passed were exceptionally picturesque and seemed exceptionally well kept. Son, grandson, and great-grandson of farmers, I knew how much work was involved in keeping a farm, even keeping it poorly. But to have land that looked like this—manicured and fertile at once—and to have whitewashed barns with straight walls, and stone and clapboard houses with neat roofs, and graded driveways, and gleaming windows—it meant laboring from morning till night, fifty-two weeks a year.

A surprising thought came to me: *These people know how to live.* Not *They know how to farm,* but *They know how to live.* I imagined a life for the man on the ladder and the woman with the bonnet—who I assumed were Mennonites. I imagined a life for the Amish folk passing in the night in their horse-drawn carriage, their children staring out the carriage's small back window at a world they would never have access to. My kids grew up with vacation trips to France, California, Cape Cod, afternoons at a friend's back-yard pool, laptops, cell phones, nice-looking clothes, the luxury of a movie now and again, a night at the mall, football and soccer seasons, an enormous variety of foods—a kind of freedom to go places and do and have things that the children of this bonneted woman and her husband would never know. If the couple was Amish, not Mennonite, then the difference would be even more extreme: Their kids would live in a house without electricity, on a piece of land tilled without machinery. They would marry in their teens and adhere to a social code that made the Pilgrims seem like punk rockers. It was one thing to live that way in Switzerland three hundred years ago—where the idea had started—but in America in the twenty-first century? Here, now, the list of things they sacrificed would be as long as Route 501. And what kind of return would there be on that? What could possibly be worth such a monumental sacrifice? Would it earn them minds as clear as drinking water completely free of sidewalk grit? After they died, would there be a special place reserved for them above the clouds, God smiling on them with a special affection, all the things they'd given up presented to them tenfold? Was that the way it worked? And, if so, what would be reserved for ordinary good folks like Jeannie and me and Natasha and Anthony, people who'd given up nothing, but who'd done little harm and a fair amount of good in our years on earth? Was it all just a game, the winners being those who could give up the most? Or were the people who gave up things only well-intended fools and nothing more? And why was it that, among my circle of coworkers and friends, arguably some of the most sophisticated and intelligent people on the planet, these questions were never even approached in casual conversation? Not once, in twenty years! Because it was simply assumed that the idea of a life governed by religion was for the unsophisticated and unintelligent? An opiate? Because they thought God was just a comforting lie? Because such questions were simply too personal?

I looked across at Rinpoche and thought about asking him his opinion on the subject, or at least starting up a conversation about it. But something blocked me. I could feel this something as if it were a thin wall between my lungs and mouth, the bricks narrow but sturdy and neatly set, the mortar hardened by years of the same pattern of thinking and living. It was just pride, perhaps. But I have never been good at finding the line where pride ends and dignity begins, and so I held to my silence.

After a couple more miles of those exquisite farmhouses and fields—and a fairly uncomfortable silence in the front seat—the landscape changed. Now there were only woods on either side of the road, steep wooded hills and narrow valleys. Along the highway we saw a dead fox, a dead possum, a dead raccoon, and Rinpoche muttered prayers over their rotting carcasses as if they were the bodies of lost sons. And then we descended and the land opened wide to right and left and the farms seemed to my eye to have a slightly different character, not quite as rich, this soil, not quite so sturdily built or well maintained, these barns and houses. There were electric wires and cars and personal billboards in front yards. WALK HONESTLY, one of them advised. And on a silo, FOR HERE WE HAVE NO CONFLICT / BUT WAIT FOR THE ONE TO COME.

No teenagers in that house, I guessed.

And then, as we neared the town I had picked out for our day's excursion, the landscape changed again, and in place of the farms there were clusters of what can only be called mansions, five- and six- and seven-thousand square foot homes with vinyl siding and partial fieldstone fronts, all of them nearly identical and squeezed close to each other on treeless lots.

Soon we began to see signs saying HERSHEY ATTRACTIONS, and I followed them. The road swept us around the center of the city and out to a dubious wonderland of parking lots, amusement rides, stadiums or concert halls of some sort, and hoards of sugar-loving, roller-coaster-riding tourists. At some point on the previous day, looking at my Rand McNally, I'd started to get a bit excited about showing my great country to the Rinpoche from Russia. It was what Cecelia had asked me to do. But even if she hadn't asked, it was the kind of thing I would have wanted to do anyway, because I have a tremendous fascination with the United States of America, the grand, swirling variousness of it, the way it siphons off the ambitious, the poor, and the abused from so many other nations, the ability we seem to have to be noble and heroic at the same time as we are being arrogant and stupid. I love my country. But I love it the way you love a wife of many years: not because you have some sentimental notion of her perfection, but because you know her thoroughly, from the courage of the maternity room bed to the pettiness of her morning moods; from seeing her sit for weeks by her dying mother's bedside, to watching her worry about which shoes to wear to a cocktail party given by a person she does not like. You know she has the capacity to get up at five in the morning and make you pancakes before you set off on a particularly arduous business trip, and you know she also has the capacity to say things, in the heat of an argument, that she should not say, to sneak the last piece of chocolate cake, to lose track of time and keep the rest of the family waiting for an hour, at the beach, on a burning hot afternoon. You know everything from what flavor of lip gloss she likes to what books she would bring with her to the proverbial desert island and what she believes the meaning of life to be. And then, always, there is a part of her you do not know.

It was like that with America and me. Though I was not an eager student of her past, I was a thoroughly engaged and captivated student of her present. I liked to read about what was happening in Utah or Mississippi or along the coast of southern California. When driving, I liked to listen to talk shows all across the political and religious spectrum. Much as I hated being away from Jeannie and the kids, I derived a profound pleasure from going to a booksellers' conference in some part of the country I had never seen, walking the streets of St. Louis or Seattle and just watching how people lived, seeing what they ate, hearing how the language of Shakespeare, Fitzgerald, and Woolf sounded in their mouths. I wanted to show some of this to Rinpoche in the way that you want to show, to a first-time guest, the new addition you've built on your home, get his opinion on the woodwork, the layout of the rooms, the color and design of the bathroom tiles, even if you know that his opinion will be coated in a mandatory politeness.

With Rinpoche, however, I knew nothing of the kind. If anything, I suspected that, being the ascetic, spiritual type, he'd be put off by the Hershey Attractions of this world, the roller coasters, the exhausted masses driving thousands of miles to see something their friends had seen, and then coming away vaguely dissatisfied. I loved it all, the bowling alleys and grungy greasy spoons, the grit and fluff, the Disney. That, to me, was the stuff and fiber of American life. It was Our Reality, and I had a somewhat perverse urge to hold Rinpoche's face to it and see if his high ideals could survive it. To prove myself right—or wrong—about something I could not even articulate.

We followed a long line of cars into the Attractions Zone, as it is called, and I looked for something that would give my passenger a taste of this particular American pie without absorbing half a day's worth of driving time. I settled on a place called the Chocolate Factory. We drove down a long entranceway. We found a parking space. We walked across the burning tar and toward a glass entrance in a sea of curious humanity and then we were encapsulated in something so clean, orderly, and purely American—the uniformed security people, the information-desk woman with her nametag and Xeroxed maps, the sound of a recorded tour echoing off the ceiling—that every particle of it might have been painted in red, white, and blue. And, of course, right there in easy reach was the merchandise area.

We opted for the fifteen-minute tour and climbed a clogged, zigzagging, carpeted walkway with the story of Milton S. Hershey, in words and pictures, on the walls. I decided that, rather than play tour guide, I'd wait for Rinpoche to ask questions. He did not. Staying close beside me in the sweaty crowd, he studied the old photographs and the tablets on which Hershey's story was sketched out. Milton was the son of Mennonite farmers, and after leaving that life he'd tried twice to start candy businesses, in Baltimore and New York, and twice failed. He'd returned home to Pennsylvania and tried again, and soon presided over an empire of sugar treats that stretched like ten million sticky fingers across the globe. Married but unable to have children, Hershey and his bride started a school for orphan boys, which eventually admitted girls, and which eventually became a school for the underprivileged, abused, and abandoned. At the time of the chocolatier's death in 1945, the school was on the receiving end of his entire fortune.

What better place for the money to end up, I thought. All the profits from all those Kisses and Almond Joy bars going to pay for kids whose parents had not been able, or willing, to bring them up.

I did not know how much Rinpoche understood. The tablets were small, a few pages of text at most, and with the crowds, we had ample time to read them. But he said nothing; his ordinarily expressive face betrayed no emotion.

The walkway swooped down toward two neatly coiffed college-age kids in uniform who guided us across a moving carpeted floor and into what might have passed for old-fashioned roller-coaster cars, clunky-looking wooden carriages with seats fore and aft. Rinpoche and I had a car to ourselves and sat side by side amid the cacophony of happy voices and stentorian recordings. Now he had an enormous smile on his face. Let the show begin!

The car swiveled and slid along through a kind of funhouse of chocolate-making, replete with singing cloth cows, screens and voices providing facts about the cocoa plant, tanks of swirling chocolate soup, and conveyor belts on which thousands of naked chocolate kisses hurried past as if anxious to find their silver coats and their place on a shelf in Bangkok or Bangalore. It was a bit like a living Food Network segment, because as we glided along we were sprinkled with facts—250,000 gallons of milk a day, 60 million kisses a day, the butterfat removed at one point in the process and then put back into the mix at another—and carried along through the rich and wonderful aroma of cooking chocolate. At the end of the ride we passed a camera mounted on the wall and were instructed to smile. We did so. And then, after we'd climbed out of the contraption and negotiated the moving floor, we were offered the opportunity to purchase these glimpses of our happy selves. To this day in my workroom at home there is a photo on the wall that shows yours truly with a man in a maroon robe who looks as pleased and excited as any child in any candy store.

And, oh, the candy store! From the photo desk we marched downstairs into a sugar addict's paradise, every imaginable chocolate confection from chocolate-chip cookies to dark chocolate, 150 different variations on the sugar vehicle dreamed up by Hershey engineers. The squeals of children spun in the air around us, the pressing of cash register buttons sang an anthem of profit. I did not hold back. A package of ROLO for Natasha, a bag of Mr. Goodbar for Jeannie, Almond Joy for Anthony, and a healthy supply of dark chocolate for myself. Rinpoche was admiring the photograph of us and saying, "How fast! How could it happen so fast?" but seemed less than tempted by the shelves of delights.

Nevertheless, I bought a bag of Kisses and pressed them into his hands, telling him, or trying to tell him, that this, all this—the gold of the ROLO wrapper, the blue and crinkled white of Almond Joy, the little twirl of tissue erupting from the Kiss's peak—was like the snap of firecrackers on Fourth of July, or football games on Thanksgiving—an essential Americana, a kind of national flag of my childhood. I wanted to ask him if he carried in his mind similar images from the early years in Skovorodino. Yak butter biscuits, maybe. Or cheap framed portraits of Lenin on the schoolroom wall. Or those fun days of setting kopecks on the rails and waiting for the Trans-Siberian Express to come along at dawn and mash them thin.

But I didn't.

After leaving the shop, we joined a river of humanity making its way at tidal speed toward a sea of windshields and SUV bumpers glinting in the hot day. A parade of fossil-fuel burners crept toward the exit. Eventually we were on the road again, at last free of the mob. After passing one farmer's field with a sign that said EVERYONE SHALL GIVE ACCOUNT OF HIMSELF TO GOD (*How do you know? I wanted to shout out the window as we passed. How is it that you claim to know?*), we saw the entrance for Interstate 76 West, curled down the ramp, and pointed the nose of the car toward the startling abundance of the American heartland.

It had been an odd morning—the dirt in my glass at breakfast, the immaculate shelves of sweets—and though I tried once or twice to start a conversation, I soon learned that Rinpoche was not in a talkative mood. To fill the empty air I turned on the radio and found a talk show where the host was waxing eloquent about the need for torturing people. I looked across at Rinpoche to gauge his response, but, though his eyes were open, he did not seem to be listening.

West of Hershey, the state of Pennsylvania turned more severe: rough rock faces, a slag pile, steep hillsides, deep valleys, unpeopled it seemed, and not as pretty as what we had passed through earlier in the day. At one point, having returned from his daydreaming, Rinpoche wrestled with the plastic Kisses bag, and when he finally managed to tear it open, the candies sprayed out onto his lap and the floor. He laughed with his face turned up, then tidied up the silvery mess. He saved one kiss and contemplated it for quite a good while, turning it this way and that, tapping the ribbon of tissue from side to side, finally tugging on it, peeling away the foil, and then spending another good while tracing a fingertip along the smooth sides of the hard little brown dollop. At last, as if he'd prayed sufficiently over this miniature feast, he popped it into his mouth. I could see him rolling it comically from one side to the other, the eyebrows up, eyes wide, lips and cheeks working. Another minute or so of rolling and sucking and making humming noises, and he swallowed it with a loud gulp, choked and coughed for a moment, laughed at himself, and then reached across and slapped me so hard on the top of my right thigh that the car sped up.

"Kees! Kees!" he sang, and when I glanced over at him, my sister's holy man was giving an enthusiastic thumbs-up.

THIRTEEN

Our driving schedule was dictated, in large measure, by our need for food. Or *my* need for food, I should say, since Rinpoche ate very little. He even managed the impressive feat of keeping the bag of Kisses open on his lap for more than an hour without ever reaching in for a second helping. It was now midafternoon and, despite three big chunks of dark chocolate, I was in need of that international tradition known as lunch. The prospect both excited and worried me. According to the map, the closest city of any size was Altoona, not exactly famous as a culinary capital, but even that was too far off the interstate to warrant a side trip. We wouldn't starve, I knew that. Every so often we saw billboards advertising food options at the upcoming exit, but these options were a murderous fare of salt, fat, sugar, and chemicals. It is true that I am particular about food. It is my profession, after all, and in my years at Stanley and Byrnes I've been lucky enough to have been exposed to some of the world's greatest chefs and a small library of fascinating books on growing, preparing, and consuming food. I guess it's as natural for me to be particular about what I eat as it is for a clothing store salesperson to be picky about neckties or dresses, or a mechanic to be fussy about the make of car he drives. Another part of my pickiness comes from the fact that I grew up on boiled potatoes and beef, sauerkraut and overcooked pork, in an environment where, if your mom put an ounce of lemon rind into the apple pie, she risked being shunned for the next decade of Volunteer Fire Department Auxiliary lunches. On our one visit to a Chinese restaurant in Bismarck, my parents ordered . . . hamburgers. And so, leaving North Dakota meant, for me, opening a door onto a seemingly limitless world of culinary experience.

To balance my love of eating, I exercise a few times a week, walking a three-mile loop with Jeannie on Sunday mornings, killing half hours on the elliptical trainer at the health club a few blocks from where I work. On the road, though, there wasn't much opportunity for exercise. Nor was there the distraction of professional and domestic chores to keep the mind away from the table. You opened the car window for a second and hunger poured in, or, if not hunger, then at least the notion of eating.

But I worried about the options there, south of Altoona and north of nowhere. Cheap, fried-to-death burgers and carbonated sugar water, a slice of wilted lettuce in the name of fiber. No, no. Not for me. And not the American cuisine I wanted for the Rinpoche, either.

At the toll booth I asked about good restaurant options thereabouts—no chains or fast food, please. The woman squinted at me as if I were a communist, then, with some reluctance, directed us to a nearby steakhouse. But I was suspicious from the first. I sensed that the place belonged to a friend of hers, or her husband's cousin, that there might be kickbacks involved. We found the steakhouse without trouble and went in. The menu posted on the bulletin board in the foyer was as unimaginative as a bad watercolor in a dentist's waiting room. I ushered Rinpoche out before the hostess made her approach. He was, understandably enough, perplexed. "Can't do it," I said to him in the parking lot. "I'll explain later. We'll just shoot down into the nearest town and see if we can't scare up something a little more interesting."

According to my map, the nearest town was Bedford, Pennsylvania. We followed a two-lane highway south and soon found it. On the left as we entered the town there stood a large Armed Forces Recruiting Center. On the right, in the windows of what looked to be a turn-of-the-century office building, JESUS IS LORD was spelled out in large capital letters, with a five-foot-tall poster of a bearded white man from a place where, to the best of my understanding, the men had been, in his day, bearded and brown. Now, I saw these things—the recruiting center and the window-sized letters—almost at the same time, but I do not mean to imply that anyone in Bedford had wanted me to do so, had tried to link Jesus and the military. But there was a linkage all the same, in the America through which I was driving my new friend. It made me uneasy. As I said, I consider myself a Christian, which means I hold Jesus up as a sort of model for how to behave in the world. My father and two uncles were decorated Korean War veterans, and a cousin lost a leg in Vietnam—so I have a pretty good appreciation of and respect for military people and their families. But something was going on in my America in those years, some wave of bad thinking that even a middle-of-the-road type like me could not be at peace with. My colleagues at Stanley and Byrnes were guilty of ignoring religion, maybe, or dismissing it. But there was another segment of Americans that used it—via a process I did not fully understand—as a springboard to a kind of aggressive ethnocentrism, as if there was obviously a God, and the God was obviously Jesus and only Jesus, and he obviously loved the United States of America more than any other nation in his millions of universes, and therefore any military action we took must have Jesus' blessing. I could not swallow this, and had become sensitized to it, and so, driving into Bedford, it was on my mind.

We pulled to the curb in front of a tourist information office. Inside, there was a poster advertising a talk by a man whose life had been altered forever when he discovered levitation, so obviously Bedford had more levels to it than I'd at first supposed. My hopes for a decent meal lifted. The couple who presided over the tourist office were as friendly as could be. The woman came out from behind the counter and listened to my short rant about chains and healthy food, smiled at Rinpoche, who was standing peacefully off to one side like an embarrassed spouse, and directed us to a place called the Green Harvest, only a couple of blocks away.

It was hot. I was ravenous by that late hour, tired from the road, big questions about war and love spinning through my thoughts.

The Green Harvest was a find. Wonderfully original oil paintings on the walls, an airy, sunny atmosphere, a screen curtain keeping out the bugs and letting in whatever cool air was to be found in that part of Pennsylvania on that afternoon. Behind the counter, a young woman presided, and it turned out that this was her first day on the job; she was backed up by a slightly older woman who seemed to own the place. Iced coffee? Yes! Hummus plate? Yes again! Hummus plate with olive tapenade, some kind of cream-cheesy pineapple spread, an excellent fresh salad, even whole wheat pita bread! A magnificent surprise! A find! Rinpoche and I sat at a thickly shellacked table, the young woman served us identical meals, and all was well.

All was well, that is, until, from beneath the mysterious folds of his garment (he had two maroon robes, I later learned; he'd wash one in the sink or tub every other day and hang it up in his room to dry) Rinpoche drew a piece of white paper. We were finished with the hummus by this point, and savoring the last sips of the excellent strong coffee, and he pulled out the sheet of typing paper, folded to one-fourth its size, and handed it across to me without comment.

"What's this?"

He shrugged, smiled shyly. I thought it might be a poem he'd scratched out the night before, thanking me for my generosity in agreeing to take him west, or for helping him in his struggles to master English. Or perhaps it was some calligraphy for me to frame and put up on my wall when I got home. As I unfolded it, another possibility came to mind: it might be some Vedantic or Kabbalistic prayer he'd ask me to memorize. Let the proselytizing begin.

But no, worse than that, it was a letter from my sister, Cecelia, typed carefully on her old electric Olivetti. I have saved it and shall quote it here in full:

Dear Beloved Brother,

You are the kindest soul to do what you are doing, and to put up with a sister like me. I hope the trip isn't going too bad, and that you haven't been cursing me. (Remember, I'm a psychic, I'll know!)

I don't know if Rinpoche has mentioned this to you yet or not, gosh I hope so, but he has several speaking engagements that we've set up on the route of your trip. He gets hundreds of requests for these things. He gets paid for some of them. Alot!!! [*sic*] And others he does for free.

Well, the first one is in Youngstown, Ohio, a free one set up by some nice people who are trying to change the atmosphere of that town. And then the second is at Notre Dame University, set up by a Catholic priest who is running a conference on crossing religious borders or something like that. Then there is one event in Madison, and that's it—unless I get some other offers while you are on the road.

I hope this isn't only another big imposition from your sister who loves you! His schedule is below. A big big kiss and a big hug from me to you, brother, and also to the great spirit in your car.

Love,

Seese

P.S. It was actually the Youngstown reading that gave me the idea to ask you to take Rinpoche. Otherwise, how could he have done it!

I read the letter four times. I read the schedule printed below it five times, and I checked the date and time of Rinpoche's first talk against that day's date on my watch and cell phone. Six times. And then looked up at my traveling pal, who was smiling at me and nodding his head in small beats.

"Rinpoche," I said, and my voice was calm. Almost calm. "The first one of your talks is in Youngstown, Ohio. Tonight. Six o'clock tonight. Youngstown, Ohio, is a long way from here, and it's after four. We'll barely make it if we go nonstop."

"Nonstop," he said, smiling, nodding.

"You couldn't have told me about this earlier?"

"Forgot," he said, and for the first time I really thought he was lying. Not evading, not skirting, not giving a sketchy account, not engaging in some Zen trickery. Lying.

I had an image of the chocolate churners, big steel arms raking back and forth through a pool of cocoa soup, back and forth, churning, cooking, in my stomach, except that the hummus and the olive tapenade and the delicious iced coffee and the salad with ranch on the side were also in the mix.

"You have a ways to go to get the hang of American politeness," I said, and I said it calmly. There was an edge, but it was a calm edge.

"Thank you," he said.

"I mean, you could have at least let me know."

"Thank you for helping me with American politeness. I appreciate. We should go now. We're late."

I just looked at him. The waitress whose first day it was came to the table and asked if everything was all right, and Rinpoche put his hand on her arm in a gesture of quintessential politeness and told her he had found the food to be better than a kiss. He had a nice one in his pocket, could he give it to her?

He meant a Hershey's Kiss, of course, but the young woman had no way of knowing that. She could not keep herself from a slight recoil, a glance over her shoulder at the boss. Was this what she'd signed on for, part of the summer job? Old bald guys in red dresses coming on to her?

She disengaged herself with some graciousness. I made it up to her by leaving a 30-percent tip.

On the highway again I brought the car up to eighty and set the cruise control. Maybe the state police would stop us, and keep us there, stewing, by the side of the road for an hour, so we'd be late for the talk. Write out a ticket for two hundred dollars, which I would send to my sister with a polite note festooned with exclamation points.

Dear Seese,

My wonderful sister, I hope it isn't any inconvenience for you to pay this ticket that we got speeding to Youngstown to make Rinpoche's talk on time! It actually came to me to send it to you as we were sitting by the side of the interstate in the heat with the trooper leaning in the window! This should be the last ticket we get, but if there are others, I'll send them, too. Hope you don't mind!!!

Love,
your brother, Otto

FOURTEEN

By the time we had crossed into Ohio and were within twenty miles or so of Youngstown, it was clear that, even though we had been going well over the speed limit for ninety minutes, we were going to be more than acceptably late for Rinpoche's speaking engagement. This bothered me about fifty times more than it apparently bothered him.

I am the kind of person who believes that punctuality is one of the columns on which a peaceful world is set. What happens to a person like me when he's running late—or when someone else is running late—is that anxiety builds up like water in a clogged sink. Six inches from the lip of the sink. Four inches! An inch! By the time we turned off the interstate south of Youngstown and began making our way north on State Route 7, the water was overflowing. "It's ten minutes past six," I said, as we crawled along that cluttered road in a frustrating stop-and-go. And I could hear and feel that my words were being squeezed up through a tight stomach, through a tight mouth, through half a lifetime of being kept waiting by my beloved and not very punctual wife. "According to this map, we have something like eleven miles to go on this road, and it's all traffic lights. No one is answering the phone at the place where you're supposed to speak. We'll never make it."

Rinpoche shrugged. By that point I was building up a small dossier of evidence to support my theory that, Rinpoche or not, spiritual master or not, foreigner or not, he was quite an inconsiderate man. I was even beginning to wonder, again, if he was using Cecelia simply to get the land and the house from her, if he was more clever than he seemed, sly, duplicitous, one of these guys who came to America, surveyed the scene, grasped instinctively the depth of our spiritual desperation and naïveté, shaved his head and bought a couple of robes, and started calling himself a guru. I had a whole string of such thoughts going.

"It doesn't bother you to keep your fans waiting?"

He didn't answer, engaged, apparently, in studying the urban landscape of Youngstown, Ohio.

And what a landscape! I've seen a good piece of America, and traveled, at various points in my life, to Europe, Asia, and Brazil. Twice a month during the school year I volunteer at a literacy center in a very poor part of the Bronx. So it's not like I'm a stranger to urban decay, or urban blight, or the slums, or whatever other word we like to paste over the raw wound of poverty. But even given all that, the part of Youngstown we saw surprised me. Once we crossed the city line we drove through block after block of boarded-up houses and businesses. Rusted signs, iron grates over the doors of dead nightclubs and bombed-out bars; side streets where it seemed that all the homes on a block—and fairly nice-looking homes they had been at one time—showed hollowed-out upstairs windows. Bottles and litter strewn about, abandoned bicycle frames, old wet shoes, a knapsack in the gutter. Rinpoche could not stop looking at it, and neither could I.

According to our directions, his talk was to be in a downtown building, right on the main drag. We found it without trouble, but things were hardly better there. You could see that it had been a healthy downtown at one time, with elegant stone buildings and a strip of greenery, mid-street. But now there were clusters of dead and boarded-up businesses, as if some kind of awful epidemic had raced through this part of Ohio—the symptoms being charred siding, torn roofs, gaping windows, sagging and untended porches—and it had reached even the brick and stone downtown and taken a toll there as well.

When, after passing through all this sorrow, we arrived at the address on Cecelia's letter, there was a beautiful woman about my age standing at the curb in front of an empty parking space, in a posture of apprehensiveness. She was tall and thin, with large, perfectly wonderful eyes, an ankle-length dress, and brown braids that reached almost to her waist. We stepped out of the car and she immediately went up to Rinpoche and bowed, so that the two braids, color of nutmeg and shining as if they'd been polished, fell down on either side of her ears. She straightened up and smiled a smile that reminded me of my sister, and then she took Rinpoche's hand in both of hers and said how worried she'd been that something terrible had happened. Saying this, she looked at me and tried to hold the smile in place, but I could see that she blamed me for the fact that her teacher was twenty-one minutes late. I said nothing.

She ushered us inside—not an auditorium as I'd expected

but a space that must have been, at one time, in a finer day, a hardware or small grocery store, or a place that sold undergarments to the wives of the iron factory executives before everything went, well, to China. It was empty now, this space, except for eight or ten rows of gray folding chairs set up on a cracked linoleum floor. It was not an overflow crowd: about half the chairs stood empty. There was a somewhat grander-looking chair up front, raised slightly above the floor on a two-foot-high homemade stage—someone had put a fair amount of work into this production. Next to the chair stood a table, and on the table stood a mug and a small teapot. The assembled audience, eighteen or twenty in all, was an all-American mix of white, black, Asian, and Hispanic. Two elderly couples sat in the front row. Behind them, a smattering of what might have been college students, or recent graduates. Then a pair of Yuppies, to use a word I dislike. And then, strangely, two rows of people with the unmistakable mark of poverty on them—cheap clothing, no smiles, an aspect to their posture and expressions that spoke of a hardness, a kind of pain, a weight they lugged through the days. Everyone knows this mark. We can pretend not to for the sake of some false politeness, but everyone knows what it looks like to be poor. And anyone with half a brain can tell the truly poor from the faux poor, the artists in their torn jeans, the college kids in dirty T-shirts. These were the actual poor.

The braided woman who had met us at the curb stood at the front and made sure Rinpoche was comfortably seated in his chair, and then she gave a brief introduction that she'd obviously memorized. "We're honored tonight to have with us the great spiritual master of our time." Standing just inside the door, I found that I was surprised. The woman's speech sounded like hyperbole to me—though, of course, hyperbole was part and parcel of the introductions of dozens of authors I'd edited. I knew the Rinpoche better than she did, after all, and while he was growing on me a bit, and while he was a perfectly nice fellow if you overlooked his impoliteness as a symptom of cultural misunderstanding, I thought that "the great spiritual master of our time" somehow didn't quite fit with a guy who, not so long ago, had nearly choked to death in ecstasy over a Hershey's Kiss; who didn't get to his appointments on time and didn't seem to care; who lied to a stranger while he was being given a ride halfway across the country; and who, perhaps, was conning a naive and good-hearted woman, herself one of the actual poor, out of her rightful inheritance.

When the braided beauty finished, there was polite applause and some fidgeting in the rows furthest from the impromptu stage. I had not sat down, was not intending to stay for the talk. Even when I saw how unenticing the options were for an hour of strolling in downtown Youngstown near dusk, I didn't feel like staying. I don't know why. When Rinpoche bowed and said he would begin with a ten-minute meditation session, I slipped out the door as unobtrusively as I could manage, went and sat in the car, and studied the map for the best route west. For all I knew they would be holding hands and chanting in there, or sitting cross-legged on the cracked linoleum and envisioning beams of energy winding up around their spinal columns like glorious serpents. Not my style.

There in the car, with the doors locked, I passed an odd hour and a half. Once I finished looking at the map—which took all of about four minutes—there was not much besides the radio to occupy my thoughts, and I'd had enough radio listening for that day. I did not have a book or newspaper to read and was, I admit, afraid of taking a walk. It was a fear I encountered every week on my trip to the Bronx, even though the tutoring sessions were early on Saturday morning and even though, in the course of six years, nothing untoward, nothing of any significance, at least, had ever happened to me there. Still, I was a well-off white man in a poor black neighborhood, my social standing stamped on my car, clothes, face, and posture as clearly as any mark of poverty, and I felt disliked, guilty, and vulnerable. Something like that feeling had attached itself to me almost as soon as we crossed the Youngstown line on Route 7. I don't know if anyone else has ever felt this; I assume so. It is not something we talk about at work, where, for the most part, the editors and marketing executives—black, white, Asian, Hispanic, and otherwise—live in Manhattan, or in the commuter-train suburbs to the north, and the shipping and receiving people, the cleaning people, the assistants, and security staff, for the most part, live in certain parts of Queens, or the Bronx, or Harlem, where the life of the street is a very different life. I realize I am on treacherous ground here. I realize I am generalizing and tiptoeing along the edge of the territory into which we never venture very far in the American national conversation: The fact that there are whole neighborhoods into which cabdrivers refuse to take a fare; that there are people among us who live in circumstances we are ashamed to talk about, children who live that way; the fact that there are huge quadrants of our cities where people like me—and not just white people like me—simply do not go, places we do not see, do not want to think about as we are sipping our designer martinis in swanky downtown bistros where dinner for two costs what these other Americans earn in a week. We excuse it by citing the laws of capital, or by telling ourselves we work harder, or that it is social inequality that serves as the motivation for our national wealth. All good logic, maybe. Still, I've always been ill at ease with the vast distance between my life and the lives of other Americans.

I sat there in the car and felt as though I were coated in a kind of thin layer of slime I couldn't name. How hard would it have been to stand quietly in the back of the room and daydream, I asked myself. How awful would it have been to hold some stranger's hand for a few minutes and chant? What, exactly, is it that you do not want to hear? And this after giving Rinpoche lectures on American politeness.

Still, I sat there. A ragged and intermittent parade of people went past, all of them men, most of them walking slowly, shuffling almost, almost prowling, looking around as if expecting some opportunity to present itself. Daylight slipped away, and then these solitary specters passed from the darkness of the abandoned part of the block, through the light pouring out of the storefront, and back into darkness again. A few of them peered into the storefront. One even stood there for a while and watched, his face close to the glass. No one went in.

When I thought most of the talk must be over, and when the voice haranguing me for my lack of courage and decency grew persistent, I unlocked the door of the car and quietly made my way back into the lecture hall. Rinpoche had finished the formal part of his presentation and was answering questions.

An elderly black man in the first row raised his hand and said, "A little earlier on you said something I never read in any of your books. You said, if I heard right, that you can only change about half what happens to you anyway. Or something like that. Could you expand on that for a minute, Rinpoche?"

Rinpoche took a sip of his tea and nodded half a dozen times, but all the while he was looking directly at the man with a sort of intimacy — if that is the correct word — that startled me. I had not seen that kind of a look from him in our time together. And when he started to speak I realized it was in a voice I had not heard from him either. His command of the language was stronger, but it was something more than that, a certain force, a charisma I had missed. To the questioner he said, "Yes, yes. It is this way: I say half but I don't mean half, exactly. But some, let us say some, okay, yes? *Some* of what you learn in this life you will learn anyway, if you do nothing, if you are not 'spiritual', if you don't meditate, if you don't care about these things. Even if you murder a person you will learn some of what you have to learn. You will suffer from the guilt of doing that, even if you pretend to yourself that you are not guilty. In the deep of you, you will suffer. If you eat too much you will suffer, and you will learn. If you put into your body drugs, you will suffer and you will learn. If you use your sex in a way that harms someone, you will suffer and you will learn.

"But also the good, you see, also the pleasant. You will love the person you are married to, or your lover, and you will learn. You will love your children, your work, your pleasures in this life, your friends, your hobbies, your sports, your sewing, or your gardening. Each of these things acts as teacher for you. You see this? Each of these things is kind of guru, too, you see? Illness, failure, sorrow, success. Yes. It is not necessary to have any particular spiritual path in this life in order to learn from these things. It is not essential to have guru, to eat this way or not eat this way, to talk this way or any way. Some part of this education of the spirit in you will happen to you in this life. That is so for every soul."

Rinpoche paused for a breath, then went on, "But if you care about your mind, you see, if you don't stir up the energies of your mind by hurting some person or some animal, by using your body in a way that is not healthy way, if you meditate, or say prayers, if you have some quiet in your life instead of keeping all the time busy with noise and errands, if you cultivate good thoughts and feelings where you can instead of bad thoughts and feelings, if you do this then you will . . . what is the word?" Rinpoche glanced back at me as if I might offer it. "*Compound.* Is that right? Yes? You will *compound* your learning. Or *increase,* maybe *increase* is the word in your language. Do you see? It does not mean you are better person than the one who does not do these things. Do not think that. Thinking that will not help you. It means you will squeeze all the juice from this life that there is to squeeze. You will not waste your time here, that you have been given, that is so precious we do not realize until the moment we die. You will not waste this precious time, do you see? This is the best kind of being an environmentalist person. This is not misusing the gifts of this world. Do you see?"

There was reverential nodding all around the small plain room. Everyone saw, apparently. I felt a twist in my intestines that reminded me of the terrible and mysterious stomachaches I'd suffered from as a boy, squirming on the couch in the old farmhouse while my mother heated dishtowels and placed them on my belly. Rinpoche sat back after his long, impassioned answer and calmly sipped his tea. From

the assembled worshippers there was a kind of glow ema-
nating out toward him. And from the back of the room,
utterly without knowing I would do so, I said, rather more
loudly than I intended, and perhaps less kindly: "And what
purpose does all the learning serve?"

Several people turned to look at me, and I cannot say
that I felt the same glow of friendliness in their faces. I had
not raised my hand and waited for the teacher to call on
me, maybe that was the reason.

Rinpoche smiled. "Yes my friend. Very good. He is my
friend," he said, speaking to the crowd now. "His sister,
too. Very good friend. Yes. What is the purpose, my friend?
The purpose . . ." he paused several beats and tapped on his
right thigh with the fingers of his right hand. "The purpose
is life itself. This is what life is for, this education of the
spirit inside you. Everyone says this. Every teacher in all
religions. Life is for to learn, to make a progress, to make a
movement toward—"

"But if you don't compound your learning, it can still be
a good life, can't it?"

There was a murmuring among the faithful. I felt foolish, angry at myself, but could not seem to simply stand
there quietly, nodding and adoring.

"Yes, of course. As I said—"

"Then what would be the motivation for someone to do
the extra work? I mean, life is hard enough, isn't it? And
what if you're happy with things the way they are? Why
change yourself? Why meditate, or pray, or go to church,
or try to alter your thoughts from bad to good if you are
happy and decent without doing those things?"

"Ah," Rinpoche said, and I thought I had him. That was

the phrase that trotted through my mind. *I have him*. He was a nice enough guy, the Rinpoche, probably harmless, but a bit of a phony, I could see that now. The people in the room were the type of people who needed to have someone to call "guru," the way Cecelia did. It made them feel better about the raw adventure that was actual life. It was a kind of safety blanket, one that people like me did not require.

Rinpoche sipped his tea calmly and deliberately, then looked up and sent a beaming smile my way. But I was not about to be disarmed so easily. "You are a good man," he said, fixing the same direct look on me that he had fixed on the previous questioner. It made me strangely angry to hear him say that. I was being worked, manipulated. "You do not hurt people," he went on. "You love very much your wife and your children and your work and your sister. I know this about you. Yes, you eat a little too much, my friend." He laughed, and by this point the entire crowd had turned around to look at me and they were laughing, too, and—this was exceedingly strange and done out of embarrassment perhaps—I found myself putting my hands on my belly as if it were much bigger than it is and shaking it. "Yes, a little too much," he went on, "but you do good instead of bad. Tell me, why do you?"

A silence fell over the room. I thought at first, I hoped, that the question had been a rhetorical one, but as the silence persisted I realized the Rinpoche wanted an answer. The problem was that no answer came to mind. When the silence became difficult to bear I said, "I'm not sure."

"Not sure," Rinpoche said. "Not sure is all right." He laughed, and the crowd laughed with him. "But when you understand why a person like you chooses the good and not the bad, then you will have your answer to your own question. Think about it now, my friend. Tomorrow I will ask you again and you will answer me, yes?"

"Sure, okay," I said, but something was burning in me, giving off an acrid, invisible smoke. My thoughts spun in little spiteful circles, so much so that I did not really pay attention to the last two questions and refused to let myself eat any of the not-too-unhealthy snacks that were offered on a side table when the whole performance was finished. I loitered at the edges of the room like a boy at a high school dance, not wanting to be rejected, or rejected again, or laughed at, feeling somehow superior in his shame and embarrassment and envy and shyness. Furious, superior, and ashamed. It was not like me at all.

FIFTEEN

By the time the final question had been asked and answered, I was anxious to get back on the road, and angry without knowing why. As if to spite me, Rinpoche lingered for a long time after he'd finished his presentation, talking to people near the refreshment table, chuckling, answering questions, putting a hand on shoulders, accepting reverent bows. After a while, I went out and stood on the sidewalk in the cooler night air, just stood there and looked out at the devastation. What had happened here? How could something like this happen in America?

I was hungry. And I felt vaguely as if I had sinned—and believe me, that is not a term I use. With their empty interiors and dirty plywood eyes, the fine old stone buildings on Youngstown's main drag somehow seemed to mirror me: nice enough on the outside, architecturally pleasing and structurally sound, but with some hollowed out places where the rats ran. Why should I have such a feeling? I was not a bad man. Standing there, waiting for the festivities within to come to their smiling conclusion, I carried on an argument with myself. I had done nothing wrong. On the contrary, with only the mildest of fuss I'd rearranged my schedule to get Rinpoche to his talk more or less on time in spite of the fact that he'd been holding on to the letter from my sister for almost two days and had not thought to mention it. True, I had pressed him a little with my questioning, but wasn't that what the whole thing had been for? What was I supposed to do, just go along with it like the rest of the people in the room? Accept everything he said because he was supposed to be a spiritual master? That wasn't my style, not at all. My style was to ask, to analyze, to question, to weigh all sides of an issue, and if something didn't seem like the real truth, to squeeze it until the lie showed itself plainly. Where was the sin in that? I had been respectful, and more honest, it seemed to me, than the other people in the room. Rinpoche hadn't seemed put off.

Yet something nagged at me, some vague guilt. *Compounding* that, was Rinpoche's reply. Why *did* a person like me do the right thing and not the wrong thing? Fear of jail, divorce, eternal punishment? A belief in heaven? Just in case there turned out to be an afterlife? And for the people who did more "spiritual work" in their lives, who not only didn't cheat on their spouse or steal from their company or condemn citizens to torture, but spent hours each week in prayer—for those people were there different, higher, more pleasurable levels of paradise?

I sensed I was missing part of the argument. What about those who didn't do good, for instance, why was that? And what about the issue of death? What was the point of it? How did one prepare for it? I was worrying these questions like a loose button on a shirt when, at last, Rinpoche and a small bevy of admirers spilled out the door.

There must have been two dozen thank-yous there on the Youngstown sidewalk, at least as many bows. The smiles, the shining faces, the childlike adoration—why was it all so irritating?

Finally, Rinpoche said his last good-byes to the beautiful woman in braids, made his last bow, and we were backing out of the parking space and heading out of town on 422, a road I'd found while stewing in the car. Rinpoche had gone totally quiet. This, in my experience, was unusual for someone who'd just given a talk. Part of my editing duties included chaperoning authors to readings when they were in town, and almost always after the more successful ones had read, or talked, after they had basked in the admiration of a group of people for an hour or two, there was a certain postpresentation ebullience, a high. It took them an hour, or a few hours, or in certain particularly egotistical cases, several days to realize they actually belonged to the level of ordinary existence, despite the fact that people periodically asked for their autograph or requested their opinion on this or that cooking technique.

Perhaps I sound jealous here. I am not. I've never really had much urge to write a book, or go on tour, to sign my name on something I've written, to have a cooking show on television and be invited to start a restaurant in SoHo. It's just that, over the years, I've noticed the effect an hour or two of public admiration has on a person, and I saw none of that in Rinpoche.

He sat staring out the window at the wreckage, dark now, of the city. In time, we passed some factories—enormous, hulking wrecks where things had once been made, where people had once worked and earned a paycheck and spent that money in Youngstown's shops and stores. Only one of these factories had lights on and seemed to be still in use. Soon we were out of Youngstown and riding through a commercial strip where things were still more or less intact.

"Hungry?" I asked my companion.

"Not so much."

"Even after all that work?"

"Not so much work, talking."

We went along for a few moments in silence, and I could feel the irrational guilt still clinging to me like a smell. There seemed to be a kind of accusation in the guru's silence. Possibly I had insulted or embarrassed him. "Listen," I said, "I'm sorry. I'm afraid I was a bit off-base back there. I came on like an attack dog at the back of the room."

"Attack dog?"

"You know, my questions were pointed. They were a bit strong. Not appropriate. I should have just kept my mouth shut."

He was shaking his head in the dark car, looking out at the street and not at me. "No," he said, sincerely enough. "Your question was the best question, Otto."

It was the first time I'd heard him use my name, and it sounded odd on his lips. "You're just saying that to flatter me, to make it so I don't feel bad."

"I do not flatter," he said, in a tone rather more forceful than anything I'd heard him use with me. "Your questions were precisely very good. Your answer to me," he chuckled and touched my arm lightly, "not so very good."

"I'll give it some thought. You said I had until tomorrow."

"Yes. Tomorrow breakfast."

"Well, I'm hungry. Do you mind if we stop? We have a ways to go if you're going to make your lecture in South

Bend tomorrow night. I thought we could have dinner and then drive another hour, so we wouldn't be in such a rush in the morning."

"Not to rush," he said.

"Never?"

"Never rush."

"Right. How about Italian?"

We were passing a place with a sign out front, ALBERI-NI'S, and the parking lot was full, always a good omen. We parked, went in, and were seated in a sort of greenhouse facing the street. The hostess who seated us, I noticed, had beautiful breasts. It was hard not to notice because she was wearing a very tight, low-cut top that seemed designed to display them. Such was my state of mind that I found myself wondering if my noticing them, my small spasm of almost reflexive lustful thoughts—that I knew would lead nowhere, and didn't want to lead anywhere—I wondered if somehow these thoughts would hurt, however slightly, my progress along the spiritual path. If there were such a path. If it led anywhere I wanted to go. Look too long at a hostess's breasts and you end up in a slightly less wonderful level of heaven than you otherwise would have.

This, I said to myself, is where all the mumbo jumbo leads. You'll start worrying about every little thing—Is the coffee free trade? The chicken free range? Should you stop looking at attractive women? Recycle the wrapper of your chewing gum? Should you go home, lock yourself in your room, and pray, as the Bible instructs, without ceasing?

From this mental morass, the busboy rescued me with a basket of fresh rolls. The waiter was attentive, the rolls warm, the menu extensive, the breasts world-class. Rinpoche had spring water with lemon. I ordered a salad to start, then the duck in a port wine sauce over risotto, and a glass of Pinot Noir. I looked once again at the hostess's chest, in a sort of childhood stubbornness—no one was going to deny me this small, harmless, aesthetic pleasure—then made myself stop. I missed Jeannie.

The salad arrived with a fine, light, somewhat sweet house Italian dressing that went beautifully with the warmed rolls. The Pinot was just tart enough, plummy and rich. The duck was perfectly cooked, if soaked in a somewhat heavy port wine sauce. But the risotto beneath it, touched with amaretto, fit the dish perfectly. It was awkward, eating in front of someone who was not, and I tried, by apologizing again, by offering him a taste of everything, to work my way free of the guilt that clung to me like a rain-soaked shirt on a humid summer afternoon.

"You are a good man," Rinpoche said, as if we had been talking about that all along.

"Please, stop with the good man remarks. It sounds false to me, to be perfectly honest. It sounds like flattery."

"Ah," he said. "You do not believe you are a good man."

"Of course I do. I don't hurt people. I'm a good father, I know that. A good husband. A decent citizen. We do our share of charitable work, Jeannie and I. We give generously to various causes."

"But something," he said, and he waved both hands around in a way that he had, as if he were playing an imaginary, upside-down keyboard with floating fingers, the notes not quite beside each other, the piano itself not quite level. "Something missing."

"No, not really. No."

"Afraid of some things maybe."

"Not particularly. I don't like flying, I'll say that."

"Of death," he said. "Of losing everything."

"I'm not a death worshipper. I don't think about it. Life is for the living. What comes with death, well, we can't control that." He was nodding and smiling in a way that profoundly irritated me. "Let's leave it," I said. "Let's change the subject." I took another forkful of the risotto, another sip of the wine, and went on the offensive. "You never had any urge to have children?"

"Of course," he said. "Sad to me I do not have children yet. I love children very much."

"Why don't you then? Vow of celibacy?"

"Sellacy?"

"Celibacy. No sex."

"Sex, sex," he said, too loudly. There were people at the nearby tables, and they all heard. It seemed we could not eat a meal in a restaurant without attracting stares. "Rinpoches like sex!"

"Really?"

"Of course. Like women very much!"

"But they would cloud the glass, right?"

He laughed at this as if I were making a joke, and tilted his chin up at the ceiling showing the sinews of his thick neck. "No, no. Women could not cloud the glass, Otto! Rinpoches would have a spiritual wife."

"Spiritual wife? No sex, you mean."

He laughed again. "A little bit sex. Not too much. Nothing too much for Rinpoches. Food, sex, sleep, business, giving talks, happiness, sadness . . . not too much."

"But why? Why only a little sex? Why not a lot of sex if there's nothing wrong with it?"

"You feel inside when you do something right or when you do something wrong, yes?"

"Yes, sure."

"I feel inside when I have the right balance."

"And too much sex would throw you off?"

"Too much anything. Too much meditating, too much talk."

At this, I fell quiet. I considered the idea of ordering another glass of wine, wanted to—I had no balance problem there—but, thinking of the drive ahead, I refrained. I did savor a piece of tiramisu and a decaffeinated coffee. And then one of the waitstaff was kind enough to suggest a town where we might stop, an hour or so up the road, and a nice inn he thought would be suitable for us. I asked him to pass on my compliments to the chef, on the meal I'd just eaten, mentioned that I edited food books, and the waiter told this to the chef and owner, a man named Richard Alberini. Richard came out for a brief chat, shaking Rinpoche's hand exactly as if he fit the profile of the typical Tuesday-night customer.

Youngstown, Alberini said, had not so long ago been a thriving place with a strong middle class and a wonderful cultural life. And then the jobs had been shipped elsewhere and the city had begun a long slide from which it still had not recovered. Business in his place had declined, he said, but they still drew customers from all over that part of Ohio. I wondered, talking to him, if the people who had moved the jobs, whoever those people had actually been, ever came back to the city now, even just to drive through. And I wondered, when they did, what kind of feelings they might have, how they would explain the situation to themselves in a way that left them feeling like good people. Profit fed the life we lived, I knew that, and saw the necessity of it. But those people had made a god of profit, it seemed to me, and according to the rules of their religion, if it was profitable to close the factory and ship the jobs overseas, then it was morally right. In order to keep from feeling guilty, they had, I supposed, devised all sorts of ways of thinking about what they did and didn't do, all sorts of clever rationalizations. It occurred to me that, in a different arena, I might be in the habit of doing the same thing.

SIXTEEN

The place where we ended up staying on that warm night—the Inn of Chagrin Falls in Chagrin Falls, Ohio—was a few miles off Route 422, down a dark road, tucked behind a town we caught only a glimpse of as we drove in. The young woman at the reception desk was perfectly welcoming, though Rinpoche flinched when he heard the price of our rooms. I resolved to find a way to take the financial burden of my luxurious tastes off his shoulders. He lingered in the first-floor library, perusing the shelves of books there. We said good night, exchanged bows; I went off to my well-heeled solitude.

Whereas, at the General Sutter Inn, which had zero pretensions and simply was what it was, the creaky floors, patched ceilings, and undersized TV didn't matter to me in the slightest, the small imperfections at Chagrin Falls nagged like an aching tooth. Unfair, of course, because it really was a very comfortable place, the room cozy and cool, the pillows abundant. But chief among the small imperfections was some kind of air conditioner or air filter machine located outside my window. It hummed loudly until midnight. I was sitting at the glass-topped desk trying to compose a letter to my son, and then, a while later, lying in bed trying to make sense of the day, wondering about internal balance and sex and food, and all the while this loud hum cut into my thoughts like a talkative neighbor on a long flight.

Just a sour mood, probably. I wrote to Anthony and tried to keep my irritation out of the letter.

Dear Anthony,

How goes it? How is practice going?

I thought that, while I am on the road, I'd take the chance to write real letters to Natasha and to you, something I don't think I've ever done in my life. I know you don't want me gushing about things like this, certainly not in person, but I just want to tell you that you and your sister mean everything to me, to your mother and to me. In these years, when the two of you are really growing into your own lives, there are going to be some tensions between you, and between you and your parents. This can be hard, but it is natural. During these moments I just want you to remember that I love you and your sister more than anything on earth, that Mom and I are proud of you both, and that you've made us happy from the moment you were born.

Aunt Seese sort of tricked me into making the drive with her spiritual teacher, I guess you could call him. Decent guy, a little weird, quiet most of the time. I find myself resistant to the type of things Aunt Seese is into, as you probably know. They are not bad things, they are just not for me. (I'd like to hear your thoughts on this when I get home.) So her friend—he's called Rinpoche, which is a term of respect, as I understand it, *RIN-po-shay*—and I have had a few moments of our own, if you know what I mean. Maybe you'll meet him someday.

Anyway, I hope school and football are going well, and I look forward to seeing you again and telling you about the trip in a couple more weeks and hearing about what's been going on with you.

Love,
Dad

I thought of calling Jeannie, but we tried to keep to an every-other-night calling routine when I was on the road, and it was late by then in any case, so I just washed up, turned out the lights, and crawled into bed. Outside the window the air machine hummed and swooshed and I felt the same small irritation inside me that I'd felt listening to Rinpoche give his talk. Or a cousin of that feeling, at least. I suppose it came simply from the world not being exactly the way I wanted it to be—my sister's quirks, my own moods and failings, the harsh laws of business, the sting of seeing real poverty and knowing I was not doing much to fix it. It occurred to me that, if I made it to old age, the chances were good that these kinds of irritations would assume a larger role in my life. The teeth, the joints, the prostate, the hardened bad habits, the behavior of those less experienced—wouldn't the world disappoint me more and more often and more painfully? The sense pleasures would fade (not food, I hoped), as would the feeling of doing something productive.

I drifted toward sleep, telling myself it had just been a tiring, long day, that this was just pessimism, not objectivity, that there would likely be compensatory pleasures—invisible to me now—to balance out future troubles. Grandchildren, perhaps. A deeper peace of mind. Tomorrow we'd make a beeline for Rinpoche's next talk, in South Bend, and maybe I'd buy a football jersey to send to Anthony, or have a nice meal, or a good talk with my wife. There was still so much to be grateful for, so much to look forward to, so much happiness waiting there in the bright American future, shelves and shelves of sugary treats in colorful wrapping.

SEVENTEEN

Next morning, after Rinpoche and I had made our way quietly through an unsurprising morning meal, we decided to take a walk through the village as a way of preparing for the long day of driving.

Chagrin Falls was a quaint little place of clothing stores with cute dresses in the windows and coffee shops where trim young women sat at their morning leisure, a Mercedes, Volvo, or BMW at the curb, sporting a Protect Wildlife license plate. There was a Smith Barney office. A local theater group advertising its next production. The Little Monogram Shop.

It was a certain kind of place, a certain piece of Americana, a certain rung on the socioeconomic ladder. And it was all familiar to me, of course, Bronxville's Ohio cousin. I wondered how my own parents had thought about my life when they visited: the lawn neatly mowed by someone else, the expensive and probably too large house, the downtown with its pricey shops, and the well-dressed neighbors cleaning up the defecation of their thoroughbred poodles. It is easier, I suppose, to be born into comfort than climb up into it. And it is easy to judge people by the externals, the make of a car, the type of shops in the place where they live.

Chagrin Falls had a river running through it, with a waterfall just beneath a bridge not far from the coffee shop. Beyond the bridge the town had built a wooden stairway that zigzagged down the steep bank and ended at a platform where one could see the waterfall close up. Rinpoche and I went down there and stood looking at the brown river as it cascaded over stone, spray flinging itself into the air, the rushing, swirling water having about it the sense of some forceful inevitability, some draw from below, perhaps even some greater plan.

We watched for a while, then climbed back up and stood on the bridge, with the roar of the falls in front of us, and behind us the hum of Chagrin Falls's minor-league traffic. "You did not ask to me your question at breakfast," he said.

"And I haven't yet answered the one you posed last night."

"Not a test," he said.

"I know. But intellectually, I guess, a challenge."

He flexed the impressive muscles of his face, without looking at me. My sense was that he didn't notice the "upscale" nature of the town, didn't care, didn't concern himself with such things in much the same way that he hadn't seemed to notice the hostess's breasts at Alberini's the night before. Maybe he just hadn't been in America long enough to read the code, to understand what a Mercedes meant that a Chevrolet did not, to know what kinds of people went through the door of a Smith Barney office and what kinds of people did not, to judge a person by the size of her wedding ring or the cost of her purse, or her license-plate frame or bumper sticker, or the newspaper she chose to read. Once you'd become aware of such things, whether they sent positive or negative signals running through you, how did you erase them from the thought process and see the world as it was, without labels and judgments?

"I want to do both," I said, over the noise of the cascading water. "I want to try to answer the question you asked me last night, and I want to ask a question that seems connected to it."

"Good," he said. "Okay."

"As to why one does good instead of doing bad, I guess it must have to do, partly, with wanting to be liked, to be approved of by the people around you. We all crave social acceptance, don't we? So I think it just makes life easier for most of us to act that way. And there might be a natural conscience at work—in good people, at least. Even in bad people in their better moments, there might be some inherent sense of right and wrong that urges them toward kindness or honesty or nonviolence, at least most of the time. Strange that there's such a wide spectrum—from Hitler to Gandhi—but I suppose you'll find that spectrum in nature to some extent, in weather extremes, in the sizes and shapes of animals within a species. Even some dogs seem so much kinder than others."

"Yes, yes," Rinpoche said, but he wasn't looking at me and did not seem particularly interested in what I was saying. I'd given the question a good deal of thought and formulated what I believed to be a logical answer, but my careful theories didn't appear to impress him in the slightest. I might have been reciting the table of chemical elements, or describing the rules of bridge.

"And I guess what I was after, in my questions last night, was very personal. I have an excellent life, a superb life. I've worked hard to achieve that kind of success, so has Jeannie, but, still, we've been so lucky. I mean, we have everything, really. We've had our problems: Jeannie's parents divorced when she was young. Her mom was alcoholic, abusive to her and not very nice to me. I had a horrible weird illness for six or seven years—insomnia, strange pains all day, not being able to eat much. No doctor could figure it out. But compared to almost everyone on earth, we are very, very lucky and we know it and we appreciate it and we try hard to be good parents, good citizens of the community. Maybe you think I'm not as kind to my sister as I might be, but we invite her over all the time, we've helped her financially. I try to be patient with her odd habits and kooky. . . . Anyway, the point is, it seems to me that we're already living the way we should live, and when I hear you talk, it sounds like you're challenging that, saying we have to do better. It's intrusive, for one thing, especially in the arena of religion, which, in this society at least, is a very personal matter. For another, why would we want to change what seems already almost perfect?"

Rinpoche was silent.

I was silent, too. A full minute, at least. I hadn't expected to give such a long answer, to ask such a long question, and, as his silence stretched on, it began to seem that he was provoking me.

"Have you seen any person die?" he said at last.

"My parents died recently. An uncle and three aunts. Two friends from high school and one from college. The man who takes care of, took care of, our lawn."

He turned and looked at me, "You saw them die?"

"Not at the moment of death, no. I feel the loss just as strongly, though, in my parents' case especially."

"I have seen many people die," he said.

"In the prison camp?"

He shook his head. "Only two there. Other places. In Europe we have one retreat center where main practice is caring for those persons who are dying."

"I didn't know that. That's fine work."

"Some people die calm and others not so calm. Why is that?"

"The lottery of life. Different personality types, different amounts of pain. Some people drive calmly, and eat calmly, are calm with their children. Others are not."

"Yes, yes, but this is dying. This is losing everything— body, family, house, job, cars, food, every pleasure, everything. How can they be calm in the moment of that?"

"That's not something we spend a lot of time dwelling on in this society," I said, in a tone I hoped would lighten the moment. "We are a people of business, an active, industrious people. We believe life is for the enjoying. We know we'll die, but dwelling on that seems like so much negativity, speaking for most Americans I know."

"Ah. And speaking for you?"

"The same."

"Ah."

"You're the only person I know who can *ah* in a way that feels like a judgment."

He laughed at that, put his hand on my back and tapped lightly three times. "My friend," he said. "My good friend . . . what means *industrious*?"

"Busy. Hardworking. We get a lot done. We work hard and accomplish things—invent medicines, build businesses, make books, roads, missiles to send into outer space, and so on. Are you calling all that into question? Are you saying it is bad?"

"Good!" he exclaimed. "Very good! Missiles into space! As far as the moon! Past the moon, yes?"

"Yes, sure."

He was laughing and chuckling and then suddenly he stopped and said, "And then you die!" and chuckled some more. I had the fleeting thought then that he was really not quite sane.

"Right. I've thought about that. And after you die, what then?"

"Don't know," he said.

"But you've lived many lives, died many times. Isn't that what you believe?"

"Of course," he said. "Obvious to me that we live many times."

"So . . . what happens afterward?"

"Don't remember," he said, and he laughed uproariously, the sound mingling with the loud swish and splash below us.

"Now you're playing games."

"No games. Tell me, why are you so good if you don't know what will happen after, if you don't believe that to be good will make a difference in what kind of thing happens in you after you die?"

"I do what makes me feel good, I suppose. If it made me feel bad I wouldn't do it."

"Exactly!" he said, as if I'd just solved the Hodge conjecture—or some other baffling mathematical puzzle. "What makes you move through this life is going for pleasure, yes? And going away from pain?"

"Of course. I've had that thought many times. It's hardly surprising."

"But I can show you a pleasure to make all the other pleasures be too temporary. Be like the little breaths that some person takes from a cigarette. Little bit of pleasures, *puff.* Little bit of *puffs* then throw away."

"Everything is temporary."

"Yes, yes. Everything but this."

"How do you know? How can you say that if you just told me you don't know what happens after we die?"

"Because people explained it to me. My father. Other great teachers. And I believed them because of the way they were, the way they lived and especially the way they died. In their faces, in their, how do you say—being?—in their being, in the way they act in certain times, you could feel that they knew."

"And I should believe you for the same reason."

"Of course yes, my friend," he said. "Of course."

Show me, then, I almost said. Show me a thing like that, a pleasure to count on when the other pleasures fade, when the candle goes out. But I couldn't. To begin with, what educated person would actually believe such an offer? It sounded too much like the advertisements on talk radio—for investments in gold, arthritis creams, jobs that paid you eight thousand dollars a month for working a few hours a day at home. Second, I could not open myself to him at that point, to anyone in that way. I paid him back then for his silences and just studied the water rushing below us, muddied in its frenzy: powerful, constant, even beautiful, but carrying a good load of dirt as it went along its preordained route.

But then I could not hold the silence, could not harden

myself to him in that way. I don't know why. There was nothing for me to lose, maybe that was it. Another few days and I'd never see him again. So I said, "I suppose I believe in heaven."

"Me also," he said. And then, "I have felt that heaven, here, before dying. As real as you feel the sound of this water. I can show you."

"Without drugs?" I said, and the Rinpoche took it as I'd intended, and laughed with his head thrown back, and then put his powerful arms around me and hugged me hard, laughing like a child, like a crazy person, there on the bridge over Chagrin Falls, with the women in the coffee shop looking out the window at us. I imagined them there with their decaf cappuccinos, smirking, superior, knowing flakiness when they saw it. Just like I did.

EIGHTEEN

Back at the inn, Rinpoche announced that, instead of getting on the road right away, he needed to do two hours of meditation. It was, apparently, a special day, the anniversary of the reincarnation of some great teacher in his lineage, Maha-Baba-somebody-ji or other, the name escapes me. He told me this with the oversized, overjoyed smile on his face and a hand on my arm, and he asked, when he was done passing along the happy news, if I would like to "sit" with him. He said he'd already set up a small shrine in his room, with pillows to sit on, and there were even enough pillows for me because it was such a nice hotel, the nicest one he'd ever stayed in, with an abundance of pillows and such a large, spotlessly clean shower.

"I'll pass," I said.

"Pass what?"

"I'll say no this time."

"I can show you the big happiness we talked about. You can believe it for yourself."

"Thanks but no. Just knock on my door when you're ready. Two hours, right?"

He held up two thick fingers, smiled, nodded, but there was something different in the way he looked at me then. The best way I can describe it is to say that there was a certain amount of authority in his eyes, and that it was perfectly mixed with what seemed to be a genuine affection. To that point in the trip—even as recently as half an hour earlier—it had been easy for me to write him off as a fool, a clown, a chuckling man, but now it was as if he'd turned some internal dial—turned it only slightly—and one layer of foolishness had magically evaporated. He still chuckled and worked the muscles of his face the way a bodybuilder works his triceps, and he still behaved, at moments, like a boy of nine. But I was beginning to think of that as his "act," and I was beginning, just beginning, to sense something beneath the act, some force, some disguised dignity that I had not been aware of during the first two days of our journey.

None of that made it any easier for me to hear about the anniversary, the lineage, the two hours of meditation. None of it made me as sure of his version of heaven and earth as he seemed to be; none of it tempted me to "sit." No, instead of sitting, I reclined. On my white wicker bed, with the TV on, the radio clock in plain view, and two of the inn's fine pillows under the back of my head. In that meditative position I spent the two hours making a study of American morning television.

God save us. God help us. If there is, in fact, a God, and if he does, in fact, pay attention to the way we live our lives (I had been brought up to believe that was the case, and still believe it, on some level), then what must he—or she, or it—think of modern life as presented on these shows? Three people are sitting on a couch with the host in front of them, egging them on. The people are, from left to right: The wife whose husband divorced her for the babysitter. The husband. The babysitter. The dialogue consists of things like this: "Well, if you'd known how to treat a man instead of being a bitch all the time, maybe he would have stayed!" And the audience is cheering and booing like Romans in the Colosseum, bursting into applause at the nastiest remarks, the host pressing his trio, inciting them, the babysitter and wife eventually, in a climax of toxic absurdity, reaching across the husband and batting at each other's arms. The husband tries to stop them from fighting, then abandons his post and flees; the women are allowed serious martial contact for five or ten seconds before the security men rush in and hold them apart. All this is done with a kind of trumped-up sincerity as if it is utterly real, and perhaps it is. Maybe there are, in fact, people so eager to see themselves on a television screen—the modern altar—that they will parade their own miseries in front of other people, also eager to be part of the drama, who will sit in an audience and cheer and shout. All this for the benefit of millions of other industrious Americans who have no greater purpose on a weekday morning than to sit and watch. And all that for the ultimate benefit of the shareholders of the companies that make furniture polish, or diapers, or laundry soap, or pills to make you sleep better or have more energy or less anxiety, and who pay to keep the whole tawdry ball rolling: new shows developed, new hosts discovered and trained, new guests—miserable, desperate, fairly nice-looking—dredged up from all corners of this great land.

Fine, let them spend their time that way, it doesn't matter to me except as a barometer of the country I love and worry over. Lying there, I remembered my father and mother taking us to a sun festival at one of the many Native American reservations in North Dakota—the Associated Tribes, I think it was, in New Town. After we'd watched the dancing and singing and were on the way home in our car, my dad remarked upon how far we'd advanced since the days when the land was ruled by Indian tribes. There were farms now, he said, where once there'd been only buffalo. Farms with telephones and TVs, tractors, airplanes, medicines . . . whereas in those old days there had been nothing. You worked from morning till night, you hunted and fished and sewed and cooked, sang and danced a few times a year, made war, made peace. "Look at us now," he said, sweeping his hand out near the windshield at a stretch of heartland. "Look at all this."

"Look at us now," I said to the TV. But I spent two hours of my life watching it.

When two hours and five minutes had passed, Rinpoche knocked on the door. I had half a mind to ask him to watch the next show with me, but it was checkout time, and we had miles to cover that day. So I got up and turned off the set, feeling strangely depleted of energy, of urge, of hope. I looked around the room to make sure there was nothing I had left behind—T-shirt, pair of socks, reading glasses . . . desire to show Rinpoche as much as I could of my beloved America.

NINETEEN

I was, naturally enough, already thinking about lunch. As an antidote to the TV poison, I wanted an especially good meal. Something different. We were checking out of the Inn of Chagrin Falls, and the kind woman there was printing out our receipts and asking if we'd had a good night, and I had the foresight to ask her if I could see the Cleveland Yellow Pages. I knew we were only about an hour from that city, and I suspected the culinary options there would be richer than whatever awaited us on the flat roads to the west. I was rewarded for the trials of the morning by page after page of restaurant listings—Chinese, Italian, Greek, Japanese, seafood, meat-and-potato. Hungarian was the most exotic of the bunch, so I copied down the number of a Hungarian place called Little Budapest, thanked the hostess, then waited until we'd put our things in the car and had our seatbelts on before making the call.

The phone was answered by a woman who spoke very softly and with a thick accent. I was sitting behind the inn, next to the air conditioner that had been bothering me the night before, with Rinpoche sitting calmly nearby, and a small device pressed up to my ear, and I was shouting into the device, trying to get directions to Little Budapest. The poor soul on the other end of the line must have thought I'd called purposely to torment her. "Four twenty-two, west," she said, though it sounded more like *"Firr-dvindy-do, yss."*

"West?" I yelled.

"Firr dvindy do, vss."

I should mention, at this point, that I am somewhat directionally challenged. Jeannie and the kids will attest to this with abundant examples of Dad walking into a building to use the men's room and then not being able to find his way out again, of Dad returning to his B&B fairly late at night, alone, forgetting which of the second-floor doors leads to his room, and walking into the bedroom of the host family's fifteen-year-old daughter (who is, to Dad's enduring gratefulness, fully clothed).

So, to be on the safe side, I took notes as I grilled the Hungarian woman. Rinpoche was sitting patiently beside me, his postmeditative calm acting as a reverse image of my posttelevision agitation. "College Road exit off 422," I thought the woman said. I asked her to repeat it and she did, and I thought she said more or less the same thing. Then there was something about a road being closed, then another left, then something about what was possibly Columbia Road, a right there I was almost certain, and then Center Reach Road, though when I asked her to spell that, she said what sounded to me like "S-E-M," and so on. I would see the restaurant up there a quarter mile on the right or the left. I waited for her to add the classic phrase, "You can't miss it." But she did not.

So we started off. I made my way carefully through the

center of Chagrin Falls, tracing carefully by memory streets that looked rather different during the day than they had at night. Somehow I made a small mistake and ended up in a neighborhood of neat modest homes, where a man was mowing his lawn when he should have been inside watching to see who had scored a knockout in the third round, wife or sitter. I thought of stopping to ask him for assistance, but I did not want to look inept in front of Rinpoche—who, after all, was entrusting me with the task of getting him safely to North Dakota. I was anxious to be on the highway in any case, and I confess to sharing, with a hundred million other red-blooded American men, an aversion to asking directions. I was hungry, too. So I stumbled on, soon found 480, or at least a recognizable road that led to 480, and we put Chagrin Falls behind us.

There is little to recommend the route that leads from Chagrin Falls into Cleveland along 480 and 422. Trees, a smattering of warehouses and low-lying office buildings, a few patches of bog. But then, truth be told, 480 and 422 do not actually lead into Cleveland, at least not if you follow them as we followed them. I became aware of this fact when, as we were speeding along, I happened to look to the right, and there I saw the skyline of Cleveland shining in the sunlight, probably fifteen miles away. We were, unfortunately, not going in that direction. I began to suspect that there had been an important lapse in communication between me and the Hungarian woman. So I picked up the cell phone, dialed again, and this time a man answered. Gruff in the classic Eastern European fashion. No-nonsense. He sounded as if he had a complicated goulash to prepare, or hungry customers to seat, and should not be expected to waste time with people who couldn't follow simple directions. His accent was slightly less difficult to parse.

"You are gong all right," he said. "Jess keep gong."

"But I'm heading away from Cleveland, aren't I?"

"All right, all right, I said! Listen! Make sure you go leff after sementy-wan, that's all. The highway goes two ways, you go leff. Then Clock Road. Then Columbia—no you can't go that way, that road closed—then right, understan? Then leff and right on Center Reach and you'll find us there. You're gong fine."

And he abruptly hung up.

We went bravely on, the top of Cleveland's silvery skyline fading away beyond the curve of the earth. I began to entertain other options. There might be something decent off the interstate, or near the lake, some little gem of an All-American Ohio diner with fried chicken, baked beans, and coleslaw, a nice piece of homemade rhubarb pie for dessert, the best coffee within a hundred miles. Might be. No doubt there was, but the difficulty would lie in actually finding such a place. Friends at work had told me to take along a book we published, *Unknown and Wonderful Eateries,* which listed hundreds of roadside eateries from coast to coast, but I had declined. If they were in the book, they weren't unknown, were they, I said. I wanted to make my own discoveries.

I then saw a sign for Claque Road, next exit. And I decided that Claque was close enough to College and to Clock that it was worth taking one shot. Claque road led us—past a Road Closed detour—to Columbia Road. "We're all right," I said to Rinpoche, who was elsewhere. But no sooner were those words uttered than Columbia

Road shrank to a winding two-lane street through a district that was painfully residential. Not a 7-Eleven, not a gas station in sight, not a Hungarian restaurant anywhere. House after house, yard after yard, lawns and garages and bicycles in the drive, and then, at last, like a mirage, an intersection with commercial buildings on all four corners. A large restaurant there, to the right. Hungarian-looking. But no, as we drew closer I could see a real estate sign in the window. Restaurant for sale, all equipment included. Instead of cooking, they had spent their time giving directions, and the enterprise had failed, and word had gotten around.

How to navigate the intersection. Right? Leff? Straight? I pulled into a gas station across the way and went into the office. Mom was behind the desk, Pop sitting in a chair reading the comic strip page of the *Plain Dealer.*

Mom. *Hungarian* restaurant? In this neighborhood?

Pop. *(Shakes his head without looking up.)*

Visitor. Is there a Center Reach Road anywhere near here?

Mom. Center *Ridge* Road, but that's all residential down there. No restaurants there.

Visitor. Okay, thanks. You've lived here all your life, right, and no Hungarian restaurants anywhere?

Pop, *looking up from the* Plain Dealer. Try taking a right on Center Ridge and going down there a ways. There are a few restaurants there. Friendly's and so on.

Mom. *(Gives Pop a squint. He has contradicted her in front of a perfect stranger. Soon they will be on the couch, the visitor between, cameras on, the audience screaming, and the host firing questions like poison darts.* Everything was fine in our marriage until my husband heard from this man about some Hungarian restaurant and then he had to go and try it, and then the waitress there . . . *and so on.)*

Without much confidence, I ferried Rinpoche down Columbia to Center Ridge, all hope evaporating as we passed block after block of suburban quietude. This is the middle of the middle of America, I wanted to say to him, but it did not seem like the right moment. In the middle of the middle of America stood two churches. In front of the first, a sign read, IF YOU ARE TOO BUSY TO PRAY YOU ARE TOO BUSY. And in front of the second, WHEN ANGER ENTERS, WISDOM DEPARTS.

"How about when hunger enters?" I said aloud, and Rinpoche turned and gave me a quizzical look. We took a right on Center Ridge—there was, indeed, a Friendly's there, to the leff. Unfortunately, I had my mind wrapped around goulash, not clam strips and fries (much as I like Friendly's ice cream sodas). I pulled into the parking lot of an investment firm not far from Friendly's and dialed the restaurant's number one final time. Again the gruff chef. I told him where I was. He said, "Korter mile on leff. You can't miss."

And I said, "Okay, I hope I don't have to call you again," and we both laughed.

And there, tucked into a strip mall that bore the grand name of King James Plaza, was Little Budapest.

Unpromising.

Immediately inside the door we came upon a bulletin board, half a dozen pages posted there with snapshots and descriptions of houses for sale and some kind of a deal where you got two hundred dollars of food at Little Budapest if you helped in the selling of one of them. CNN giving the news of the day to an empty bar—soldiers crouching as they ran past the black skeletons of bombed cars. Relief maps of Hungary on the wall. The skin of a wild boar. And a dozen black plastic tables with windows looking out on Semter Reach Road.

Not promising.

Rinpoche and I took a window table and were handed menus by a blond waitress whose voice seemed familiar. We opened the menus to a great variety of offerings from the banks of the Danube, everything from Transylvanian Cabbage to Veal Paprikash to Breaded Goose Liver. This made me happy. Just seeing these things written on a page made me happy.

When the waitress returned, Rinpoche asked for some noodles and a salad. I had already eaten the free appetizer of sliced cucumbers in vinegar with a garnish of sour cream and paprika and it had not made a dent in my hunger. So I ordered and ate chicken crepes in a cream and chicken broth sauce, with diced chicken and diced red and green peppers in the filling, the crepe itself light and perfectly made. Delicious Hungarian coffee with chocolate in it and whipped cream on top. Then a huge portion of lamb stew and mashed potatoes. And then, to finish, an apricot- and walnut-stuffed palascinta, which turned out to be a thin pancake stuffed with apricot-walnut cream.

I was at peace, the sour film of daytime TV washed from the lenses of my inner eye, the belly full, the road ahead promising only good things.

Rinpoche was smiling at me and patting his midsection in a way that seemed gently sarcastic.

"I know, I know. But the breakfast at the inn just wasn't

enough for me, or not interesting enough. And it's almost one o'clock."

"Ah," he said.

"The judgmental ah."

He laughed.

"You have your meditation pleasure. I have my food pleasure."

He laughed again.

"Your meditation pleasure lasted two hours. My food pleasure was what, twenty minutes? See how much more ascetic I am?"

"Ascetic?"

"Giving things up. Living the lean life."

"Rinpoche could never give up his meditation."

"Ah," I said, and he laughed again.

"Rinpoche went three years without speaking. Two times."

"You're kidding."

He shook his big head and reached across with a finger to scoop up the last dollop of the apricot cream. "Retreat."

"Is that a tradition?"

He nodded. "Two years in prison eating kasha and bad bread and tea."

"What did they arrest you for?"

"For being the son of my father. My father was a great, great Rinpoche, famous everywhere for as far as you could travel on a horse. A great teacher, and so . . . to jail."

"Threatening to the powers that be," I said.

"But why?" He seemed sorrowful.

"Do you miss your dad?"

"Father, mother. Very sad. My mother died when I was in the prison."

"It's hard when you don't have a chance to say good-bye," I said. "My parents died in a car crash. In February. No good-byes there either."

"Yes, very hard," he said. "When we go outside I show you something."

I paid and thanked the waitress, stepped into the kitchen to get directions back to the highway from a heavy, happy man, and then found Rinpoche waiting on the sidewalk. He had been gardening again and held in one hand the kind of wide-bladed, lime-green grass that grows at the untended edges of sidewalks and lawns. He shook the dirt free, pulled out a half dozen of the longer strands, smoothed them, then twisted them into a flimsy green braid.

"Time," he said, holding up the braid to me. He indicated one end, then the other, "Maybe one thousand year." He touched the individual stalks of grass tenderly. "Souls. Spirits. You see? You, your father, your mother, sister, wife, children, you see? Your spirit is together with their spirits like this, tight against each other. That is why you were born into this wife together." He pulled one strand out and tossed it up into the sunlight. "Maybe one of these people, or two, not so close after this wife. But people you really love, spirits that are close to your spirit, you see? They tie around tight to you, wife after wife."

"*Life,*" I corrected him. "L."

He paid no attention. "You see them, you live with them, you meet them now as son or daughter, next as mother or father, next as friend, maybe sometime as enemy, you see? You go through time with them."

"A nice idea," I said. "Comforting."

And in response I received a hard look and felt the power in his eyes, in his being. It made me think of the power in the hands of a gentle-seeming karate master, and in fact, at that moment, Rinpoche did poke me fairly roughly in the center of the chest with one finger. He glared at me fiercely for a three-count, then smiled. But this time the smile was only a thin coating of velvet over stone. "You have the good life," he said harshly, emphasizing the *l*. "Easy life this time, Otto. Do not waste, okay?"

TWENTY

Well, I may not be open-minded about the illogical and inexplicable, as my sister claims, but I have long had a great curiosity about what we call "coincidence." You are thinking about a person you have not seen in years, and then, on that very day, the person calls; you dream of something, and that something happens the next afternoon. You are sitting in a bar in Manhattan with your young live-in girlfriend, broke and pretending not to be, without prospects, without patrons, your dream of life in the big city you love starting to fade, and just at that moment a man twice your age sits down nearby and orders a vodka martini, and you start talking to the man, and it turns out that he works as an editor for a well-respected publishing house in Manhattan, and they specialize in books about food, and you start to talk about how, in the city, even on a tight budget, you can eat pretty well, and you tell him you come from North Dakota, and the dining options in even four square blocks of Manhattan make you feel like you've died and gone to heaven, and the conversation goes on for an hour and at the end of it the man takes a business card out of his wallet, says he happens to have an editorial assistant job just coming open, and it doesn't pay much but the work isn't that rough, and there are some good books coming in, and interesting authors, and if a person is really sincerely enthusiastic about food, it can help, and there might be a future in the publishing business. And so on.

Mere chance? Or the hand of fate, or karma, sketching dormers and trellises into the architecture of some grand plan? I have always wondered.

On the way out of Cleveland (or, I should say, on the way out of the far western reaches of the suburbs of Cleveland) there were a couple of small moments like that. Minor coincidences, really. I'd noticed that Oberlin, Ohio, was more or less on our route. A coworker's daughter had gone to school there and liked it, and she sounded, from her mother's description, a lot like Natasha. In the interest of future considerations, I thought we should make the ten-mile detour.

So, with thunderclouds gathering in great purple knobs above and to the west of us, I took the Oberlin exit. Here's the first half of the coincidence: I happened, on this short drive from the interstate to Oberlin, to look up and see a street called Russian Road, on our right. And then, when we pulled into town past the green lawns of the college, we happened to park in front of a coffee shop called the Java Zone, and we decided to go in—Rinpoche for green tea, yours truly for iced coffee. It was quiet at that time of year, but you could imagine how, in the other three seasons, the tables would be occupied by students with their laptops and professors with their reading glasses and stacks of essays to grade. From what little we'd seen, the town looked to be a quintessential college town: quadrangles, classroom buildings, and a couple of commercial streets lined with small shops. Natasha would love such a place, I thought.

The woman who served our drinks in Java Zone (Rinpoche was treating) had a thick accent, and soon Rinpoche was rattling on with her in a language I took to be Russian. I sorted out a "*dah*" and a "*nyet*," remembered Russian Road. And then, as they went deeper into their conversation (the young woman seemed much taken with him), I wandered next door, where there was a combination department store and bookstore. In the spirituality section, on the middle shelf, just at eye-height, stood three thin volumes with the words VOLYA RINPOCHE on their spines. One was titled, *The Greatest Pleasure,* so I bought it, asked for a paper bag, and then, reason not clear to me, slipped it into the trunk of the car so the author would not see.

While I was waiting for Rinpoche to come back out of the Java Zone, I checked the map again and saw that Ohio Route 20 ran parallel to the interstate toward the Indiana border. There weren't any large towns along it. We wouldn't lose much time, taking that route, and I might be able to give Rinpoche a better sense of the American Midwest and give myself a respite from the highway madness.

He came out smiling, of course. When he was settling into the car he told me that the woman in the Java Zone had been from Irkutsk, which, in the scale of things, was not really all that far from Skovorodino—maybe two thousand miles—and she spoke what he called "clean Russian," whereas Russian was actually his second language, as she could tell by his accent.

"What is your first language?"

"Ortyk."

"Ortyk? Never heard of it."

"The Ortyk people are my people. Descended from Mongolians, and before that, Tibetans."

"Buddhists, then?"

"Not so much," he said. "They were, what do you say? Close off? Close off from main lineage of Buddha's teaching by big mountains there, and then by politics there, and they made their own lineage of teachers, and the teachers made their own way of thinking, their own practice, and so, now, to say Buddhists . . . not exactly right."

"And you are part of this lineage?"

"Small part."

"But you're famous. You have books out."

"I will give you one," he said.

"No, I wouldn't hear of it. I'll buy one."

"There is a bookstore right there," he said, pointing.

"No. I'll buy one in South Bend. I'm sure there will be stores there, too. Which one should I read first?"

"For an advanced soul like you," he said, "I think the best would be the one called *The Greatest Pleasure*."

TWENTY-ONE

Ohio 20 proved to be as flat as a Hungarian palascinta but interesting nonetheless. To the northwest, the clouds were angry and swirling, and we saw great spidery fingers of lightning flashing there. But the territory we traveled was untroubled. There were farms by the side of the road, uniform and flat and fertile, a sign at the edge of one field that read, GET U.S. OUT OF THE UNITED NATIONS. The John Birch Society. On the radio, the so-called Christians were going on in stentorian tones about the spiritual decay of America.

I have to admit that I often agree with them. I have moments—watching wife and babysitter punch each other on daytime TV, or reading about two-year-olds left alone by crack-addicted moms, or hearing radio loudmouths fomenting hatred, or seeing thirty thousand dollars spent on our neighbors' daughters' sweet-sixteen parties while my sister's friends in Paterson work for five dollars an hour—when I wonder if we have, in fact, started in on a moral decline that will end with our extinction, the flag in tatters being run down the pole for the final time, the Great American Experiment lying in pieces like a beautiful broken vase, weakened from within and then smashed from without. But when I listen a bit longer to the so-called Christians, it sounds to me as if their cure for what ails us is more and stricter rules, more narrow-mindedness, more hatred, more sectioning off of the society, and it has always seemed to me that, if Christ's message could be distilled down to one line, that line would have to do with kindness and inclusiveness, not rules and divisiveness.

Even so, as I mentioned, I have a sort of perverse fascination with the whole spectrum of talk-show nuts, and on the drive down Route 20 I made myself—and Rinpoche—listen to a long "Christian" call-in show. The host was ranting about the Sacred Sabbath and all the things you shouldn't do on the Sacred Sabbath and all the people in this country who are "loathsome to the eye of God" because they don't observe the Sacred Sabbath. Then the host started in on the righteousness of spanking, or "biblical corporal punishment," as he called it. A caller wanted to know if it was appropriate to spank his fifteen-year-old daughter, who was straying from the Christian path, and put off by his "witnessing," and did the host think it would be appropriate to render biblical corporal punishment to her?

The host thought that would be just fine. Spank on, my brother! So what if she's fifteen? Toss her over your lap and spank on! In the name of Christ our Lord, amen.

Ordinarily, as we drove, especially when I had the radio on, Rinpoche would go into a kind of half-absent zone, studying the passing scenery, occasionally asking what a particular building might be used for, or how he should pronounce a name—Lido, Toledo. But on this drive he seemed to be paying close attention to the prattle about punishment and hell and God. When it ended—in a long flurry of commercials for tapes, CDs, donations to keep the word of God alive—he turned to me with a perplexed expression on his face and said, "Why so angry?"

"I don't know."

"Anger, anger. Why so much in America, tell me."

We were passing through Monroeville at that moment, a tiny little burb. In a parking lot to our left there was a police car with blue lights blinking and a policeman standing on the tar, and, opposite him, there was a large man with reddish hair and sideburns and a goofy, drunken smile on his face, as if what awaited him was not handcuffs, the local hoosegow, and a DUI conviction, but an invitation to the officer's home for dinner with the wife and kids.

"They think the country's gone to hell," I said. "They think America isn't living right. They think God is going to punish us if we don't straighten out, and that, until God himself arrives on the scene, they are the ones who can do the straightening."

"Ah."

TWENTY-TWO

We pulled into South Bend, Indiana, in early evening and not far from the highway came upon our lodging for that night, a place called the Inn at Saint Mary's. If nothing else, my chauffering of the Rinpoche was giving me a look at places I otherwise would have whizzed right past. Plus it was saving me a bit of cash here and there: the people who'd invited him to talk at Notre Dame had set us both up at the Inn at St. Mary's with very nice suites, all paid for, thank you. Accustomed as I had become to the high-finance accounting that goes with suburban life—the bills, the donations, the taxes, the cash outlays for ballet dresses, football cleats, and granite countertops—I found myself wondering how Rinpoche, as we say in the book business, worked his numbers. I knew from Cecelia's letter that he had not been paid for the Youngstown talk, but would be paid handsomely for this one. Did he demand cold, hard cash for the dispensing of his wisdom? Or did he get paid by check and just walk into a bank and say, "Hi, I'm the famous Volya Rinpoche, would you mind cashing this for me even though

I don't have an account here?" and then fold the *dinero* into the sleeve of his robe and produce it whenever he wanted to chip in for gas (which he did, against my objections) or buy a postcard (over which he would lean, and with great concentration inscribe a message to my sister)? Did he have a nonprofit foundation? Patrons? An inheritance stashed away in a bank in Ulan Bator, from which he periodically ordered drafts? I wondered what percentage of my interior life was spent thinking about money and what Rinpoche would have to say on the subject, but I did not ask.

By this time he and I had developed a traveling regimen. When we stopped for the day, if we were both having dinner, we'd first go to our separate rooms and give each other an hour of alone time, one of us meditating, the other flipping through TV channels, taking a shower, or lying on the bed and going through a long-ago-memorized routine of stretches designed to ease an aching back. My suite in South Bend was on the first floor, two large rooms, two televisions, a couch, desk, and king-sized bed, very clean, fairly quiet, with a strong shower and tan striped wallpaper marred only by not very original drawings of Notre Dame dormitories and classroom buildings. Probably they got a lot of ND alums at the inn, down from Michigan or over from North Carolina for the big football weekend, and the drawings of Father Mahoney hall, or whatever, summoned memories of the good old years. It occurred to me in one of my many fruitless musings that if the term *religion* were defined more broadly—and I believed it should be—then the real religion of Notre Dame would be not Catholicism but football. After all, did they get a hundred thousand screaming fans for Mass on a Sacred Sabbath morn? Did the parishioners come early for the service and set up bar-

becues in the rectory parking lot? Return year after year to
relive memories of a favorite sermon? Buy pennants, sweat-
shirts, and bumper stickers with the name of their church
emblazoned on them?

And then, in the midst of this somewhat irreverent
reverie, I wondered what my own religion might be. If I
defined it that way, that broadly, as the primary focus of
my thoughts and passions, what would it be? Family life,
perhaps. Our sacred rituals would include eating meals
together, going to Anthony's piano recitals and Natasha's
soccer games, walking Jasper by Sprain Brook, the annual
trips to the Green Mountains in winter and Cape Cod in
summer; like the so-called Christians on the radio shows,
we were engaged in a continual debate about rules and
transgression.

Or maybe I belonged to the First Church of Good Eating. Or work. Or sex. Or money. What occupied the very
center of the stream of thoughts that ran through my
gray matter night and day? What was the deepest pool in
which the largest fish cruised and fed? Or should I use the
Hindu model, with dozens of gods and goddesses—Jeannie,
Natasha, Anthony, my parents, my boss, my tennis part-
ners and friends, my sister, sex, food, swimming, work,
bank balance, reading—each presiding over their precinct
in the Greater Realm?

Joke about it, fine, a little voice in me chirped. *But try
answering the question, Otto. What is the main current
in the river? If you had your own talk show — God save
America from that — what would you rant about? What
do you care about most?*

Lying on the bed in the nice suite, with the hot Indiana
day easing into evening beyond the curtained windows, I

gave the matter some serious thought. And what I came up with, to my own surprise, was love. It was the only answer that held up. Love—of Jeannie and the kids, of Jasper, our wonderful mutt, of work, of eating. There was my next career. I would be the national radio voice of the Love Party, somewhere left of the Democrats and right of the Republicans, far out in space.

I'd be the Rush Limbaugh of Love, the Jesse Jackson of Love, the Michael Savage, the Jerry Brown. Callers would dial the 800 number and tell me how much they appreciated the show, how I was the only voice in the country talking any sense, how those awful, no-love types had ruined the America we adored, and how it was our duty to take it back from them. Twenty minutes out of every hour there would be commercials for medications, for investments, for enlistment in the Peace Corps. We are the few, the proud, the volunteers in Zimbabwe.

But can't you, the voice chirped, *answer the question in a serious way? Isn't mockery the province of the insecure? Isn't that what you do with Rinpoche and Cecelia, in your heart of hearts, make fun of them because something in their way of thinking threatens you, or at least challenges your assumptions?*

Instead of dealing with that question, I started thinking about food. I took a shower, wondering the whole time what we might find for dinner there in the flat cornfields north of Indianapolis.

Rinpoche's talk wasn't scheduled until nine p.m., which I thought was an odd hour. The other strange thing was that he'd agreed to go out to dinner with me. I'd expected him to skip dinner entirely and leave me to venture out into the culinary wilderness on my own. But on the drive in from Ohio he'd said he wanted to find a restaurant and have the evening meal with me before his talk. It was the latest in a series of curveballs.

"Do you really eat meat?" I had asked him.

"A little meat, not too much."

"Do you mind spices?"

"Spices very good. In Skovorodino we never had spices. When I went to India I discover my tongue."

I laughed and thought: *What is called for here is Thai. Not too much meat, spicy as you want it. Probably some more-or-less Buddhist statuettes on the walls.* So, at check-in, I'd inquired about the possibility of finding a Thai restaurant in the vicinity, and the young fellow at the desk (who looked as though he appreciated a good feed as much as I did) told us, with a big, proud smile, that there was a place called Siam, right here in downtown South Bend.

"You can't miss it, really," he said.

"No, trust me. I can."

He laughed, and for the first time I really digested the fact that I was back in the Midwest. Not so many good eating choices, maybe (I hoped that had changed), but there was a kind of ease and unself-consciousness between people that seemed to grow like corn in this soil. "Take a right out of the driveway. Follow that road. No turns. You'll come into downtown and it will be there on your right."

When I thanked him, he said, "You bet."

So I was thinking about that as I showered and dressed and ran from the questions of the chirping internal voice. And then I went to knock on Rinpoche's door. Green curry, I was thinking. Thai iced coffee. Basil fried rice. Pad Thai. Tom yum soup.

Running. Running.

Rinpoche and I went down the first-floor corridor side by side, and through the large, sunlit, sofa-and-chair-filled lobby, where we attracted some not entirely friendly gazes from the dads of freshmen football recruits, in town to watch the August double-sessions.

When we were settled again in the car, stopped at a light on the way to Siam, I said, without planning to: "I bought one of your books in Oberlin when you were talking with the woman in the coffee shop. I didn't want to tell you. I hid it in the trunk so I could read it when you weren't watching. I'm a bit ashamed of that."

Rinpoche liked to ride with his oversized cloth purse between his ankles (I sometimes wondered if it was filled with cash), even though I'd suggested several times that he keep it in the trunk or back seat. It was resting there now. He reached down and unclasped it, fished one hand in, and brought out a paperback copy of *Mending Your Life with Food,* by Jersey L. Rickard Jr., a book I'd edited. It had been released two summers earlier, sold 88,000 copies in hardcover, and earned the author close to a quarter of a million dollars in foreign rights sales alone. I looked over and saw him holding up the book—one of my biggest successes—so I could see it. There was an enormous sly smile on his face. My astonishment must have shown because, when the light turned green and we started forward, Rinpoche began to laugh and did not stop laughing until we found a parking space on Jefferson Street, two blocks from Siam.

TWENTY-THREE

My experience of Thai restaurants, from Miami Beach to Massachusetts, is that the food served in them is of a universally high quality and that the interiors tend toward the Nouveau Plastique. There are exceptions, of course. But Siam was not one of them. A storefront on a crowded stretch of business block, in the flat, staid, if—in a midwestern way—somewhat alluring downtown South Bend, Siam was filled with evening light from tall sidewalk windows and presided over by a crew of waiters and waitresses who seemed to believe that if the water in a customer's drinking glass fell below the three-quarters-full mark then King Padinpathanrananan himself would appear magically in the doorway and give them a bad time.

They were a friendly, gentle sort, the women black-haired, slim as saplings, and beautiful, and the food they served Rinpoche and me had a healthfulness and tang to it that made *me* realize I had a tongue. What a wonderful cuisine it is! Rinpoche was partial to white rice and ordered a half-portion of vegetarian Pad Thai to accompany it. After the spring rolls and a full portion of chicken satay, and after flirting for a few minutes with the idea of a green curry, I at last settled on a main dish that included tender pieces of chicken, carrots, cabbage, green peppers, and onions in a gingery sauce.

At the table closest to ours sat a man with one of those ear buds, and he was talking, apparently, to his young daughter, going on and on with her, obviously very much smitten with fatherhood. "Sure, sweetheart. And I'll be home day after tomorrow. I miss you more than anything. Here's a kiss for my little pumpkin." And so on. It reminded me exactly of my younger self, precell days, standing at a payphone outside a conference in Dallas, with booksellers from all over the Southwest waiting their turn, and Natasha on the other end of the line, asking how many days till I came home, how many hours, how many minutes was that, Daddy? And me thinking nothing else mattered, not sales, not marketing, not publicity, not anything at all but keeping this innocent happiness in her voice for as long as we possibly could.

The interesting part was that Rinpoche could not see the ear bud, and so, from his angle, the happy and well-dressed father appeared to be talking to himself, or to his Shrimp Pwangathang, saying, "Yes, sweetheart, I love you, Daddy loves you," in a low voice. I could see that Rinpoche was watching, and I knew him well enough by then to understand that he was struggling between his ordinary urge to laugh at everything and some sense he was beginning to have about Americans, that there were places and times where laughter might be deemed childish, even offensive. The muscles of his face were working as if his skin covered a colony of ants under siege. "My little pickpocket," the man beside him went on, stirring sticky rice with the tines of his fork. "Daddy's going to come tuck you in tomorrow night."

Rinpoche could barely contain himself. His lips were twitching. There were tears forming at the corners of his eyes. At last, he could no longer stand it. A one-syllable laugh escaped him. The man looked over, the ear bud peeking out, but it was too late. Without excusing himself, Rinpoche got up and left the table, made straight for the entrance, and I saw him there on the sidewalk beyond the glass, doubled over, his wide maroon ass pointing back at me and the happy dad. Laughing and laughing, hands on his knees, folds of the robe shaking, passersby stopping to see if he needed assistance. . . . He really was not quite normal.

By the time the entire Siam experience was finished, it was twenty-five past eight, and I thought it made sense for us to get over to the lecture hall so Rinpoche could see if he liked the setup. Out on the sidewalk, I took Cecelia's letter from my pocket and checked the name of the hall and the time. The event was being sponsored by an organization called Catholics for Interfaith Dialogue, which sounded promising, though I wondered, as we drove to the sprawling green Notre Dame campus, what kind of organization would have their feature lectures at nine o'clock at night.

We drove down a long driveway onto the campus, parked, and asked the first person we saw how to get to O'Malley Auditorium. It turned out to be a five-minute walk from the neat, bland, pale-brick building in front of which we stood. When we arrived, the door of the auditorium was locked and there were no lights on inside. The entrance was rather grand—three glass doors, carved stone archways, trimmed shrubs to either side of the cement walk.

"We're pretty early," I said to Rinpoche, by way of explanation, but something felt wrong. Someone should have been there, setting out the doughnuts or aligning chairs. I unfolded Cecelia's letter and went over it for the twentieth time: "August 9, 9:00 p.m. O'Malley Auditorium on the Notre Dame Campus. Catholics for Interfaith Dialogue. Contact: Marie Desjardins," with home and cell phone numbers.

We waited another ten minutes, checking with a passerby to be sure there was, in fact, only one O'Malley Auditorium, and that we were standing in front of it. Then I dialed Marie Desjardins.

"Hi, this is Otto Ringling. I'm traveling with Volya Rinpoche and we're here at O'Malley Auditorium for his talk and no one else is."

"You're there now? You didn't get my message?"

"What message?"

"We had a conflict—another important event on campus tonight—and we decided to move the Rinpoche's lecture to tomorrow at eleven."

"Eleven p.m.?"

She laughed. "No, eleven in the morning. It's the last event on our morning session and the conference ends with lunch. You weren't told?"

"What number did you call?"

"I don't know. I called the person with whom we set it up originally."

"Was it a woman with a bit of a singsong voice? In New Jersey? She made you repeat everything twice to be sure she wrote it down correctly?"

"That sounds right. She said she would pass on the message. I'm so so sorry."

"Not a problem. We'll be here tomorrow at eleven. And the hotel rooms are very nice, thank you."

Rinpoche, of course, thought this was most amusing, and I have to say that, after sixty seconds or so of my usual line of internal sister-criticism, I managed a smile. I had made a vow to myself that there would be no more tantrums in front of the holy man, and to that point I had been good. "Well, you'll want to get back to the inn, I guess, for the nightly meditation."

Rinpoche was smiling and shaking his head . "No, tonight we go out, my friend."

"Out where?"

"Out for American fun."

"American fun? Have you been watching TV?"

"You choose, my friend."

American fun, I thought. American fun meaning what, exactly: A movie? And if so, what kind of movie? *Lethal Mass Destruction IV*? Or should it be pocket billiards? Or should we drop a few hundred dollars at the Gentleman's Club? "What do you have in mind?"

And then my thoughts swept back around into the past like a middle-aged man at dusk on an August night, standing at the edge of his swimming pool with the long-handled net, and the children inside in their rooms, at peace, and the woman of the house doing yoga on her mat on the study's hardwood floor, and he reaches out, far out into the shadowy blue middle of the deep end of his overcrowded mind and manages to catch a piece of leaf floating there. In that light, he can barely see the leaf, perhaps he cannot see it at all, but he somehow knows it is there, remembers seeing it there a few minutes earlier, when the light was better, and he reaches out as if by instinct, sweeps the net under it, and carries it back, and the water is now clean, his work complete, duty accomplished, and he can rest.

"Rinpoche," I asked, "would you like to go bowling?"

"Yes," he said, with a smile so huge that it wrinkled his skin all the way to the top of his shaved head. "Very much like." And then, after a short contemplative pause. "What is this bohling mean?"

TWENTY-FOUR

The Chippewa Lanes can be found on South Bend's south side, and if you go there, try to rent your shoes from a pleasant young man named Jeremy, who refers to himself as "Jeremy the Counter Guy" and who, on a busy Wednesday night in late summer, could have made things difficult for a visiting Rinpoche with no socks and no clue as to his American shoe size, but did not. In fact, with his sunny disposition and tendency to see the humor in everything, the young fellow reminded me just a bit of Rinpoche, and that made me wonder if half the people we encountered had, by some sort of Ortykian magic, been set in my path to help me understand the strange monk.

Jeremy assigned us to lane one. There were seventy lanes at the Chippewa, and probably thirty were free at that hour, but he assigned us to lane one, which wouldn't have mattered to me except for the fact that lanes two and three were occupied by the Association of Tattooed and Felonious Motorcyclists of the Midwest. Four men and two women, marked as belonging to a certain tribe by the tattoos and

cable-tight muscles of the men and the tight-shirted tough-
ness of the women, the fact that they would all curse loudly
and without embarrassment when they missed a spare, and
that their laughter contained in it the sound of cigarette
smoke, booze, and a lifetime of small humiliations.

There was music leaking out of the Chippewa's ceiling
speakers. Nine Inch Nails, Limp Biskit, or something along
those lines. Natasha and Anthony would have known for sure.
Rinpoche had chosen from the rack a twelve-pound ball—
pink in color—and, after watching me manage a strike in
my first frame (I had been All Stark County in junior high,
and then given up the sport for other pursuits), he stood
up there with his thick fingertips in the holes and tried to
mimic what he saw: the long smooth strides, the ball drawn
back and then swung forward in a pendulum motion, the
crouch as the ball rolled, and then the fist pump when the
pins pinged and rattled. Except that, in his case, things did
not go so well. In fact, the ball slipped out of his hand on
the way back, banged hard on the polished maple floor, and
skittered sideways into the ankles of one of the women sitting and tapping her cigarette ash in lane two. She looked
up, snarling, saw Rinpoche, took in his bald head and the
hem of his maroon robe, which ended an inch or two above
blue bowling shoes. A couple of the men looked over as well.
Rinpoche shuffled toward them in his unfamiliar shoes to
retrieve the pink sphere, saying, "Sorry, sorry," and laughing in a way that might have been taken wrong.

I got up and walked over to go to his assistance. The men
stiffened at my approach. I could feel my hands sweating.
I knew a little bit about the world they lived in, or thought
I did. There had been some rough characters in the North
Dakota of my youth, guys in grade school and, later, on the

football and hockey teams, to whose homes I was occasionally invited, who'd lived in a kind of soup of incipient violence, in hardscrabble neighborhoods where the adults had about a fifty-fifty chance of losing a hand or an eye in the factory conveyor belt or meat-packing mash line or eventually going to jail, and those adults, whose futures consisted only of more work like that, came home and tried to drink away the memory of the day, and so they lived their lives hour by hour, just getting by, getting through, finding any way to kill the pain of it. It is hard to be a child in a home like that and then grow up to be kinder and gentler and cherish the idea that people are basically good.

In my experience, some of those adults had not been good. They had been mean and even vicious. I'd once seen a friend's father slap his wife across the face as casually as you would swat a fly, with a nine-year-old guest sitting right there at table, and for nothing, for some domestic oversight that had to do with the kind of bread she'd brought home, or the way his beer had been poured or opened. But many of them were just coated in a thick skin of roughness, as if they needed an armor to survive their lives, and had fashioned the only armor that came to mind. For some of them at least, underneath all that—the tattoos, the cigarettes and cheap canned beer, the loud laughter, bad language, and obvious prejudices—was the usual tender soul, and if they sensed that you saw them as human beings, if they sensed a basic respect, or decency, or that you were at least not going to mock them, then the armor melted. I hoped, as I went to Rinpoche's aid, that the people in the next lane fell into the second category. "His first time," I said to the man nearest us. And then, in my nervousness, I added, "He's a spiritual master."

The women turned away. The men looked at me for a few bad seconds, and then one of them said, "No shit?"

"No shit. He's giving a talk tomorrow at Notre Dame. He gives talks all over the world."

"No shit," the man said again, not a question this time. He was looking Rinpoche up and down and, after a second, shifted the bowling ball to his left hand and held out his right in a strange gesture of supplication, as if he were about to bow. We could see the tattoo of a snake curling around a sword up the inside of his forearm. "What about a blessing then?" He said to Rinpoche. "You know. For good luck. What about it?"

I thought, for a moment, that he was being sarcastic, and that now the real trouble would come. Behind him, his friends were smiling, but they were the kind of smiles you see on the faces of scarred young children who are about to pull an insect apart, leg by leg.

Rinpoche did not notice any of this, or gave no sign of noticing, at least. He reached out and shook the first man's hand vigorously, smiling, nodding at the others.

"Yeah," one of the women said, "he needs his sins to get forgiven."

This line caused the man with the snake tattoo to smile and the others to go into paroxysms of hacking guffaws.

Rinpoche let go of the man's hand and looked at him, moved half a step closer—I was going to try to stop him—and then he put his palms on the man's shoulders and started in on some kind of a prayer in some language—Ortyk, it must have been—that sounded like a cold Siberian stream running over stones. No one understood it, of course, but that didn't matter. What mattered was the tone, and the tone was like honey, like love made into a song, a quiet, utterly fearless little chant that would have calmed a wolf with her back to the cliffside and three pups on her teats. It went on for maybe twenty seconds. When it was finished, Rinpoche took a step backward and bowed. The man with the snake tattoo stood frozen in place. And then across his jagged features bloomed the smile he must have had as a young boy, before anything had been taken away from him by what he saw and heard, before the world had shown him its teeth and bitten him. He smiled like that, watching Rinpoche, and then he remembered who he was supposed to be and shifted the bowling ball back to his other hand and said, "Hey, thanks, man. You're all right." And the woman behind him lifted up the pink ball and handed it over.

For the rest of the evening—Rinpoche and I bowled two strings—things went along without incident. The cursing beside us ceased, and I thought the laughter was less raucous, too. Best of all, Rinpoche turned out to be absolutely crazy about tenpin bowling. By the end, he was doing fairly well. He'd take one step and send the ball away with a small bounce, and then crouch with his hands on his knees and watch intently as it grumbled slowly down the alley. When it banged into the pins he would straighten up, almost jumping (he was extraordinarily limber for a middle-aged man), and clap his hands, and then turn to me with the most beatific smile on his face and come over and let me explain the scoring.

The motorcyclists finished their evening a few frames before we did. Three of the men and the two women just carried their shoes back to the counter, but the guy with the snake tattoo stepped over to me when Rinpoche was bowling and said, "Hey, what's his name anyway?" I told him, mentioned that he had books in the stores. The man's green eyes shifted once to Rinpoche and then back, and he said, "He's the real thing, man, ain't he?"

And I said that I thought he was.

IN THE CAR on the ten-minute ride back to the Inn at St. Mary's, Rinpoche seemed almost to be giving off light, he was so happy. At a stop sign, I glanced over and saw that he was looking straight ahead with a joyous grin on his face. I thought he must be pleased at the way the encounter with the tattooed man had turned out, but as we pulled into the lot he said, "Bohling is excellent American fun. Thank you, Otto."

I wanted to ask him what he had said to the man, what kind of blessing he'd given, but I managed only, "Knock on my door on your way to breakfast," and then we went inside and I watched him go down the hall to his room, and waited to make sure his card key worked.

When he was settled in, I slipped back outside, took his book from the trunk, and carried it back in. I lay on the bed and started reading. The first couple of chapters were interesting enough, but, I thought, mostly unsurprising. And then on page 19, I came across these paragraphs, and read them four times.

For many people, many, many people, the spiritual situation is like that of a young boy who decides to take up the piano. This boy likes the piano, likes the sound the keys make when he touches them, likes the feel of the ivory against his small fingers. Perhaps he knows someone, or has seen someone, who plays well, and this inspires him.

As he grows older, he continues to play and to practice. As he practices perhaps someone criticizes him in an unkind way, or perhaps he begins to see that he cannot play as well as the person who inspired him, that he makes mistakes, that his hands do not always work the way he wishes them to work, that it requires effort and sacrifice to improve.

By the time he is a young adult, he is somewhat accomplished at the piano—some of this came from natural ability, some from his love of music, some from practice. He plays well, sometimes at gatherings of friends or family. But then, as he grows older, he decides that, even though he can play well, he will never play *very well*. He will never play *perfectly*. He is not good enough to be a concert pianist, just as, in the spiritual realm, on this complex earth, he believes he will never be good enough to satisfy his idea of a God who looks over him, so he stops really trying to do so, stops thinking about such things.

Probably he does not even form these thoughts in such a way. He just sets up, between him and the next level of piano playing—the next level of his interior life—a kind of invisible barrier. He makes a limit where there is no actual limit. This is not bad. He is not an evil man. Just the opposite, he is a good man, but he builds this limit the way you would build walls around a room, and then he lives there, within that room, not completely satisfied but not knowing what he can do about his dissatisfaction. He grows old. He waits for the end of his life, for God to pass judgment on him, and chases as many decent pleasures as he can while he waits. This is just the way life is, he says to himself. This is as good a player as I will ever be. He would, in fact, like to play the piano better, but what keeps him from venturing outside that room is a kind of fear, the idea that he might fail, that people might mock him for his ambition, or that he would then not be the person he believes himself to be. But where did this idea of who he actually is come from? In the spiritual realm, or, if you prefer these words, in the emotional or psychological realm, what is he denying himself by staying inside these walls?

I set the book on the night table, turned off the light, took off my clothes, and lay on the bed looking up at the patterns of shadow on the ceiling. It was late, and I had promised to call Jeannie, and I knew I would do that. But I lay on the bed caught up in a vague notion, not thinking, exactly, just musing on something, circling some idea, pondering. The metaphor of the piano-playing boy seemed imperfect to me. If I had been editing the book, I would have written in the manuscript margins, "Work this," meaning that the author should take the general idea and sharpen it, make it clearer to the reader.

And yet, the general idea, the plight of the piano-playing man, would not let me go. I thought back to the encounter between Rinpoche and the tough guy, to the pure joy on Rinpoche's face when he bowled. I leaned over and reached for the telephone and dialed my home number.

TWENTY-FIVE

I am not a fan of the so-called buffet breakfast, or of buffets of any kind, Chinese, Indian, or American hotel. But the buffet at the Inn at St. Mary's was better than average, and I made myself a decent meal of waffle, fruit, and coffee. Rinpoche ate only an apple, which he sliced expertly with one of the inn's plastic knives and washed down with two cups of water.

"Don't you want more than that before the big talk?" I asked him. "Don't you want to fill up the tank so you'll have some fuel to run on?"

"Fuel last night," Rinpoche said. "Bohling."

Between breakfast and the time we left for his talk we strolled over to a nearby shrine of Mary that was surrounded by beautifully groomed lawns. I suppose I shouldn't have been, but I was surprised when I saw Rinpoche get down on both knees in front of the ceramic Virgin, bow low so that his forehead touched the grass, and stay in that posture for a long while. Mary—any holy woman, really—had never been an important part of the Lutheran pantheon of my formative years, and I'd come around to the opinion that, though Catholics were stubborn in their resistance to woman priests, they didn't get enough credit for keeping a female figure so close to the heart of their worship. The shrine was dedicated to something called the miracle of LaSalette, which, according to a plaque on the grounds, referred to Mary's appearance to three schoolchildren in western France in 1947. It was a peaceful spot.

O'Malley Auditorium was, too, though there must have been 150 people there when we arrived, at quarter to eleven. Marie Desjardins, an elderly woman with a gorgeous Jamaican accent, greeted us warmly and then introduced Rinpoche with a few simple remarks that avoided hyperbole. He was, she told the assembled conference-goers, which included a good number of priests and some nuns, a man who had devoted his entire teaching life to breaking down the barriers between people of faith in all traditions. With that, she yielded him the podium, and he stood up there, looking relaxed but completely out of place in the wood-trimmed room, his shaved head and maroon robe in stark contrast to the priests' neat haircuts and dark suits and the nuns' white-and-black habits.

I sat near the very back again, but this time had no urge to flee.

Rinpoche began his presentation by talking, in a fairly general, inoffensive way, about the Bible, about Jesus, about a rabbi friend who spent all the holy days in prayer and fasting. From there he moved on to the Hindu idea of At-man, or soul, and the power, or Brahman, that infuses it; and then to a Sufi master who counseled a steady, patient approach to spiritual practice rather than a "materialistic" one, where there was something to be chased after and caught; and then to a Vedantic yogi whose central idea was that the mind's impurities tricked us into believing we were our bodies and not something greater: an essential part of the sacred whole. Toward the end he touched upon Buddhism, with its emphasis on personal responsibility, and said something I'd never heard before: that the Buddha's last words to his disciples were, "Work out your own salvation with diligence."

It seemed to me he made a convincing case that, though these belief systems were not identical, they had a large area of overlap, a huge demilitarized zone, as it were, where people of good intention could meet and converse in an atmosphere of mutual respect. The talk was, as I said, inoffensive and no doubt designed to be that way. But in the question-and-answer period he came under attack—I cannot find a more accurate word—from a nun who'd been sitting in the second row. She approached one of the microphones that had been set up in a half dozen places around the auditorium for those who wanted to ask questions.

"Is there, Mr. Rinpoche," she began, in the tone of a district attorney, "in your tradition or any other that you know of, besides Christianity, an instance of one of what you call holy figures rising from the dead?"

"Yes, in my tradition there is," he said calmly, happily.

The district attorney had not expected this. "There is?"

"Yes. In the ancient times we have reports of people who appeared to have been died and then came back to living. We have stories of people whose bodies turned into rays of light at the moment of their death. These stories, to me, are inspiring. Inspiring, yes? That is the right word?"

Priests, nuns, and editors nodding all over the place.

"But, to me personally," he continued, "there is no need

of proof of some Creator, of some Magnificent Ones, that they rose from the dead or made miracles. For proof I look at you, all of you here, and I think: Your hearts are pumping now, when we sit here and think and talk and question to each other. The blood is going. Outside, the trees are drinking in the sun and growing. Beyond them, the planets are spinning. These are facts. No one disputes—disputes, yes?—these things. More proof of God, or some Greater Being, why is it necessary?"

The nun was not assuaged. "Who, then, do you say Jesus Christ was?"

"Very, very, very great spirit!" Rinpoche answered, without a missed beat. And he laughed, the high chuckle. I smiled. No one else in the room seemed even slightly amused.

"And that's all?"

"That's all? That is very much, isn't it?"

The nun frowned. "He's not God?"

"Yes, yes, of course. God. Yes, he is. You are God, too. I think Jesus Christ said that you are God. He said that his father is your father, yes? That makes you his sister, yes? I think Jesus Christ wanted not so much that you worship him but that you act like him, that you be like him inside. I think he came here to save us by showing us what we could be like inside. He said, 'The kingdom of heaven is within you,' so we should ask the question to ourselves what this means."

A few people in the room were nodding thoughtfully, but the good nun was holding her ground against this onslaught of heretical wishy-washiness. "Another question," she said. "You used the word *enlightenment* during your talk. I, personally, do not like this word. What exactly do you mean by it? Is it a kind of supposed heaven on earth? A kind of null, or sensual bliss? Help us to understand, please."

"I will help you," Rinpoche said, and then he laughed again, as if either she was beyond help or he was not the right guy for the job. "I will try. And thank you for the questions. I like these questions. . . . I think it is maybe that you are correct to not like the word. I think it is possibly not a very good word because it implies . . . implies, yes?" He was looking at me now, I was nodding vigorously. "Implies, what did you call it, *null*." He laughed. "I do not know what this *null* exactly is, but maybe it means not changing. The end. I do not think heaven means the end. I do not believe enlightenment means the end. How can there be this end? What would the end be? What would God do after the end, he would be bored, yes? He would have to start over and make the worlds again. No, no end, I think. End would be no more hearts going. All right, maybe so. But no more sun? No more trees growing? All right. But no more universes? No more dust, no more light, no more atomic particles? How could this be? This would be *null*, I think. Yes?

"We are humans, and we have human minds, and we try, with those minds, to understand something that is very beyond us. Like trying to swim like a fish underwater without breathing, or flying like a bird with our arms. Or seeing in the darkness without a flashlight. Or . . ."

I watched him struggle. Metaphors were, it seemed to me, not his strongest suit.

"Or like knocking down bohling pins with a small marble. No, to me, enlightenment is a big shift inside your eyes, a different way to use your mind so you can understand some of God, some of Jesus. But it is maybe not one shift,

but many small shifts. You change your spiritual condi-
tion—by prayer, by meditation, by the way you live, the
way you decide to think, by the lessons you learn in living
this life with a good intention—and then, when this happens, after a long times or a short times, the way you see
the world changes. Physically. I think that if you are a bad
person, maybe a thief, then the way you see the world is
What can I steal? You see everything that can be stealed.
And that changes the way your mind works, and makes
you blind to see what is really there, all the good things you
cannot steal—the sun, the hearts—and so on." He paused
and laughed, as if he was about to make a fine little joke.
"And if you are a person who loves sex very much, then you
are always seeing sex in the world, always looking at bodies and thinking about sex. There is a shop here in the city
near the bohling house that sells sex things, sex pictures.
You would know where this shop is if you were a person
like that. You see . . . I know where it is!"

A few people laughed, but not many, and the nun continued to stand at rigid attention before the microphone,
fixing the visitor with a look that would have sliced an ordinary man in two.

"And if you are a person who has had bad things happen
with you, and who is angry," Rinpoche went on, resting
his eyes on her, "then you are always seeing in the world
reasons for you to be angry about. You see? Even, you get
angry at yourself when you are not perfect.

"But if you can clear this out of your mind a little
bit—that you want to steal, that you want sex all the time,
that you want to eat very much all the time, that you want to
sleep many hours, that you so much want money, that you
want to win the argument with someone to show that you

are right, or be angry at someone because you know they are wrong, or that you are a bad person because you are not perfect—then your mind clears like a clear, clear water. When that happens, you have a small waking-up. You start to see the world as the world really is. And after many small waking-ups we begin to see the world a little bit, some little bit, the way Jesus sees it. You see? That is the 'kingdom of heaven.' You see? This, I think, is what he wanted and why he came to us here on this planet, to teach us this."

He was addressing the nun in her own spiritual language now, individually, personally, even intimately, and she was narrowing her eyes further and looking like she was ready to scream. For a few seconds, there was this awful standoff: Rinpoche watching her with a patient look, waiting for her to have a small waking-up, and the nun pressing her lips together, about to explode. But before she could get out another word, Marie Desjardins stood up and said, with a graceful forcefulness, that Rinpoche would take one more question from someone who had not yet asked a question, and then there would be a reception in the adjacent room.

The last question was not a question at all, it turned out, but a comment from the elderly priest who'd organized the whole conference and who was sitting in the back row not far from me. This man was close to eighty, I guessed, but trim and alert. It seemed to me that the best word to describe him was *happy*. He was a happy man, at ease with himself, at peace, with a certain, mildly amused expression on his face that planted in me a small seed of envy. The old priest thanked Rinpoche for coming and said that he was obviously a man of God. And the Rinpoche thanked him in return and bowed with his hands pressed together, and there was polite applause.

I turned my back on the sweets and coffee and went outside and stood there, in the heat of the midwestern day,
looking around at the lawns and buildings, the billowing
clouds, the smattering of people strolling the paths, professors, young lovers, other conference-goers, other beating
hearts. I found myself remembering the expression on the
old priest's face, and then, for some reason, thinking about
the day Jeannie had given birth to Natasha. It had been a
long and difficult labor, and at one point in the midst of it,
the fetal heart monitor had made a sudden change. It had
been going along for ten or twelve hours by then, the con-
sistent *beep-beep-beep-beep,* with the numbers of beats per
minute showing on a digital monitor: 168, 181, 176, 177.
And then something happened, and the beeps weren't coming so close together, and the numbers on the monitor had
crept down: 183, 159, 140, 122, 107, 88, 71, 51. The nurses
literally leapt into action, rushing up to my wife's bed and
turning her to another position, putting an oxygen mask
on her, calling the doctor, alerting the operating room. I
wanted to lift up the hospital on my shoulders and shake
the whole building to get that beeping sound back to where
it had been, to get those numbers—49, 41—to change.
But then the heartbeat began to climb steadily back to
the proper level. The nurses relaxed. I sat down and held
Jeannie's hand, but for the rest of her labor—another eight
hours—even when I went out into the hallway for a bathroom break, I thought I could hear that beeping sound, as if
it measured the pulse of the universe and was as fragile as a
single thread. We learned, later, that the umbilical cord had
wrapped itself around Natasha's neck and nearly choked
the life out of her.

I had forgotten the feeling of that day.

TWENTY-SIX

As a parting gift, Marie Desjardins presented Rinpoche with a Bible, and as we walked to the car in the steaming Indiana heat, he held it reverently against his chest. I was thinking about his presentation, and I was thinking about the previous night's conversation with my wife, and I was starting to feel there might be something I had been missing all along, some primary color of the interior world that had simply been—and still was—just outside the spectrum visible to my inner eye.

And I was hungry.

Rinpoche said he wouldn't mind a little something to eat, too. The night before, as we'd been driving south on South Bend's main drag, searching, in a kind of wilderness of warehouses and small office buildings, for the bowling alley to which we'd been directed, we had, in fact, passed an Adult Emporium or something of that nature. Rinpoche had noticed it, naturally, and asked about it, and I had done my best to explain the place—which was not, as you might imagine, an easy task. And then, on the way home, we'd passed a store with a bright yellow sign that read: TAQUE-RIA CAMICERIA. The place seemed somehow outside the realm of everything else we'd seen on that night, as if it had been plucked out of a parallel universe and dropped down in urban Indiana. When we left the campus, I retraced our route of the night before, found the yellow sign, and turned into the lot.

There, we asked an ancient and very small man selling Popsicles from the back of a truck if it was possible to get lunch in the store.

He turned his sun-dried face up to me in a puzzled way and smiled at Rinpoche.

I made an eating gesture with one hand, pointed to the glass door, and he nodded and said, "*Sí, sí,*" but did not understand when I tried to tell him we would buy our dessert from him on our way back out.

Inside, we found a sort of Mexican American Woolworth. Sandals, bottles of guava juice, heads of lettuce, and boxes of laundry soap for sale in eight musty aisles, and off against the left wall, a six-stool counter behind which two men worked, frying meat. Rinpoche and I sat there beside three T-shirted, black-haired, brown-skinned construction workers who were finishing their lunches and who gave us a thorough inspection—frank, unabashed, neither smiling nor sneering. It seemed that people who looked like us, like me at least, did not often take their midday meal in this place.

The fellow behind the counter had a scar running from his jawline up to the outside corner of his left eye. Above our heads were four handmade signs with the offerings. I asked for a chicken and bean burrito, and Rinpoche did the same.

"What do you have to drink?"

The cook pointed to a cold case nearby, but the only offerings there were of the sugary carbonated variety, so while the man prepared our food, Rinpoche and I made a tour of the little store and found, among the guava and pear nectar, a large bottle of apple juice. We carried it back to the counter.

The cook's helper was much younger, still in his teens, and on the side of his neck he had an elaborate tattoo in Gothic font that read CHICO. I asked for a cup and he shook his head. No cups. He watched me a moment, then pointed to his own cup and his coworker's. Cheap blue plastic, large, and sitting upside down on a dishcloth, obviously just washed. With his hands and facial expression he indicated that we could use those cups if we were willing. We were. The men to our left finished their meal with another round of stares, and then we were the only customers, with the meat and beans and onions and cilantro spitting on the grill, and then tortillas there beside them, like the thinnest cross-sections of a paler earth. We asked for ice. No ice, but the juice was cold, and soon the burritos were served and they were enormous. Pinto beans and flakes of cilantro spilled out from the cut; the chicken was tender as cream cheese and almost sweet.

"Ever been to Mexico?" I asked Rinpoche.

He shook his head.

"We went there for our honeymoon. Jeannie speaks Spanish pretty well, you know, and I had two years of it in school. We spent most of our time in Mexico City. Then a place called Mazatlan, on the Pacific coast."

Rinpoche said a prayer over his food, took one deliberate bite, chewed thoughtfully, nodded, looked at me, swallowed. "When you say the names it sounds like you were happy in that place."

"Hard not to be happy on your honeymoon," I told him, but even as I spoke I knew there was more to my feelings for Mexico than sweet memories of love. It had been loud in the capital, I'd gotten sick. And then, in Mazatlan, we'd shared our hotel with a bunch of beer-guzzling Yanquis, down for a week of sun and superiority. Still, something about the people we met there, the real Mexicans we went out of our way to meet, had touched us in a certain way. Some of them seemed, to Jeannie and me both, to live by a different set of assumptions. Smaller, poorer, they walked and talked as if the world were enormous and mysterious—which, of course, it is. I'd felt some of that from the Popsicle man outside. I'd felt some of it in O'Malley Auditorium, too, listening to my new friend talk about his idea of enlightenment and studying the old priest's face. I watched the men behind the counter and ran through my mind a series of questions, for Rinpoche, that I was almost ready to ask.

It took him as long to eat one of the halves of his burrito as it took me to eat the whole. He asked for the second half to be wrapped up to go. We left a generous tip, exchanged nods with our cook—who seemed pleased and proud that we'd ventured into his world—and then we went out into the parking lot to discover a police car parked where the Popsicle man had been.

Up Michigan Street we drove in a slow, full-bellied silence, past the Glo-Worm Lounge, past a bar with a sign outside that read, NOTRE DAME STOP IMPORTING CRIME, DRUGS, AND HOMELESSNESS FOR MONEY, past the Hope Rescue Mission, then, after a few blocks, past the shrine to the miracle at LaSalette, the Inn at St. Mary's, and then into a gas station where we stopped for a fill-up and where the newspaper headlines read FORTY-ONE KILLED IN BAGHDAD BLAST. And then onto the superhighway headed west.

TWENTY-SEVEN

It was at this point in the trip that something in my interior world began to break open. The shell cracked, the thick whitish fluid started to leak out, though I had not yet taken the drastic, untakebackable step of pulling the brittle halves apart and dropping the egg into the pan. It was the passage I'd read in Rinpoche's book, and the angry, proud resistance of the nun reminding me so much of myself. And then that sense of having stepped, for half an hour, into the Mexico I remembered from our honeymoon. "No one runs away from anything here," Jeannie had said as we boarded the plane for the trip home, and though it wasn't precisely true, I have always remembered that remark.

And then, just as we merged onto the interstate and turned in the direction of Illinois, I spotted three white crosses by the side of the road, with flowers and an inscription I could not read. It made me think of my parents, naturally, of the feelings I'd been having since their death, that puzzled emptiness, that sense that the ground had slipped out sideways from beneath our secure, rich life. There, on that highway, I felt something change inside my mind, and it was a physical sensation, though very small, as if four tiny walls had been moved outward a few inches, or a door cut in one of them, a sliver of light peeking through, nothing more.

As we rode along the flatlands of northern Indiana, Rinpoche fell into one of his quiet reveries, those stretches of time during which he did not speak, and seemed not to move and, almost, not to be breathing. In order to relieve the monotony of the landscape—and possibly to put a temporary halt to the breaking of the eggshell—I turned on AM radio. Rinpoche wouldn't mind, I knew that, we'd talked about it. AM radio did not reach the place he traveled to.

It did not take more than a minute of hitting the seek button to come upon another religious talk show, the kind of thing I'd been listening in on, during odd moments, for as long as I could remember. This one turned out to be a Catholic show—unusual in my experience—from a Chicago station. The name of the host was Colleen or Eileen or Irene, and her subject was gluttony. I am not making this up for narrative convenience. My belly was full; her subject was gluttony. The first words I heard her say were: "Remember, gluttony is the sin that brought sin into the world."

I pondered that, took it personally perhaps. I assumed she was talking about Adam and Eve and the apple, and I started talking back, as I sometimes do. "I thought their sin had been a sin of *pride*," I said, too loudly. "I thought they were kicked out because *they were sure they knew better!*" Stirred from his contemplation of the internal alfalfa fields, Rinpoche sent a curious look across the front seat. Eileen or Colleen or Irene went on about gluttony for so long I felt myself starting to get hungry again, and then she took a call and moved on to one of the other great areas of sin.

The caller was a mother, concerned and upset because her twelve-year-old son had been told in school that it was okay to fantasize. About sex apparently, though that incendiary term was not explicitly mentioned. Eileen told her that what she had to do was to take her son out of school on the day sex classes were given and have a talk with the principal.

"Sure," I said to Rinpoche. "The kid's twelve, bursting with hormones. Keep him out of school. That'll do it. That'll fix everything!"

Rinpoche said nothing.

"Let his mom keep him home on the day of the sex lecture, so all the other kids can give him a hard time for the rest of the semester. He'll turn into a . . . a . . . a glutton, for God's sake, Mom. Cut the kid a little slack, Irene!"

But there was no slack to be had from the direction of Colleen. She started to go on about how bad the schools were for making kids think it was okay to be "selfish" and "do selfish things with their bodies" when sex was supposed to be "a selfless act for the pleasure of husband or wife."

I was, by that time, squeezing the steering wheel with both hands and wondering who it was we were talking about, which twelve-, fourteen-, or eighteen-year-old boy or girl on American soil—bombarded with erotic images from every angle—who was going to think of sex only in terms of giving pleasure, ten or fifteen years down the road, to his wife or her husband? Why was it always the middle-aged and old people, their sexual urges barely a shadow of what they had once been, their own guilt and regrets ballooning as they aged, who insisted on telling the young to abstain? And why was it that the loudest and most public religious types always sooner or later circled around to sex: talking about the "filth and whoremongering," and the evils of birth control, and going on about abstinence, and then everyone expressing such shock when teleministers were caught with prostitutes of both sexes and priests went after little boys and pregnancy rates shot through the roof. Sure, kids were having sex too early—we'd talked about it at length with our own children. Yes, the act of lovemaking ought to have some meaning attached to it—it was the source of life, after all—ought to be more than a release of some thoughtless, mutual lust. But sex was natural and wonderful, an essential part of life, and I hated this overlay of guilt and terror, hated to think of my children growing up to think it was somehow filthy in the eyes of God.

There were a lot of Catholics in Dickinson, and senior year in high school I had dated a Catholic girl. She was, in fact, my first real girlfriend. And I remembered, with a kind of agonizing vividness, the things she would and wouldn't do; the way, in the grassy field behind her uncle's house, she'd tiptoe around the Catholic definition of sin and somehow manage to suspend us both in a state where sex was all we could think about, for days. Her mother told her I'd end up in the flames of hell after I died, simply for being Protestant, and that she would, too, forever and ever, if she married me. I remembered sneaking into St. Patrick's Church in downtown Dickinson and attending Mass with her one time, and how wonderful it had been—the stained-glass saints and gilded altar—and how terrifying and old and marvelous the ritual had seemed.

I have a real affection for Catholicism; I make that claim in all sincerity (believe me, not all my Protestant brethren share that feeling). A deep respect for real Christianity. But these radio shows were making me want to strangle somebody.

The last straw came when Colleen took the subject and ran with it, going on about couples who had their "two token children." When those words registered I slapped my fingers down hard on the dashboard and yelled out, "They are not token, goddamn it!"

And Rinpoche put his hand on my arm until I calmed down.

"Listen," I said to him, snapping off the radio. "I want you to tell me something. In your tradition, is pleasure bad? I mean, sex, eating, and so on, does it keep you from holiness? Does it keep you from God?"

"It leads you to God," he said in a simple way, as if he were a chemistry teacher answering a question about the molecular weight of calcium.

I had an urge to reach out and shake his hand. "Now *that* makes sense to me. I want to convert. Where do I sign up?"

He was smiling and nodding. After a while he said, "But when you get tired of those things, your tiredness leads you to bigger pleasure."

"What if you don't get tired of them?"

"You should get a little tired of them," he said.

I was suddenly not so sure about converting. "But what if you don't? What if you like to eat, and you always like to eat; it never gets boring. Does that make you evil somehow? Not as good as these goddamned, self-righteous —"

He held up his hand, smiling, smiling, smiling. "Sex, food,

anger, violence, greed," he said. "Dirt in the glass. Then if you give up sex and food and anger and greed and you feel so proud about giving these things up, better than people, all about you, *you* gave this up, *you* are good, other people are not as good as *you*. That is more dirt in the glass, that's all. No big fuss, just that."

"You're talking about the golden mean," I said hopefully. "The middle way."

"Middle," he repeated. "Little this side of middle, little that side of middle. No fuss. What matters is how you treat people."

"Not what you believe about what happens after death?"

He laughed. I had made a joke, apparently. "What difference makes what you believe? What happens will happen anyway, exactly same, no matter what you believe. What you do makes the important part, what you do."

"But if some people believe one thing, and you don't, then what they'll do is tell you you're wrong. They'll try to change you, judge you. Maybe kill you, in extreme cases. So what you believe and what you do are connected, aren't they?'

"Do not worry so much all the time, my friend, about the other people, what they say. And do not have so many strong opinions, so many strong judgments. What *you* do matters. And what you think matters. . . . Here is Buddhist prayer," he said, and he rolled off a few sentences in what must have been Ortyk, then struggling just a bit, translated them. "All that we are is the result of what we have thought: It is built on our thoughts, it is made from our thoughts. If a man speaks or acts with evil thought, pain follows him, just like the wheel follows the foot of the ox that draws the . . . cart. . . . If a person speaks or acts with pure thought, happiness follows him, like a shadow that never leaves."

"So you can control your fate, then, to some extent."

"To every extent."

"So is there a life after death, then, in your belief system?"

"Not a system," he said.

"But there is what we call an afterlife?"

"After this, yes," he said. "How could there not be?"

"Well, plenty of people think it's obvious how there could not be. You die, your body rots, end of story. Couldn't that be the way it's set up?"

"Of course."

"You've just contradicted yourself. You're playing Zen games with me. I hate that."

"When your mind is clear you see it, that's all. You know what is and what is not, what will be and what will not be."

"You sound like my sister."

"I like very much your sister," he said. "Very, very much."

"But she claims to see the future."

"In some way she does see it. In some way you see it."

"But you see it differently than I do."

"Little bit different," he said.

"But you talk as if you are sure, and the people on the radio talk as if they are sure, and how can you both be right when your ideas of how things work don't match at all."

"They match. Of course they match."

"Oh, man, this is the worst conversation we've had, do you know that? Do you know how much I hate this kind of going around in circles?"

"Maybe you hate it because you like very much your thinking mind, one plus one is two. Always one plus one. Always B after A and then C after B. Dostoevsky—you know Dostoevsky? My father in Russian liked to read to me Dostoevsky. Then I read it, too, later."

"Of course I've heard of Dostoevsky. In college we—"

"In one book Dostoevsky said two plus two makes five, not four. What does this mean? My father asked me this question for many years until I get the answer right. What if you had another mind, maybe even for a few seconds? What if you knew how to make it so your mind did not think for a few seconds, or for a minute? What would happen then to your ideas and your opinions and your judgments?"

"I have not the slightest urge to make my mind stop working."

"Not your mind, your ordinary mind that thinks so much all the time for no usefulness. What then? Then maybe you see something new. But you cannot do that because all the time you are thinking about food, about sex, about worries, about who is saying something in this radio, about who is rich and poor, who is smart, who is good, who is right. Good, think like that. Very good. Not bad. You do that all the day and even when you are at sleep. But what about a few seconds or a minute or a few minutes of not thinking? Then what happens? Then what do you see? But you don't do that, my friend. You are afraid to do that, my good friend."

"Who on earth *could* do that? Even if they wanted to."

"Many, many peoples."

"Who? You? How? What does it feel like? How do you learn to do it?"

"I will show it to you if you want," he said.

I very nearly said, *Okay, we have a deal.* I wasn't ready to start taking not-thinking lessons, but I didn't hate the conversation so much anymore. I didn't resist him so much anymore, down in a deep part of me. It wasn't as if I'd suddenly turned gullible in western Indiana, but the raspy hard edges of my suspicion had been worn down, and I have to admit that it frightened me. This was not a physical fear but something else, a shakiness at the base of who I thought I was.

TWENTY-EIGHT

We let the conversation die there and soon we were leaving the corn-carpeted countryside of the heart of the Midwest and being drawn into the windy steel tangle of its greatest city. The first sign of that approach was the huge factories near Gary. I pointed through the passenger-side window and passed on a tidbit of Americana: "There's an important place in the history of American industry, that city right there. It was founded by the U.S. Steel Company and named after the chairman."

"Ah. Very good place," Rinpoche said.

Soon we could see the lake spreading northward like a blue sea, and then the skyscrapers of downtown Chicago. And then, on I-90 after we'd paid our toll, we became embedded in one of the most stupendous traffic jams in recorded human history, worse, even, than the one in Pennsylvania. The radio said the White Sox were playing that afternoon, that was the reason, and when I mentioned that to Rinpoche, he said he'd heard about baseball, and was it possible to go see the men play?

At last we crept into the city proper and parked in a lot on Harrison and Clarke streets not far outside the Loop.

Walking north from the parking lot we were presented with the magnificent variety of the American metropolis: a man sitting in a doorway with a fistful of scratch lottery tickets, checking them one after the next as if his happy future lay hidden there beneath a thin silvery layer; the imposing public library; the overhead trains on their rusty steel supports; people jaywalking; five muscular boys drumming on upside-down plastic buckets and accepting money from passersby; businessmen in suits and businesswomen in black shoes; lovers holding hands. There was every sort of life here—people who looked rich and people who looked poor, who seemed happy and who seemed miserable; mothers and fathers walking contentedly with their children; and men and women who appeared to be addicted to drugs, or to be suffering from mental problems, or who were ill, or whose lives were a walking nightmare.

As we moved along the west side of State Street with a warm, wet breeze stirring off the lake a few blocks to our right, I saw a billboard for the Cystic Fibrosis Foundation, with pictures of the two biggest individual fund-raisers in the area. Jeannie and I had friends who had two children with that illness, and over the years of knowing them we'd watched the children struggle and fight against it, and their parents worry about it, and we'd sent thousands of dollars in donations. "From the time I was a boy," I told Rinpoche, "I've always been obsessed with the way lives can be so different. I mean, even if you just take the people we've seen in the past ten minutes, a tiny sampling of the spectrum of good and bad fortune on this earth, look at how different they are. Some of them are so miserable and some so happy.

Some people seem to have an enormous burden set upon them at birth, and others seem to cruise right through with very little pain. I've always wondered why it's set up that way."

"Yes, yes," he said, fixing his brown-gold eyes on me as if he were seeing not my face and features but something buried beneath that, beneath the personality. It had been unnerving, at first; now I was almost used to it.

"'Yes, yes,' isn't much of a reply to such a profound question," I said.

He smiled. "It was a question?"

"All right. In your belief system, is there an explanation for that?"

He kept smiling. He said, "Yes."

"All right. Cut it out. What is it? What is the theory of the Ortyk non-Buddhists, or Sufi-Christians, or whatever it is you call yourselves?"

He laughed. By this time we had reached Marshall Field's, the wonderful old department store where Jeannie and I had gone for lunch on our first real road-trip-adventure, the start of our love affair. Rinpoche and I suspended the conversation temporarily and walked through the revolving doors, through the perfume and makeup department, and into an elevator that carried us up to the Walnut Room on the seventh floor. It was exactly as I remembered it: a sea of white tablecloths, large windows looking out on the city, the elegant walnut paneling with its brown and black swirls. The hostess led us to a table by the window and we were greeted immediately by a waiter carrying a pitcher of water, menus tucked under his arm.

When the waiter left us, Rinpoche said, "If you want to know why this life is like it is, you should know that it is because of your last life. If you want to know what your future life will be, you should look at the way you are living in this life."

"So it's a punishment, then. If you're straggling down State Street addicted to heroin, and you have AIDS, and you're poor as dirt and squatting in a doorway scratching lottery tickets you bought with a few dollars someone put in your hat, that means you were a bad person in your last life."

"Absolutely not," he said, and for once he was not smiling. "It means you are given that for your practice in this life."

"Practice for what?"

"For your next life," he said.

"You're playing the Zen game with me again. You know I hate it."

The waiter was back. Since it was my second lunch of the day, I decided to have something light—scallops on a salad, decaf coffee. Rinpoche asked for mint tea.

"They have the smallest banana splits in the world here," I told him, trying to simultaneously find a conciliatory note and change the subject. But Rinpoche was having none of that.

"My good friend," he said. "You want A-B-C like the alphabet, and two plus two make four. But you are asking about something so far past ordinary human thinking mind. How can I put together those two things in an answer?"

"I don't know."

"I can't make those things be sense in words, in the logic way of thinking, so I play Zen game. But it is not a game. It is the only way to begin—begin—to understand. I am trying to teach you, but you don't want to accept the teaching. You are very proud. You have a good life, you have worked hard for that life, you are very intelligent man, and in this society, intelligence like yours gets a good job, a good house, a good life for you and your family.

"There is nothing wrong with that. But you should try now to stop using so much that kind of intelligence, and stop thinking about punishment and sin and good and evil. I am telling you that your kind of intelligence makes you have a good job, but your kind of intelligence does not make you able to answer these questions. For that, you need a different kind of mind. And I am telling you there are people—maybe like that man in the doorway, maybe like that man sweeping the street in the city where your sister lives, or that man sitting outside the gas station the other day, or a woman we will meet soon—who can answer these questions better than you can, though maybe they do not have the fancy words. I am trying to tell you this, but you are proud of your intelligence, and your good job, and you will not let me teach you, so I play games." He sat back. "Is that answer better to you, my friend?"

The food arrived. For a little while, I buried myself in the pleasure of it, not answering the good Rinpoche. In truth, all during the main course, my mind was running frantically this way and that, trying to find a logical refutation. I finished the salad and ordered one of the World's Smallest Banana Splits and an extra spoon for Rinpoche, who tried two bites and smiled politely.

"Is that answer more pleaseful to you, my friend?" he asked, when the meal was finished.

"Yes," I said. "Somewhat more pleaseful, and massively confusing."

He reached out and touched my forearm in a kind way. Against a background of the rich brown paneling of that room, waiters and waitresses swirled and hurried, balancing trays at their shoulders, leaning in to take orders from elderly matrons whose eyes wandered out the floor-to-ceiling windows and down the length of State Street, where the traffic clogged and loosened like blood in an artery, and the world of business, of endless busyness, hurtled on. That busyness holds such an appeal, their eyes seemed to be saying. Such a strong appeal.

The light of the city of Chicago has a certain quality to it—because of the proximity of the lake, probably—and I was pondering that quality, and pondering the world of busyness, and thinking about my family, and feeling, just below the place where the meal I'd eaten was now at rest in its acidy bath, a kind of tearing open. The feeling reminded me, in a visceral manner beyond thought, of the way I'd felt in the moment I realized Jeannie and I were about to make love for the first time, an event that had occurred only a few miles from where the good Rinpoche and I then sat. In that hotel room there was the sexual excitement, of course (absent now, naturally enough, in the Walnut Room), but there was also something else surrounding it, a kind of terror-ecstasy balance, as if I were stepping off the sill of a tenth-floor window with the smallest of parachutes strapped to my back, a young man making a severe break with the familiar comforts of his past.

Exactly at that moment, as I was lost in that improbable comparison, Rinpoche said, "Ask any question now."

I looked up and for an instant the image of him seemed to flicker. For a second or two he seemed about to morph into someone or something else. Just nervousness, I decided, just a twitch in the optical nerve. Too many hours on the road. I looked at him more closely and he stabilized, if that is the word, and I hesitated for a moment and then hesitated some more and then said, "All right, my question is this: Assuming I wanted to find out about the greatest pleasure, as you call it . . . assuming I was open to that . . . what would the next step be?"

A smile the size of Lake Michigan. The no-longer-wavering Rinpoche saying, "How many days do we have now, you and me together driving?"

I pictured the route I'd planned out for him, north and then west so we could see the lakes in Wisconsin and Minnesota rather than the dry, flat, featureless grazing land of eastern South Dakota. "Maybe three days more."

"Not enough," he said.

"Maybe four, then, at the very most. I promised Jeannie and the kids I'd be back in time to — "

"Four days," he said.

"All right."

"Is it possible to show me to understand America in four days, Otto?"

I laughed and shook my head. "Fifty years, maybe."

"Fifty years to teach you, also."

"But you keep saying how advanced I am, what a good soul."

"I am advanced, too." He slapped himself in the center of his chest. "Rinpoche is not stupid," he added, and let out such an uproarious laugh that people at tables on all sides of us interrupted their meals to stare. "Rinpoche can understand America in four days."

"Not stupid at all," I agreed, quietly. "All right. I'll try to show you America in four days. You try to show me enlightenment."

"Maybe a little enlightenment. Maybe one piece."

"A fair exchange. One piece of enlightenment for one piece of the American experience."

"My good friend," he said, and I could see that I had made him happy, and it was not an unpleasant feeling, though the twisting in my intestines, the pinching at the bottom of my lungs, the sense that I was somehow going back on an old, old promise I had made to myself many years before—all of that abated only slightly.

TWENTY-NINE

At the Marshall Field's information desk I made an inquiry about baseball tickets and Chicago's other options for American fun. We retrieved the car and made the stop-and-go drive up North Michigan Avenue to a side street, where I pulled the car down and around the corner and back up in front of the Knickerbocker Hotel. I handed the keys over to an eager and clean-shaven young valet, and then, inside the lobby, was hit with such a wave of nostalgia that I stumbled and bumbled through the check-in like a college senior on his first overnight trip with his first serious love. After agreeing on a schedule for the rest of the day, we went to our separate rooms, the Rinpoche and I, and even then, when I was lying on the bed in the stately old room I'd requested, with the quiet hum and whistle of the city pressing through the window glass, and the soft pillow beneath my head, even then memories knocked and glided through the blood in my brain.

I dialed the number of my wife's cell phone. It was the middle of the afternoon, too early for my customary call, and when she heard my voice she said, "What's wrong, Otto?" with a small note of panic.

"Absolutely nothing. Guess where I am?"

"Bismarck. You drove all night. You're frustrated, you can't take it anymore and drove all night without sleeping, risking your life, because—"

"Chicago," I said. "Knickerbocker Hotel. Room 721."

She paused a beat. "You're joking."

"Not at all. I'm lying on the bed farthest from the window."

"You're really there? Since when did you become such a romantic?"

"Next anniversary we're coming here."

"I'm not opposed. Only not by bus this time. And with more than eighteen dollars in our pockets when we leave. That was such an extravagance."

"They've redone the wallpaper and the curtains, and the TV is different."

"They had no right to make changes to that room without consulting us. We should file suit."

"Do you remember that day?"

"Minute by minute. I could recite our conversations verbatim. I remember what we did. I remember what you were wearing—those awful double-knit maroon pants your mother had given you. I remember reaching down to undo the clasp and my hands were shaking so hard I thought you'd laugh at me."

"Grandmother. It was my grandmother who gave them to me."

"I remember taking a shower with you, hours after that, and feeling like a wild girl, and thinking what a nice muscular body you had, and feeling so self-conscious and so excited, like a whole new world had opened up. I remember the hockey-stick scar on your neck."

"You'll scandalize the children."

"They're out. I remember everything."

"You're the romantic," I said.

"What possessed you?"

"I don't know. I just wanted. . . . You should have come with me on this trip. You should meet this Rinpoche guy, he's not what I expected."

"Has he converted you?"

"Not exactly."

"Not *exactly*?"

"I did go into a barber shop in the Loop and have them shave off all my hair. I wear a robe now, I've sworn an oath to remain celibate, and I—"

"You're scaring me."

"I think there's something to what he says," I told her then, in a different tone, and she noticed it, naturally— we've been married long enough for her to detect that small change in my voice—and there was a silence. "It's not bad," I added, foolishly.

"Tell me what's happening."

"What's happening is that he's worn down my cynicism a little."

"What cynicism? You're the farthest thing from a cynic: you're a romantic."

"He's made me think about things from a different angle, that's all. Life and death, you know."

"What does he have you doing?"

"Nothing. We just talk. I'm trying to give him a sense of

America, and he's promised to try and give me a sense of . . . I don't know what to call it . . . another dimension of the interior life, I guess it would be."

"It doesn't sound like you."

"I know it."

"Dimension of the interior life . . . it doesn't sound like something you'd say at all."

"I know. I just have a feeling there's something I'm not paying attention to, and I'm willing to spend a couple of days exploring it."

"Should I put a FOR SALE sign on the house?"

"Just FOR RENT," I said, and she laughed, and I knew there was no problem between us, and wouldn't be, that the cord of our affection for each other was strong enough to allow me to venture out of the safe territory of our ordinary patterns without either of us pushing a panic button. I can't overstate what a feeling of freedom and love I had then, how calm that made me, how suddenly the whirring in my belly ceased to worry me.

Jeannie and I talked for another few minutes without discussing Rinpoche and his ideas. She had always been slightly more open to such things than her husband, and I knew we'd both hang up and think about what had been said and have a longer conversation about it at some point, but I did not want to go there yet. We talked about the children—the strongest fibers in the cord that linked us—and then simple things, domestic things: repairs to the front gutters, her plans for the rest of the day. When I hung up I lay back on the bed more contentedly even than I had twenty-four years earlier, my first real love there against me, skin to skin, and the future opening out in front of us, a vast prairie of possibility.

THIRTY

Both of Chicago's baseball teams were at home, as it turned out, so that night I took Rinpoche to see the Cubs at Wrigley Field. We rode the subway out there, rumbling and roaring beneath the city in an eclectic crowd of fans, troubled urban souls, and late commuters. It is such a great thrill to step out of the train and see the banks of lights above the walls of an old ballfield, to smell the popcorn and beer, to cross paths with scalpers offering tickets, and dads with their excited children. If you are late, as we were, it is at once exciting and frustrating to listen to the crack of the bat and the roar of the crowd swelling and ebbing just on the other side of the wall and to want so badly to be among that crowd. There is no feeling like walking through the old cement bowels of a place like Wrigley or Fenway or the House That Ruth Built, then emerging into the artificial light, seeing the flat, perfect emerald city of the playing field, the players themselves like gods in their white uniforms and fluid movements, the alert ushers, the families in rows, making the long climb up gum-stained concrete steps, sidling into seats, watching the way darkness falls gradually beyond the banks of lights as if the world there is a separate, sadder thing, and you have temporarily loosened its hold on you. The Cubs were playing the Phillies that night, and our seats were behind home plate but far up under the overhanging upper deck, almost in the last row.

For dinner, Rinpoche had popcorn and bottled water; I went with a hot dog and a beer and convinced him to try a few bites of cotton candy. He seemed to enjoy the cotton candy and the stadium atmosphere, but the game itself perplexed him. I tried to explain the immeasurably complicated pageantry of strikes and balls, umpires hooking their hands and making their war cries, the illogical shape of the field, the bases, the white-clothed young supermen spaced out on the greensward. Impossible. Try explaining, for one small example, the infield fly rule to someone who has not grown up with it. After a while I gave up and just submerged myself in the ocean of noise around us, standing and cheering when the home team scored, sitting in a muttering angst when the visitors' third baseman smacked a home run. In the bottom of the fifth I turned to Rinpoche, intending to explain the meaning of a double play, and I saw that he had fallen asleep there with the bag of popcorn clutched tightly in his hands, his big square head tilted slightly to the left. On his face was an expression of the most profound peace, cousin to the peace you see in the Buddha's smile. Even the next inning's home-run roar didn't wake him. From time to time I would take my eyes away from the elegant existential distraction that is baseball and look at the expression on Rinpoche's face, and I'd imagine myself pointing to it and saying to Jeannie, "See that. That's what I was trying to explain on the phone. That is what I want."

THIRTY-ONE

The next day, because I wanted to show Rinpoche a bit
more of the city before we moved on, I signed us up for an
architectural cruise on the Chicago River. I suppose I felt
the need to add some cultural or intellectual component to
his American tour. We could have gone to a museum, but
it was a glorious midwestern summer day, not too hot or
humid, the sky blue and endless. Plus, as much as I enjoy
paintings and sculpture, I like buildings more. For a time,
in college, I even thought of majoring in engineering, with
a minor in design, imagined myself going on to architecture
school and then transforming the nonexistent skyline of
Grand Forks, Fargo, or Bismarck with a series of startling
glass-walled masterpieces that people would be marveling
at hundreds of years after Otto Anthony Ringling was gone
from this earth.

But all that had been decades earlier. By the time
Rinpoche and I walked down to the Chicago River on that
perfect summer morning, my desires had been pruned, my
architectural ambitions narrowed to this: I just wanted to

soak up a little more of the big city. There would be nothing like it for the rest of our trip, I knew that. What awaited Rinpoche now, at least along the route I'd planned, was the pleasant, corn-fed humility of Madison and then the green-and-brown expanse of nature for eight hundred more miles.

So for an hour Rinpoche and I sat on the hard bench seats of a diesel-powered boat and listened to a fellow with a microphone talk about the great fire, and the deep-set pilings of this or that ninety-story building, and the million-dollar condominiums with river views. We looked out and up at the intricate cornices and massive steel walls, and down at the eddies of plastic cups, twigs, twisted tooth-white prophylactics, and the rest of the river filth. "At one time," our guide said, "the river flowed west to east, emptying into the lake. But people took their drinking water from the lake then, as they do now, and every year so many people fell ill and died from waterborne diseases that the city actually reversed the flow of the river so that it now empties in the other direction."

At last we disembarked, grabbed a quick Chinese appetizer at Jia's on Sterling Street, then retrieved the car again and made our way north on Highway 12, out of the city, out past the airport with its chain-link fences and cargo warehouses, out through the sedate suburb of Des Plaines, and then into the countryside and across the Wisconsin line.

I noticed, of course, that since our conversation in Marshall Field's, Rinpoche had not brought up the subject of my spiritual re-education. I was at peace with that. Somehow, overnight, the flame of my curiosity had dimmed. Looking around at the thousands of faces in Wrigley Field,

I'd had the thought that they were, most of them, good solid midwesterners, good fathers, mothers, and friends. How many of them meditated? Went to church, temple, or mosque every day? How many of them worried excessively about what might happen to them at the end of their lives? If all these thousands of good people weren't troubled by such things on an hour-to-hour basis, then why should I trouble myself? The thought had some power, and it carried me through that night and half the following day on a happy, easygoing mood that wasn't conducive to deep questioning.

As we followed small highways into the greenery of the Badger State and toward the capital, I said, "You have a talk this afternoon, don't you?"

He nodded. Rather somberly, I thought.

"Not looking forward to it?"

"I am thinking about the nice boat ride," he said.

"Some remarkable buildings in that city."

"Yes," he nodded, looking out at the silos and fields. "They made the river go the other way."

"Amazing, isn't it?"

"People were getting sick, so they made the river go the other way. Why didn't they just clean the river and make it go the same way?"

"Too hard, I guess."

He nodded again, let out one of his judgmental *ah*s, and after a mile or two of silence I realized that he'd probably been using the redirecting of the river as a spiritual metaphor: Why not just alter your life instead of changing its direction 180 degrees? And then I wondered if everything he said and did was meant as spiritual metaphor, and I was already becoming vaguely uneasy when he said, "I would like you to be in the front row this afternoon, not at the back."

"Okay. Sure. It's just a talk, isn't it?"

"A talk and something a little else."

"What's the something a little else? Group meditation?"

"Meditation makes you afraid," he said flatly, and out of the side of my vision I could see him turn his big head and I could feel his eyes on me. "Doing nothing for half an hour scares Mr. Otto."

I lied then. I said, "Not really."

"Good," he slapped the top of my leg. "First row, then. We will have more fun."

"Can't wait," I told him. After sitting there quietly for a few minutes, he started chanting, the same kind of thing I'd heard in Seese's back yard. It was a quiet chant, a low-octave mooing, almost as if he were singing to himself, mourning or celebrating I could not tell. It went on for nearly an hour and I did not feel it would be appropriate to turn on talk radio during that time. Later, when I asked, he told me the chant was the Ortyk way of praying for people who were in danger.

THIRTY-TWO

In downtown Madison they were having some kind of festival that included the placement of brightly painted, life-size ceramic cows on the sidewalks surrounding the white marble capitol building and along the adjoining streets. There were neon cows, art-deco cows, impressionist cows, and cows of no particular artistic style, around which small children stood and giggled. We followed a bovine trail of them along State Street, past a row of tourist shops, and into a district that seemed to offer every imaginable style of cuisine. It made me so happy, this World of Food, that I temporarily let go of my anxiety about Rinpoche's talk and "something a little else." We paused for a moment at a corner. Across the busy street I saw a maroon awning with the words HIMAL CHULI, AUTHENTIC NEPALI CUISINE on it.

"We have to try that."

"Yes, yes," Rinpoche said with one of his mysterious smiles. "I think this place is very good for you."

Himal Chuli had eight or ten tables set too close together and exotic prints on the walls featuring gods and goddesses with many arms. We were near the college, and you could sense that from the other diners: bearded young men with laptops and somber faces, studious young women in hand-me-down shorts and small tattoos. The menu listed the vegetarian dishes first, and I decided to try one of them as a kind of gesture toward my adventuresome new interior life. True, to that point, the adventuresome new interior life was identical to the staid old interior life, but I felt I'd made some kind of commitment . . . for a few days at least, and I was proud of myself for doing so.

"Khichadi," Rinpoche said, pointing to the first page of the menu. "We used to eat khichadi very much in our house when we were small children. Khichadi is a magic food, it makes your any sickness go away."

The menu described khichadi as "a fresh and light mixture of mung beans, Jasmine rice, fresh ginger, cilantro, tomatoes, peas, and ajwan seeds, favored for its nourishing and healing properties," and I decided it didn't sound half bad. Our order was taken by a child-sized woman of seventy or so with raven black hair and that same beatific smile on her face that I'd seen on the features of the sleeping Rinpoche at Wrigley Field. Rinpoche spoke to her in what turned out to be Nepali; I don't know why I should have been surprised.

"So how many languages do you speak?" I asked him when she'd headed off toward the kitchen.

"Eleven."

"Eleven!"

"Some of them, like English, not so good."

"You speak eleven languages?"

A professorial type at the next table looked over and smirked.

Rinpoche changed the subject: "Khichadi will heal a person if he is sick."

"I wished I'd known about it a few years ago. I had this awful mysterious sickness where I slept only a few hours a night, burping constantly, twitching. It went on for eight years, actually. I couldn't exercise much, had trouble digesting foods I'd eaten all my life. There were periods during the day when I was so exhausted I just wanted to sleep, and then when I tried to sleep I couldn't. It was a kind of torture, and I don't use that word lightly. I had every imaginable test and procedure and no doctor ever found anything. Even chronic fatigue syndrome didn't fit the symptoms. Eventually it just went away, but for a while there, after all those bad nights and miserable days, I just wanted to die."

"But you were strong," Rinpoche said.

"Strong? I felt weaker than an infant."

"You didn't die."

"I had thoughts of killing myself, to tell you the truth."

"I know that," he said, and I pretended not to hear him because I had never told anyone that particular secret, no one, not even Jeannie, and because, although I was now determined to be open to him and his ideas, mind reading was not yet on the list of things I was ready for.

"I don't think I would ever do that, but I had the thoughts. Some nights I'd wake up and sit on the side of the bed and cry, or curse. It wasn't easy on Jeannie and the kids."

"You were strong," he repeated. And then, after another waitress had brought us an appetizer of cucumbers in sour cream and soup for Rinpoche, he added, "All sickness comes from your spirit."

"Yes, I've heard that. We published a book on the subject—it was the book you showed me in Indiana. But I have to say I've never really believed in that idea."

"Good book."

"Yes, and helpful to some people, I suppose, but I believe that most illnesses are purely physical."

He was shaking his head and looking at me with some amusement. "All from the spirit. Past lives, this life, all from that. When you had that sickness, it meant that inside yourself you were trying to decide a very important thing. To go this way or to go that way . . . in your spiritual life. Big strain in you. And so, because of this strain—your sickness."

"Really?"

"Of course. All from the spirit. Except sometimes people take for themself a bad sickness so another soul will not have to, or so people will find for it a cure. Those things can be very complicated, taking someone else's karma."

"Jesus dying for our sins," I said.

"Yes, very much. Exactly. But, in the Bible there is no part about Jesus being sick. And Buddha was not ever sick until the very end of his life. Their minds were clean to the deepest level."

Without really intending to, without really thinking about where it might lead, I said, "How does one get one's mind that clean?"

"That is the very best question, my friend. The answer is a simple answer, but very hard also: Live a good life. Help people. Meditate. Live another good life. Meditate some more. Don't hurt. Don't hurt. Don't hurt." He chuckled and sampled his soup, smacking his lips loudly.

"You were going to teach me about, you know, that kind of thing."

"Yes, yes. Today lesson one."

"Good. When?"

"Now, soon."

The khichadi was bland to my taste, I'm sorry to say, a soupy stew of rice and vegetables. I ate half of it, tried the yogi tea, which was a milky concoction loaded with cinnamon, and then a delicious dessert called peda, made from ricotta cheese, pistachio nuts, coconut, honey, and cardamom seed.

Rinpoche finished his khichadi. He sat there savoring his tea and looking around at the wall decorations as if he'd been away in prison and had just returned to his parents' cottage on the Ortyk River and his mother had made him his favorite lunch and he was seeing the ordinary household objects he'd grown up around, but with a grateful, fresh eye. "Let me show something," he said, standing. He gestured for me to step with him into an alcove and he took hold of my upper arm and pulled me in close to one of the works on the wall there, a print of a bluish goddess with pointed breasts and dozens of arms. Her various hands were all holding something, vases, a flower, a skull, a serpent. As I looked closer I noticed that, floating above the head of the goddess, at the very top of the print, was another being, sitting cross-legged, its head surrounded by a blue halo. Other creatures, rather androgynous, occupied the bottom tier, below the goddess, against a background of plains and mountains, and these lesser souls did not have halos and were kneeling sideways rather than sitting in the lotus position. But they had similarly calm expressions on their faces, and they were wreathed in floating ribbons the color of the highest creature's halo, robin's-egg blue.

"It's interesting," I said, and Rinpoche laughed. There

were times when I suspected he was laughing at me, but this was not one of those times. This time I knew he was laughing at me.

"Here is the big world," he said, as if it were the most obvious thing. "Here is all creation. And here," he pointed to the goddess who occupied the large central circle, "is the god who watches over all of this part of creation, this earth."

"Fascinating," I tried. In fact, the print seemed odd to me. Odd, crowded, overly complicated, not particularly beautiful.

"This being is the greatest teacher of our age. She will soon come down to this earth and help us. She will soon be born."

"We need help," I said in a neutral, agreeable way, but now I was beginning to feel, again, something akin to that anxious twisting in the intestines that I'd felt with Jeannie in the room in the Knickerbocker Hotel so many years before. It was very strange to feel such a thing there, at that moment. It was deeply unsettling. And, really, it almost completely muted the old mocking voice in me that was trying to reassert itself.

Rinpoche said, "There is a prophecy that this goddess will come soon to save us from something very bad. Maybe she is your niece."

"I don't have any nieces, that I know of."

"Maybe she will be. . . . See, there are symbols in this painting—to know them you have to study many years—but the symbols say it is so that she is coming now."

"I'm glad," I said. Like everyone else I knew, I'd had moments when the apocalypse seemed imminent—the start of another war, the arising of another nuclear-armed despot, the boiling over of yet another ethnic conflict—but these were always followed by something like the feeling I'd had at Wrigley Field: everything was going to be fine. This was America, we were going to move forward, always, toward some greater, richer, more pleasurable future. Things could shake us—wars, riots, demonstrations, assassinations, terrorist attacks—but the enormous momentum of our settled and well-fed middle class, and the enormous reservoir of our goodness, generosity, brains, and energy, these would pull us through.

"Very dangerous time now," Rinpoche went on assuredly. "Not dangerous for our bodies, you know, to die, not that. Dangerous for us in the other way. Spiritual."

You've been watching daytime TV, I almost said.

"But now, soon, it will be better."

"Good, I'm glad."

"Do you want me to show you where you are in this picture?"

"What?" It was suddenly difficult to be standing. It sounds foolish, I know, but I have promised to say what happened, foolish sounding or no, improbable or no. Rinpoche said what he said, and my legs started to shake.

He let out the small, mucusy chuckle I'd heard from him in the car in our first hour together. He was still gripping my arm. He moved me another inch closer to the print and pointed one thick finger at a being I had not noticed before, a berobed fellow perched on one of the blue hillsides to the right of the lower-tier types. It was difficult to be certain, but the fellow seemed to be reading, or writing, to be holding in his lap a book or a sheaf of papers. I looked at Rinpoche and he had the enormous lippy smile on his face, but there was something utterly somber behind it.

"Can't be," I said. "That person has black hair and my hair is brown."

He threw back his head and laughed. His grip on my left tricep was like iron. "But he has a smile like you. Look!" he said when the laughter had subsided.

If the fellow was smiling it was the world's smallest smile, all of a sixteenth of an inch.

"You don't believe," Rinpoche said.

"No, frankly."

"Very bad, Otto!"

"Well, I'm just telling you the truth. The painting from which this print was made was probably painted a hundred years ago."

"Eight hundred! Eight!" He let go of my arm and held up eight fingers.

"Even more so, then. I wasn't around. How could that person have known about me?"

Rinpoche's face was only a few inches from mine. It was a frightening face at that moment, hard and honest, un-clothed by the usual social niceties. He seemed to be trying to tell me something about himself, about me, about life, but without using words. "You don't see, do you?" he said finally.

"No."

This seemed, momentarily, to sadden him. He nodded without breaking eye contact, and then, oddly, reached his arm around me and pulled me hard against him in a quick embrace.

Upon my release from this embrace, I was going to tell him that he had been overestimating me from the first. That I wasn't a particularly good soul at all, that I wasn't special, that it was exceedingly unlikely I would ever have an amazing niece or be chosen for any particular spiritual work, essential to the world's salvation or otherwise. Perceptive as he was, he had the wrong man, that's all. Maybe Cecelia had misinterpreted one of her visions, inserted me when, in fact, the Rinpoche should have been introduced to the man sweeping the sidewalk in Paterson, or the guy sitting near the gas station in Pennsylvania, the Popsicle seller outside the Mexican restaurant, the nut-brown woman who'd taken our order today. It was all a mistake, I was going to tell him, and it was time to stop the foolishness. I should pay and get him over to his lecture. *Forget the lessons,* I wanted to say. *Now you know who I am. I'm just one of the yelling crowd at Wrigley Field. Ordinary. All-American and proud of it. Too rich and soft and flawed to make any spiritual mark on anyone other than my own dog and children . . . on a good day.*

Just at that moment the nut-brown woman appeared at my left elbow, close to us in the small alcove where the print hung. I thought she'd come to ask why we were still taking up the table, why we hadn't paid and moved on so other customers could sit there. But she had something in her hands, and I saw that it was an expensive-looking necklace of robin's-egg blue beads. On her face rested the tiny, peaceful smile, but it was wavering as if she was excited, or nervous. She bowed deeply to Rinpoche and said something to him, and though I didn't understand a single syllable, it was clear from her gestures that she was asking permission to place the necklace over his head, and that she revered him in much the same way my sister did. Rinpoche nodded. The woman went up on her tiptoes, he bowed his head, and she placed the necklace over him in a gesture of such reverence that, I tell you, I began to shake almost violently. Rinpoche took her tiny hands in his large ones and spoke to her, and it was as if they were mother and son, or sister and brother, such was the intimacy. After another few words she turned and looked at me, searching my face with her chocolate eyes. She shifted the gaze to Rinpoche, who nodded, and then the woman bowed to me with that same reverence, that same otherworldly calm. *No, no,* I wanted to tell her. I wanted to take her by the shoulders and say, *No! Wrong guy! This is Otto Ringling. Look, I can take out my wallet and show you my tennis club membership. I like sex. I like food very much, too much probably. I yell at my kids once in a while and I have opinions, very judgmental opinions, about everything on earth. This is a mistake. I don't know what he said about me but it wasn't true. It's a mistake!*

But—who knows why—I accepted her bow and nodded my head in return. And then Rinpoche had his arm around my shoulders and was leading me out—we never did pay—across State Street, through the door of a building. We went single-file up a narrow set of stairs to another door, which opened into a room that had no furniture in it, just mats and pillows, and fifty or sixty faces staring at us with a frightening expectation.

THIRTY-THREE

To my shock, to my dismay, it turned out that the "something a little else" Rinpoche had referred to was a yoga class. If I had felt like running away during the strange scene in the Nepali restaurant, now I felt like sprinting to the door, crashing through, and knocking over a dozen ceramic cows on my way to the car and freedom. Only the fear of embarrassment kept me from doing that. The fear of embarrassment and the fact that, as we stood around talking with the yoga instructor (a part-Asian woman who looked, it seemed to me, something like the supreme goddess in the print across the street), more and more people came through the door. This was a problem, the instructor said quietly, there was not going to be room for all of them, enough mats, enough floor space. "I'll just stand in the back," I volunteered. "Don't worry about me."

But Rinpoche laughed. He had a hand on my arm. It seemed that he'd had a hand on my arm for the past week. The instructor, whose name was Kaylee or Molly or Kali or Paula—I was much too uncomfortable to hear it clearly—was standing two feet away in her yellow leotard, with her short black hair and clear-as-air green eyes. She seemed to think I was making a joke. When she realized that I wasn't, she said, "But, Mr. Ringling, your mat is right here, in the front row. We've saved this place specially for you." She pointed to a mat that lay between the mats of two women who looked as though they had one thousandth of one ounce of fat on their bodies. And these were not college-age women, either. They were loosening up (though why one loosened up for a yoga class, I could not imagine), sitting with their legs spread in a V and pushing their chests flat to the floor between their knees, or bringing their arms behind their backs—one arm from above, one from below, clasping the hands there and rocking this way and that. It was awful. It was a nightmare. I looked at Rinpoche with what must have been a pleading expression, because he squeezed my arm harder and told me I shouldn't worry, that I was a good man, that I was his good and special friend.

When the class began, Rinpoche and Paula sat up front on their mats, and it took me about a minute to understand that the man who had been riding with me all these days, the thickset, muscular guy who looked like he could pass for a Chicago Bears linebacker coach, was as limber as a ramen noodle all cooked.

The room was filled: thirty or so shapely women in tights, a couple of long-haired men in the back who were built like the circus guys who catch female trapeze artists in midair, and behind them, lining the wall now, a crowd of mostly college students in nonyoga wear, standing reverently and watching Rinpoche's every move. I was wearing chinos and a jersey, not exactly the uniform of the day. As instructed, I took off my shoes and socks and belt and set them at the side of the room. I unfurled my blue mat. My heart was thumping so violently I thought I might be saved by some kind of minor infarction.

But no, there was no salvation for me. Molly introduced the Rinpoche as a great holy man and yogi and then introduced me as his associate, "first student," and traveling companion. My face was the color of a persimmon. Behind me I could feel four dozen sets of eyes, and there I was, in all my clunky middle-aged glory, fit only for the occasional two-mile walk and friendly game of doubles tennis, the chinos, the jersey, the sweat already plastering my hair to the back of my neck. We knelt, sitting on our heels, and began with a few minutes of silence, "to quiet the mind," as Molly said. But my mind was about as quiet as Grand Central Station at five p.m. on a Tuesday. When the meditation was completed we chanted "Om" once and then stood. We began with a bow, simple enough—even I could manage a decent bow—and then went into something called "whipassavana," or something of that sort, which, of course, every single other matted soul in the room was familiar with. I looked around, spying desperately. The lithe creature to my left was crouching down and extending one leg behind her, planting her palms on the mat to either side of her bare foot, and arching her back so that she was looking at the ceiling. It was as effortless for her as reaching across the table for another handful of honey-roasted cashews was for me.

But I tried it. Rinpoche was watching me, smiling broadly, one knee poking up through his robe, and his new necklace glinting in the natural light. I managed not to fall over. We put our hands briefly on the knee, then raised them to heaven, palms pressed together, eyes up, and I did fall over. I fell sideways and knocked into the woman next to me. "Sorry," I managed. I was breathing very hard. I tried again. This, Kali said, if I heard her at all right, was called "keepassona." We were to breathe into our stomachs. My stomach was full of khichadi, yogi tea, and the sweet dessert. But I tried. We were to bring the hands down, thank God. Then put the other leg back also and hold ourselves in the higher push-up position—"allassoavana," or something like that, also called "the plank." This I could do. But Kali held us there until my arms were shaking, all the while telling us in a depressingly calm voice that, to get the most out of the pose, we were to turn the muscles of the upper arm out and the muscles of the forearm in and the muscles of the inner thigh up and breathe through a relaxed throat. Then we were supposed to sink slowly, almost—*almost,* she repeated—to the mat, and hold ourselves one inch above the floor for eight slow breaths. I collapsed. I looked up at Rinpoche. His body was as rigid and still as a piece of metal, an inch or two of air beneath his chin.

Soon we were doing what sounded like "sikovara," which entailed sitting on the tailbone, bringing one knee up, and twisting over it so that the eyes were facing the back of the room. I was sweating profusely. There wasn't the smallest sound from anyone. Sikovara the other way, slowly, watching the breath. Then forward bend—achinarrassavana. Then achinarrassavana left, achinarrassavana right. I was, by this point, furious at Rinpoche for having tricked and humiliated me. Even a person who *did* belong in the print in the alcove across the street would have been furious. But I *did not* belong there. It was a case of mistaken identity! He smiled at me. I did not smile back. I vowed to press on. I would show him. I would show Kali, or Molly, or

Paula, and the woman to my left whom I'd knocked over, and the trapeze artists in the back of the room with their steroid shoulders and long hair, and the students against the wall staring. I would make it through, if nothing else. I called upon every ounce of will developed in my 135-pound days on the Dickinson High gridiron, every bit of courage from the rink at UND jayvee hockey tryouts, when I was similarly outmatched but managed to be the last man selected. Ognipassineh. Silsa rannawathana. Boothanagan masi. Standing on the left leg with the right foot pressed into the left thigh, hands high, palms together. Downward facing dog. Upward facing dog. Dog facing death. My arms were trembling, my legs were violently trembling, perspiration had worked its way through my shirt and down to the top of my chinos and I worried that I had not sufficiently washed my feet that morning. On and on and on it went, standing, lying, twisting. A torment.

At last, after what seemed like the better part of a school year had passed, Molly called for something named, appropriately enough it seemed to me, corpse pose, or death pose. The lights were dimmed. We lay on our backs and tried to relax every cell in our bodies. For the first minute I bathed myself in a kind of triumphant fury. I had made it. Stumbled a few times, given up on a few poses, but survived. And Rinpoche would pay. Forget my lessons, my open-mindedness, his three- or four-day tutorial on America. We were going to get in the car and race to Bismarck and I was going to drop him at the farm in Dickinson the next day, do my business, and be done with him for all time.

But then, as I lay there, the fury subsided. What caused it to subside I'm not sure, perhaps just the fact that my body was no longer in pain. Or, at least, not in severe pain. I was pretty certain I'd pulled my left hamstring—which meant no tennis for six weeks—and that I'd torn a small muscle in midback, which meant a few hundred dollars in chiropractic visits. But after several minutes of stewing, I noticed that a wonderful whole-body calm was coming over me. I had not relaxed like that in decades, if ever. Every fiber of my body, every cell from the soles of my feet to my scalp, had been worked, and now they were at rest, and my mind slowly joined them. It was not like sleep, I was not drowsy at all, but a kind of sunny calm descended over my thoughts. And then, for a short while, a few breaths, there were no thoughts at all. I had never experienced anything remotely like that, had believed it impossible, in fact. But there was a short stretch of alert thoughtlessness and it was unimaginably sweet, stunningly sweet. When it passed I found that I was thinking of my children and wondering if they had ever given yoga a try, and if not, why not.

Then Kali was calling us to our feet for a final bow, a thank-you to Rinpoche. Mats were folded up, the crowd at the back swelled forward, and my friend was surrounded as if he were Elvis come back to Graceland for the summer season. I shuffled over to my shoes and leaned against the windowsill in a state of exhaustion. My shirt was drying. I could feel it going stiff against the skin of my belly.

In a moment, Molly herself stepped free of the crowd and came over to me, not walking exactly but floating along an inch above the floor. She could have been a model for the anatomy charts, the muscles defined, the posture perfect. I looked at her with what wasn't even sexual admiration—it transcended that. She was somehow beyond sexual, überhuman.

"You made it through okay?" she said, rather coyly, I thought.

"You're laughing at me."

"It was hard, wasn't it."

"Hard? It was like being inside a washing machine."

"But you feel good now, right?"

"Differently good," I said, and she laughed.

"And mentally?"

"Calm there for a minute."

"Going to keep at it?"

"I don't know. Probably not. Maybe. I don't know."

She smiled, touched me on the shoulder, said, "Drink lots of water," and glided away. "You might be a tiny bit sore tomorrow," I thought she said, as she went.

It was the better part of an hour before the crowd around Rinpoche dissipated. Even then, Molly had to chase them off. I don't know if they were asking for his autograph, or plying him with questions, or what was going on. Who could see through the dreadlocks and backpacks, the torn T-shirts? This, I supposed, was his talk, though I could not hear him talking. Leaning there, resting, I watched the goings-on, and as my mind does after sex, a particularly good meal, a fine symphony, or any other joy it wants to touch and touch again, it kept circling back to those few seconds when it had been blank. But *blank* was not the right word for what it had been. *Stillness* was not the right word. For the space of eight or ten seconds, something, some process or interior habit, had been suspended, and in those seconds, wordlessly, I thought I had seen or understood something, and I kept reaching back to retrieve that understanding, and my mind kept tripping over its old habits and bouncing away.

THIRTY-FOUR

That night we stayed on the outskirts of the modest city of Eau Claire, Wisconsin. On the drive north out of the capital, Rinpoche said not a word. A fair portion of my anger had returned, but alongside it ran the memory of those few seconds on the yoga mat in the death pose. I felt as if I had been shown a kind of essential secret, something so subtle and quiet and small (and yet so important) that I could have gone my entire adult life and never even imagined such a thing existed. As I reflected on it, I realized that I'd experienced somewhat similar moments—watching the sun go down from a beach chair on the Cape; taking a first sip of hot chocolate after a morning of skiing; just lying in bed on a Saturday when the children were small and safely asleep on my chest. But those flashes of peace seemed somehow accidental, and they bore a resemblance to what I'd felt in that overheated yoga studio in the same way that a kiss on the cheek by a nice aunt bears a resemblance to an orgasm with the person you love. A lush new field had become part of my interior world, and it was difficult to sustain anger under the open sky.

Rinpoche was quiet, quiet, quiet, not mooing, not asking, not chuckling, just staring out the side window, buried in thought. Or, perhaps, buried in no-thought. I wondered if he had somehow found a way to remain in that airy, sunny field for long stretches at a time, and I wondered what that would feel like.

Just at dark we pulled off the highway and immediately found a place called the GrandStay. Still riding a kind of yoga high, I went in and asked the young man at the desk for his most expensive suite. And what a nice room that turned out to be, out there on the edge of the Wisconsin wilds. Two large bedrooms with their own TVs, and a huge central room with fireplace, full kitchen, sofas and chairs, two baths.

When we were about to begin the ritual of going to our separate rooms and giving each other some alone time, I felt I had to break the silence. "I'm angry at you," I began.

Rinpoche nodded without smiling. He seemed to be standing perfectly still, as if he were not breathing, his heart not beating. He was not blinking.

"Just when I was starting to trust you, to really listen to you, you tricked me into doing that yoga class."

He nodded again, waiting.

"At least you could have let me be in the back row so everyone couldn't see me make a fool of myself."

Another nod. More attentive stillness. At last he spoke, "Is Otto finished being angry now?"

"Pretty much, yes."

Nod number four. "Are you ready to become the new Otto, or do you want to stay the old Otto?"

"The old Otto wasn't half-bad," I said. "Some people liked the old Otto. Loved him, even."

"Today, you had a little bit of while when you were the new Otto."

"Where? When?"

"Corpse pose. A few seconds."

"How would you know that?"

"I see it."

"How do you see it? Where? My aura?"

He chuckled and shook his head. "It was pleasure-making to you, yes?"

"Yes."

"New pleasure, yes? Different."

"Yes, I admit that."

"Then I will show you more, but if you want to be angry with me I can't show you. Anger is like hands over your eyes when another person is trying to show you."

"All right. I'm done with it, then."

"Good," Rinpoche said. "We are not eating tonight, you and me. Tonight no eating, and tomorrow no eating. Tomorrow, dinnertime, we eat. Okay?"

"How about just a little snack before bed? Health food? Celery sticks or something. Popcorn."

He sat on the couch and patted the cushion beside him. "Sit like me," he said. So I sat there, separated from him by a few feet of motel sofa. He took one of the small throw pillows off the sofa, put it beneath him, and crossed his legs. I did the same, my recently overworked muscles protesting painfully. "Now," he said, "listen to me with all your mind and all your self."

"Okay. Trying."

"Close your eyes, Otto, and listen to my voice."

"Okay. Are you going to hypnotize me?"

"The opposite of hypnotize. The very different."

"Okay."

"Now. Do you hear that noise of tapping?"

"Yes, I do."

"That is a bird hitting with his mouth against the edge of the window where he thinks it is wood."

"Okay."

"He is trying to make a house there. I saw him when you went inside to buy this room. He can't make a house there because it isn't real wood. It is pretend wood of plastic, but he is trying, do you hear him?"

"Yes. But it's vinyl, I bet, not plastic."

"Do you hear the noise of the refrigerator now?"

"Yes."

"Do you feel this chair against your back and your legs."

"It's a sofa. Yes, I feel it."

"Do you feel your breath going in and coming out?"

"Yes."

"Now, we will sit here for two hours about. If your legs hurt, or if you have to, you get up and walk a little bit, but don't get up at the first time you feel like it. You will be thinking about food. Every time you are thinking about food, now and tomorrow, I want that you think about the feeling that food gives you on your tongue. Think about exactly that feeling, the food on your tongue, in your mouth. Take one breath thinking about that feeling, and then let that feeling go away when the breath goes out. That is what meditation is: You see the thought and you let it float away, see the thought and let it float away. Maybe you say to yourself, *That is only a thought.* . . . After a while, listen again to the bird, to the refrigerator, feel again the sofa on your back and your legs, feel the pain in your legs. You will think about food again. Breathe in and breathe out. You will think about your family, your work, about me sitting beside you, about many, many things that are interesting to think about. This is like the bird knocking. You cannot make a home in those things. They are not bad, they are just not the right home for Otto. Do not get upset because your mind thinks about them. Do not push the thoughts away like they are bad things. Let them go away from you but do not push them, yes? But always come back to the feeling on your mouth, and breathe in and breathe out. Yes?"

"I'll try."

Rinpoche went quiet. And shortly after Rinpoche went quiet, my mind became a combination circus/symphony/rock concert. Seven television stations on at once, in the same small room. Grand Central Station but with a band marching through it now, advertisements being read aloud, the babbling of fifty voices. I thought about food, at first, and tried to do what Rinpoche had advised. I heard the bird tapping. I thought about food again—a good steak, in fact, medium rare. I could feel myself salivating, feel the gnawing in my belly, feel a twinge of anger at him for making me abstain and a twinge of anger at myself for being foolish enough to agree to abstain. I heard the bird, the refrigerator. I thought about Jeannie. I thought of Anthony playing football, imagined him sitting on the bench, with the first-string players muddy and manly on the field, and the cheerleaders cheering, and Jeannie and I and Tasha in the stands. This particular scene played itself out in elaborate detail for what must have been several minutes: Natasha sitting a few feet away from us in the cold bleachers, texting and frowning, barely paying attention; Jeannie watching her son's back to see what his mood was; me hoping for a lopsided score either way so that Anthony might see two minutes of playing time. It wound and spun, this scene, and then I heard the bird knocking and remembered to focus on the sensation of eating, remembered my breath. Then I thought of Rinpoche and actually even opened my eyes to peek at him, though it was like peeking at a stone to see what it is doing. I closed my eyes. Refrigerator. Bird. Rinpoche. Rinpoche. The steak. What were they doing at work? What would my assistant, Salahnda, say if she could see the boss now? Then, of course, my legs began to hurt.

On and on the circus went. Four or five times in the two hours, I got up and took one loop around the room, watching Rinpoche be perfectly still. By the last half hour my legs were starting to stiffen and ache terribly—the yoga was catching up with me—and I was anxious to be done with this exercise, and I sat there in a more comfortable posture, feet on the floor, eyes closed, the circus going, spinning, whirling.

And then, five minutes or so before Rinpoche tapped me on the knee, I began to settle into a kind of quiet that was very pleasurable. There were thoughts, but they came and went without carrying me away. There seemed to be spaces between the thoughts—that's the only way I can express it. Thoughts and images floated across the sea of my mind with spaces between them. I could watch them come and let them go. The bird had stopped tapping, gone elsewhere for the night. The refrigerator hummed. I thought about eating, of course, but even those thoughts were small sailboats out on a placid bay, harmless and interesting but not particularly enticing, wending their way across the calm waters of my new mind. Rinpoche tapped on my knee, and when I opened my eyes he was studying me. Then he was smiling. "Good, yes?"

"Yes, partly. I felt—"

He held up a hand. "Now," he said. "Go to sleep, and just every little while in your sleep if you remember, breathe in once and out once and sleep. Okay?"

"Okay," I said. "But can we talk about what happened?"

"Just sleep now instead of eating, instead of talking."

"All right. Thank you. Good night, then."

"Good night."

THIRTY-FIVE

In the morning, I woke to the realization that I could not move. I discovered, in my postyoga agony, that there are hundreds of tiny muscles—back of the neck, armpits, pelvic area, front and back of the legs—that we do not pay the slightest attention to in the course of our normal waking activities. During the ten or fifteen minutes I spent lying there, trying to work up the courage to move, it occurred to me that yoga was all about becoming aware of those muscles, training them, feeling them, and that the misery I was then experiencing must be a kind of payment for four decades of being half-oblivious to my own body. I wondered, too, if this physical situation was a metaphor for my spiritual one: Maybe, surely, there were whole areas of the mental landscape that I had been blissfully unaware of all these years.

When I tried to sit up in the bed the silent crying out of my muscles turned into a full-throated screaming. On top of everything else, I was ravenously hungry. I lay there and concentrated on the hunger, imagined the pleasure of food in my mouth (for some reason that morning I had a particular inclination for a bran muffin, grilled and slathered with butter, a plate of fresh fruit, and hot black coffee), then breathed in and out slowly, once. Again. A third time. I tried to move just my feet and found that I could twist them in circles, very gently. Then I moved my hands the same way. Not too bad. In this fashion, after fifteen minutes, I was able to sit up on the edge of the bed and hold myself there on locked arms so that my stomach and back muscles would not have to do any work. Outside the window I could hear the bird at its fruitless tapping. I breathed in and breathed out. I pushed myself to a standing position and let out an involuntary groan. Getting back and forth to my bathroom for ablutions and medication and getting dressed was another fifteen-minute process, but as the muscles warmed, and as the ibuprofen kicked in, they hurt slightly less. When I stepped out into the main room I found Rinpoche waiting for me, standing at the sink, big smile on his face, glass of water in one hand.

"So we can drink, at least," was my morning greeting. "I'm glad. I worried I was cheating because I already had a few sips with my ibuprofen."

He filled a second glass and handed it to me.

"You didn't tell me you were a yoga master."

He laughed happily, kindly. "Otto has muscles that hurt today, yes?"

"Otto hurts. His selfhood hurts. The innermost essence of who he is has become pain."

He kept laughing. "Next time not so bad," he said, and when we were done drinking he hoisted my suitcase and carried it and his famous oversized purse down the stairs.

In the lobby, checking out, I tried to keep my back turned to the breakfast buffet, but I could smell everything—the apples, the toasted bagels, the sugar-dusted raisins in the Raisin Bran in its vacuum-sealed packet in its cardboard box. I could hear the morning news: a number of men had been arrested in Great Britain because they had been planning to blow up airplanes in midair. New restrictions on carry-on luggage were to be put in place. To distract myself from the food smells and bad news, I filled out one of those comment cards, telling the GrandStay management how nice I thought the room was, and soon we were in the car, driving away, filling up with gas, and starting north on Route 53, in the direction of Lake Superior.

Every half hour or so, Rinpoche would tell me to stop, and I would get out of the car by the side of the road, stretch for ten minutes, and drink from a bottle of water, then get back in behind the wheel. It made for a long and very slow trip. Duluth was the next big city on our route, and I had cell phone service, at first, so on one of those stops I called information, selected a massage therapist at random, and made an appointment for the next morning.

All this time I was thinking about eating. In a not very serious way, I wondered if, by not sticking to my body's usual routine, I might be doing myself harm; if some organ—spleen, maybe—would cease to function because of the lack of caloric intake and be damaged forever. I pictured Jeannie and the kids eating. I pictured myself at work, taking my time with a raisin scone and coffee at the midmorning break, or walking around the corner to the Taj Raj for chicken korma and gulab jamon. Every time we passed an exit I looked at the signs for chain restaurants and thought about all the people there with their burgers, their fries, their slices of factory-cooked cherry pie. Was God angry at those people? Was the creator of the universe sitting in judgment on them for indulging their appetites? It seemed only right and natural to eat and a kind of violence to be refraining. A very logical interior voice kept nagging at me to sneak a bit of chocolate and break Rinpoche's fast. But I did not.

Somewhere in the middle-north of Wisconsin, where the fertile cornfields had fallen behind us and we were traveling through a stony terrain of weatherbeaten houses and shaggy farms, I said, "I have to say I don't see the point in this not-eating stuff."

"No point," Rinpoche said.

"Then why do it? Is eating evil? Is it sinful? I don't understand."

"Not evil."

"What, then? Tell me."

"Eating. Sex. Movie. Bohling. Nice things. Not evil. It makes you think about itself, though, yes?"

I thought of the days when Jeannie and I were first married, and the great sense of anticipation I'd always feel as we climbed the stairs to our third-floor Chelsea walkup, arm in arm, knowing we would make love. I thought about it then, and thought about it afterward, and the next morning, and the next afternoon, and the next night walking up the stairs again. "Yes, I suppose so. Of course," I said.

He nodded. "And this always thinking about the next pleasure, this is not so bad. Except it keeps your mind from how it could be calm in this moment. This can happen on a very subtle level, or not so. If you don't eat for a little while when you can, or don't sex for a little while when you can, then you see better the way the mind makes the world for you."

"And that does what, exactly? Abstaining, I mean."

"Makes the glass more clear. When your mind is more clear, you see the true way the world is made. When you see the true way the world is made, you feel at peace inside. You see how you make your own world, so then you can make it different if you want."

"But that's just another pleasure to anticipate, isn't it?"

"Yes, very much."

"You're Zenning me. I've been Zenned."

He laughed but did not say anything else. By the side of the road I saw a barn with IT'S A GIRL! in faded white paint on one side.

"At the end of the meditation there, last night, and at the end of the yoga, there was a short period where my mind seemed to be functioning differently." I glanced over at the Rinpoche, expecting a smile, a word of praise, or encouragement. He seemed bored. "It was a wonderful feeling, a kind of quiet. Do you know that feeling?"

"Of course. I am in that feeling all the time."

"All the time?"

"Of course."

"When you were in prison?"

"When I was in prison I prayed that the people hurting me there would know that pleasure."

I glanced back and forth between the road and his calm face. A lie? Self-delusion? A sweet rewriting of history? I tried to recapture the mental landscape of the few minutes in the corpse pose, the few minutes on the hotel sofa. "Why is it so pleasurable?"

He pondered this question for a while, looking out at the unspectacular scenery. "Remember the painting on the wall in the restaurant?"

"The print of the eight-hundred-year-old painting with me in it? How could I forget?"

"Remember around the heads of the goddess and the gods was a circle, and in that circle a blue space with nothing inside?"

"Yes."

"That is the blue space, what you felt."

"All right. It's a nice blue space. I liked it. In the picture it reminded me of the halos around Jesus and Mary and the saints in a lot of the Christian paintings I've seen."

"Yes, exactly so. The people who made those paintings of Jesus and Mary could understand this, what I am saying. In that space there is no anger, no killing, no war, no wanting food or sex all the time. And no fear of dying."

"How do you know?"

"Forget me!" he said, rather roughly. He had turned to face me now, and his voice held that note of pure authority in it and not so much kindness, not so much patience. "Many peoples have written about it. Catholics and Protestants and Sufis and Hindus and Buddhists and Jews and Muslims and Baha'is, many great teachers. Not my idea, Otto, not me, just a fact. Is the sky my idea?" He swung an arm up in the direction of the windshield. "If I say, there is the sky, do you ask me how I know? Do you think I'm the crazy man that thinks he invented the sky?"

"Well, I have only a few days, I want to learn as much as I can. . . . And I admit to a certain skepticism that—"

"You should underlearn," he said.

"Underlearn? You mean unlearn?"

"Unlearn. You learned already too much. Don't think so much now, just whenever you want to think so much take a nice breath, listen to the tires' noise on the road, look at the trees, look at the lake, look at the other cars, feel inside when you are breathing, feel the pain in your muscles. That is what yoga does for anyone, makes you to pay attention, not to think. Do not force information into your mind. You are smart now, you will always be smart, but if you think too much it pushes you from God."

"All right. God here I come. Watch for my halo."

He didn't laugh. "Life is very fast, Otto."

"I know that. I've seen that with my children—they were infants in diapers a couple days ago; now they're ready to leave the house."

"This is a way to make it slow."

THIRTY-SIX

At one point, I remember, we turned off Route 53 and wandered around in the sandy territory to the east, taking two-lane highways that ran along a lake and past plain-looking cottages. I thought, maybe, we could pull over and take a swim, or hike down a side road, but, in spite of three doses of anti-inflammatories, my muscles were as sore as if I'd just had my first week of high school football practice. Swimming would hurt. And I suspected that Rinpoche had seen enough trees and cornfields, so a dirt-road hike did not seem the wisest plan either. We passed a small town, then the Fisherman's Hall of Fame, marked by a hundred-foot-long plastic pike or muskellunge suspended on stilts, but even that didn't tempt me. I decided not to think about it, to just drive back to the big highway, observe, calm my mind, and let any American fun in the area come to us as a gift of the gods.

I had hoped to stay that night in downtown Duluth—a place I remembered well from half a dozen childhood trips—but a series of phone calls gave me to understand that all the grand old waterfront hotels there were full up, so we had to settle for a motel on Barker's Island, on the Wisconsin side of the lake. With the stretch breaks, semicircular detour, a stop for gas, and another stop for tea, it was late afternoon by the time we pulled onto Barker's Island, the air hot but not particularly humid, my stomach clenching and muttering. Steak, I was thinking. A nice rare steak with garlic mashed potatoes and grilled asparagus, maybe just a salad beforehand, a couple of glasses of cabernet. Then cheesecake for dessert.

Our lodging on Barker's Island was adequate, a sort of resort motel with an indoor pool. Rinpoche and I were given two rooms on the first floor at the far eastern end, just past the pool, which was filled with squealing, happy boys and girls, their parents sitting at nearby tables reading the newspaper or paging through magazines. There was a moldy smell to my room. I opened the window and looked out across the parking lot and lawn, to the edge of a body of water that seemed to be some kind of bay or inlet, not the huge lake itself.

Rinpoche was meditating. We'd agreed to meet up in an hour. I soaked my aching muscles in a hot bath, flicked through the television channels—golf, cooking, news, romance, celebrity fascination—and, for a moment at least, saw them the way I imagined Rinpoche saw them, as just more pleasures to think about, more information to crowd out the blue sphere, more distraction from some essential path. I supposed it was true that certain distractions were better than others. Looking at a great painting or reading a great book might turn your mind in the direction of the pleasurable emptiness; watching babysitters and jilted wives fighting on a TV show probably would not.

Drying off and dressing for dinner, I thought about my parents and wondered if they had, in fact, been living out a kind of meditative existence there on the vast plains west of Bismarck. When my mother swept snow off the boards of the front porch, with a bank of storm clouds speeding east and leaving a bare blue sky above her, when my dad spent all day in his tractor riding back and forth along the endless rows of soybean fields, could they have been sensing something like what I had sensed in my two brief glimpses on the yoga mat and on the GrandStay couch? Some sweet, charged emptiness they knew intimately but could not find words for? Was that why they urged me and Cecelia so persistently toward the farming life? It seemed possible but unlikely. It seemed to me that their spiritual urges were confined, by habit and a kind of Protestant peer pressure, to the plain church where we worshipped on Sunday mornings. Their contract with God was a simple and straightforward one: Don't do anything evil during the week, go to church on Sunday, God will take care of the rest. Yoga classes optional.

It seemed to me that Rinpoche was making the opposite point: that I was in control of my spiritual situation, not God; that we had been given the tools for an expanded consciousness and it was up to us to use them, not simply wait around for death and salvation. I thought about this in my moldy motel room—just what Rinpoche had advised me not to do. Thought and considered and pondered and held the idea up to the light so I could examine it from several angles. I couldn't stop myself from approaching the question this way because, after all, thinking and learning had been my path out of the unadorned monotony of Stark County, North Dakota. Once I turned eleven or so, my father had started taking me with him to his regular Saturday lunches at Jack's, in town. He and three or four other farmer friends would sit over their fried chicken, mashed potatoes, coffee, and pie, and their conversations would be about beans, wheat, soil, insects, weather, feed, the hundredweight price of Angus heifers at Stockman's auction that week. Those conversations had frustrated me in a way I could not explain: My mind was already looping out into the wider world. Late at night I'd twist the dial on my transistor radio and find stations from Calgary, Montreal, Seattle, Saskatoon, Boise, St. Louis. The people on those radio shows were talking politics, art, the state of the world. They were really *thinking*. Meanwhile, my father and his pals were stuck in their overalls and hard-skinned hands, trapped in a way of life that seemed to me like a beautiful library with one book in it. I did not want to read that book over and over again forever. Rinpoche was telling me not to think, but it was my thinking, my thirst for learning, that had led me to break the mold of my parents' expectations and go off to college in Grand Forks, then to graduate school in Chicago, then pack a suit and some city clothes and, with Jeannie, head east for New York City, capital of the thinking world.

Now, Rinpoche seemed to be encouraging me to go home, back to a calmer, slower world, and it was not an easy trip.

THIRTY-SEVEN

The odd pair of us—I in my sportcoat and chinos and Rinpoche in his robe—walked through the motel parking lot and down the access road a few hundred yards to a restaurant I'd seen on the way in. The Boathouse, it was called. The warmth of the day had dissipated somewhat. We could feel, but not see, the cold mass of Superior off our right shoulders, north of the inlet. As we approached the Boathouse we saw an old freighter tied up there, some kind of museum, it appeared, and in its shadow, a miniature golf course with throngs of moms and dads and kids and young adults on dates out in the cooling lake air, hitting their putts and marking their scorecards and shouting in delight.

"A circus," Rinpoche said.

"No, golf. Miniature golf. It's for kids mostly."

"I see the adults, too."

"Yeah, some adults, but mostly for kids. We can try it after dinner if you want."

"Try it now," he said.

I was very hungry. My shoulders and thighs ached. "It's really crowded now," I said. "Look at the line of people waiting on the first hole."

"Now we should try it," he said, and he put a hand on my shoulder and looked into my eyes as if spying out the little whining man there who'd been imagining his steak and asparagus for two hundred miles and had to have it NOW! "What you say?"

"I say: After is better. But if you want to play now, well, let's give it a shot."

"Shot," he said, with a big smile. Even with the hungry voice calling out its interior complaints, chastising me, lecturing me, mocking me, upset at the Rinpoche for his games, even with all that, it was impossible not to like the man.

Once we'd paid our small tariff (Rinpoche's treat) and joined the line waiting to tee off, we found ourselves standing next to a middle-aged couple dressed in casual summer clothes.

"Aha, we have the possibility of making a foursome with a man of the cloth," the male half of this couple remarked to his wife as we took our place just behind them. "Would you join us? Do you mind?"

"Happy to," I said. "I'm Otto Ringling, and this is my friend, Volya Rinpoche."

"Ah, Ringling," the man joked. "And Volya Trapeze, how are you? This is my better half, Eveline, and I'm Matthew Fritton. We're caught here in line like the rest of the proletariat and would be happy to have your company. Monks, are you? Tibetans?"

"Rinpoche's the monk. I'm just chauffeuring him around."

"Giving a talk at the university on the hill, is he?" Matthew asked.

"Not that I know of."

Matthew and his wife turned to see how the line was moving. We were two or three groups from the first hole. They shuffled up another yard or so and turned back to us.

"We're both professors," Eveline said. "English," she pointed to herself. "And philosophy," to Matthew.

Rinpoche was smiling and nodding at them, as was his custom. When there was a break in the introductions he said, "Is furniture golf American fun?"

"Beg pardon?"

"Miniature," I said. "Miniature golf, not furniture golf."

"A lot of fun," Eveline said. "Matthew takes it a tad overly seriously—look, he's brought his own two-hundred-dollar putter—but for the rest of us, it's fun."

"Ah, marriage," Matthew countered, putting his arm around his wife's shoulders and giving her an ironic squeeze. He bent down and kissed the top of her head. "And what religion do you profess, sir, if I might ask? Buddhism, is it? The philosophy of the great Gotama? Many lives that lead us to the blessed nothingness, is that right?"

Rinpoche was smiling up at him, a small smile, a curious smile. "Almost," he said. "Almost right. I am a Rinpoche. I sit. Sometimes I talk. And what is your work?"

"Well, Eveline has just told you, so this must be a Zen question. If you work at the university and you fall over in your office and no one is there to actually hear you, do you make a sound?"

Eveline made a small laugh at this, a nervous giggle. But the joke struck me as slightly off key, almost as if Matthew was assuming a defensive posture without realizing it, and then trying to coat his defenses in clever humor. I caught a whiff of gunpowder from the academic battlefields. A few years earlier, I had been asked to teach a course at Columbia University, just one course, one term, as an adjunct, as someone who knew the world of publishing firsthand. I'd made some friends there and liked the students quite well. But I'd also encountered people like this uneasy fellow in the Hawaiian shirt and toothy smile. In the faculty lounge over coffee you'd greet them with some pleasant, innocuous remark like, "Nice day." And it would be as if you'd sent a lob over the net. Instead of volleying it back, they'd smash it, or spin it, or slice it, say something like, "Well, *'nice,'* I don't know, not *nice,* exactly, more like *decent,* or *cosi-cosi, mezza-mezza. Seminice* would actually be more accurate, wouldn't you say?" It was all a joke of sorts, but the joke had nails and pins and poison in it.

"No, I didn't understand," Rinpoche said. "Sorry. For me, you talk very fast."

"We teach," Eveline told him. "There is a large university here, in Duluth, actually. I teach English and Matthew teaches philosophy."

"Ah, very good. English I need a teacher for. And philosophy, very good. Many ideas about living, yes?"

"Thousands."

"And it helps you live, yes?"

The line moved up another group. The Frittons shuffled another yard away from us; we closed the gap. Matthew's hands twittered on the handle of his expensive putter. "Yes," he said. "It does. I find it a wonderful exercise to ponder the wisdom of the ages, yes, I do."

"Good, very good," Rinpoche said, and he reached out to pat Matthew on the shoulder but then pulled his hand back, as if he'd thought better of the idea, and folded his arms beneath his robe.

"And you," Matthew asked, "do you find your almost-Buddhism helpful in living? Does it enable you, as they say, to just drink a cup of tea when you are drinking a cup of tea?"

"It helps me miniature golf."

"Really? You're proficient then?"

"What is this proficient?" Rinpoche turned to me.

"Good at it," I said. "Talented."

"An aficionado, are you?" Matthew pressed on. I had the feeling he couldn't help himself.

"Honey, these aren't words he understands, you can see that."

"I thought he might intuit," Matthew said.

And at that I could not stop myself from saying, "He speaks eleven languages."

Matthew drew his head back in surprise, actual or feigned, I could not tell. "Really. Say something, then, in Italian, or Russian, or Greek. Or are they languages none of us might know, your eleven?"

Rinpoche looked at him for a long moment, until the silence grew awkward around us, and then he said, "Kindness is one language I know." And he spoke the phrase kindly, too, as if it were simply a statement of fact.

Matthew did not take it that way. "Am I being unkind? Mea culpa, as they say in Latin. Forgive me, Rinpoche. I don't mean it personally, really. It's just that I find the whole Buddhist, or *almost* Buddhist philosophy patently absurd. If nothingness is the point, why bother? If we must strain, struggle, and contemplate our thought processes in this life with the goal of the obliteration of our own ego, our self, well, it hardly seems worth the trouble to me, though I suspect you'd disagree."

I thought Rinpoche would say then that he was Sufi, or Catholic. I thought he might ask the Frittons if they'd ever seen anyone at the moment of death, or if they could sit still for two hours every day watching their brains work, or go three years without speaking. Instead, he said, "Buddhism is not something I think you like very much," another simple statement.

"It's not a question of like or dislike," the professor said, taking the lob and smashing it back across the net. "It's a question of a sound philosophy or some kind of antisolipsistic shoddiness."

"He wouldn't know the word, dear."

"Nonsense, then, some kind of nonsense," Matthew said.

"Could be nonsense." Rinpoche put a hand on Matthew's arm as if to calm him, or to turn him back to facing us. "Could be. How do we test?"

"In our tradition," Matthew said, "the test for thousands of years has been something we call *logic*."

"Ah."

"And, frankly, I've never found Buddhism to be able to pass. No offense, please."

"You could not offend me."

"It's just not every day you find a Rinpoche out miniature golfing and have the chance to . . . and give him the chance to defend the ideas his religion is founded upon."

"Not a religion," Rinpoche said, smiling happily. "Not Buddhism, and not me."

"Bah, mere semantics."

Rinpoche turned to me, puzzled, and I said, "Wordplay."

And Matthew said, "Not exactly."

By then, thankfully, it was our turn to begin the game. I pointed this out to Matthew and he indicated to his wife that she should be the first to hit. I'd played some miniature golf in my day—on the Cape, when the kids were younger, we'd go out for a game almost every night after supper. But I'd never seen a challenge quite like the one we faced: a long, narrow, green-carpeted track with four, foot-tall humps spaced probably five feet apart. The hole sat between the third and fourth hump. "This one's a killer," Eveline said happily. "I should probably just write down a six and pick my ball up."

Matthew laughed. "No, no, sweet. We count all our strokes in this family."

"Do you play for money?" I asked.

Matthew swung his eyes to me and there was something pained and terrified in them. "A challenge?"

"No, just a question."

"Sometimes, yes. Would you like to?"

"Not particularly."

"I play," Rinpoche said.

"While you're practicing your eleven languages, no doubt."

"Honey!" Eveline interjected. "Why are you being so mean to the man? He's done nothing to us, and it was you who invited him to join us, after all."

Matthew seemed surprised and even hurt by this, which surprised me. It occurred to me then that he was partly or mostly unaware of the effect he had on people, of the dark, hidden places his words came from. I could see, in his angular face, something like the expression I'd seen on the features of the nun at Notre Dame, something like the emotion I'd felt in myself during the first few conversations with my traveling pal. Rinpoche's way of being—his personality or his voice or his face—brought out a kind of terror that lurked inside people like us, thought-full people. The terror had been sleeping peacefully until he showed up with his bald head and maroon robe, his calm demeanor. When it awoke, we had to cover it over as quickly as we could—with piety, with wise remarks, with intellectual superiority.

"What say the Rinpoche and I have a match?" Matthew suggested. Prompted by his wife's question, he was trying to bring himself back to a tone that sounded less aggressive, and halfway succeeding. "A duel of sorts. We'll be like Barban and McKisco in *Tender Is the Night*. Or Bazarov and Uncle Pavel in *Fathers and Sons*. Do I have my references in line, Eveline?"

"He wouldn't understand those references, sweetheart."

Matthew didn't seem to hear. He focused his wide-set blue eyes on Rinpoche's face. "What say you, sir? A duel. Western rationalism versus the filly-fally of the East, played out upon the transcendental field of the miniature golf course. The winner gets to ask the loser a koan—that's fair, isn't it? And the loser cannot eat his evening meal until the koan is answered to the winner's satisfaction."

"Let's just play a friendly game," I said.

Rinpoche's wide face had gone unreadable. I was trying to get his attention, to give him a signal: *NO! In case you lose. . . . We* have *to eat. . . . So don't!* "Yes," he said, after a moment. "Yes, okay."

"Aha, excellent. Go ahead, dear, show us how it's done."

Eveline took her stance, waved the club awkwardly at

her bright yellow ball, and pushed it halfway up the first hill. It rolled back to her feet.

"Honey, come on now."

She was forcing a smile. She waved at the ball again, harder this time, and it squirted sideways, bounced off the board there, and made it over the first hill. "Now me," Matthew said. "I'll give his holiness the benefit of watching my ball fly into the hole." He bent down over it in imitation of the real golfers I sometimes watched for a few minutes on TV on Sunday afternoons. He gripped and regripped his club, studied the shot, reset his feet twice, and at last made his stroke. The ball climbed over the first, second, and third hills a bit too fast and ended up beyond the fourth hill, far from the hole.

I stood up and made a similar shot, my green ball coming to rest an inch this side of Matthew's brown one.

It was Rinpoche's turn. The way he set his ball on the carpet and stood over it reminded me of the way he'd moved at the bowling alley—as if he had absolutely no idea what he was doing and was just trying to mimic what he'd seen. I worried we'd have another confrontation like that, Rinpoche's ball flying wildly right, into a family of vacationers, Rinpoche chasing after it, more apologies, the match dragging on and on, with Matthew cruising to an easy win and crowing about it, spewing cluster-bomb quips like a sad clown with a grenade launcher. The whole thing would end in disaster: Rinpoche unable to answer the professor's koan, yours truly unable to eat.

Rinpoche was playing with a pink ball, of course, his favorite color. He made a quick little swing and the ball climbed smoothly over the first hill, then over the second, losing speed and just barely reaching the crest of the third, and then it dropped down in a straight line right into the cup. I let out a shout. A dad on the next hole had been watching and he gave a small ovation. Even Eveline raised her arms above her head for a second.

"Ah, is that good?" Rinpoche inquired.

Eveline and I managed to get the ball into the hole in three hits, but Matthew, wielding what indeed appeared to be an expensive putter, knocked his shots back and forth over the hills, playing more and more poorly as his frustration mounted, trying for casual laughter, as if it didn't mean anything to him, as if there were no bet, no ego involvement, no attitude. He scored a seven.

From there, the game dragged on with exquisite slowness. We played a hole and waited, played a hole and waited, an awful tension forming between the Frittons and us. Either Rinpoche had played golf before, had a natural aptitude for the game, or, my personal theory, was working some kind of yogic magic, because he made two more holes in one. Matthew was behind by nine strokes at the halfway mark, seven behind with four to play. By then, Eveline had adopted a neutral silence. Matthew made a hole in one, finally, on the last hole, earning himself a free game next time around, and the Rinpoche made an awkward four. Still, the pro from Skovorodino had won the bet.

"So," Matthew said as we were returning our borrowed putters and he was enclosing his in some kind of protective sleeve, "congratulations to the holy one. And now I shall take my medicine."

"You're a good sport, honey," Eveline said.

"I'm ready to pronounce the correct answer or begin my fast," Matthew said.

Rinpoche was studying the angular face as if it were a painting. "You want a question?" he asked.

"Yes, a koan."

"But in my lineage we do not use koans."

"Make something up then. Surely you have a test for me."

Rinpoche was nodding. "Yes," he said. "I do. But you can eat if you don't answer it. It maybe takes you a little time. I don't want you not eating. Not eating is very unhealthy in our tradition." He looked at me and one of his eyes flickered. It might have been taken as a wink. "I have the small question," he said, turning back to Matthew. "My question is," he freed his right hand from the cloth of his robe, held it up, and brought the thumb and third finger together in a circle. He held the circle for a moment, then opened his hand. "If I think *make a circle* and my hand does not, what is happening?"

"I don't follow."

"Look, my hand is open now, yes?"

"Yes."

"But I am thinking to my hand: *Make a circle.* But it is not making a circle. What is happening?"

Matthew frowned. "That's obvious. Another part of you is overriding the order. You are *thinking, Make a circle,* but another part of you, call it the will, is not going along with the order."

"Excellent," Rinpoche said. He reached out and warmly shook the professor's hand. "You may eat. You and your wife may eat tonight. With us, if you want to. Rinpoche pays. This restaurant right here. We go there now, we're very hungry. Will you come?"

Eveline was smiling and starting to nod when Matthew cut her off. "Not possible, I'm sorry to say. Other plans, you see. But it was a pleasure, really. I'm sorry if I was a bit competitive. Sports bring that out in me. My apologies."

"*Niente,*" the Rinpoche said with a respectful bow, a smile, a friendly squeeze of Matthew's forearm. "*Nichevo.*"

THIRTY-EIGHT

I can tell you that the wood-grilled prime New York strip steak served at the Boathouse Restaurant on Barker's Island was one of the finest pieces of meat I have ever had the pleasure of putting into my mouth—and that, for a North Dakota boy, is saying something. Rinpoche contented himself with a fillet of whitefish, caught in the big lake just to our north, and watched with evident pleasure as I made my way through an appetizer of lobster, oyster, zucchini, and hazelnut tartlet in a champagne sauce; a superb salad of mixed greens with herbs and buttermilk dressing; and then the steak, which arrived with roasted shallots, fingerling potatoes, asparagus, and marrow sauce. All this was accompanied by two glasses of cabernet. After my long fast, this was such a satisfying meal that I did not even order dessert, just a cup of coffee. Rinpoche had tea. We sat there contentedly in the start of a long northern dusk.

"You've played miniature golf before, haven't you?" I said, when the hot drinks had been served and sipped.

"In Europe," he said, "at my center, I have a very rich

student, and this man sometimes takes me to play golf. Big golf. On his very nice course."

"Somehow I can't picture it."

Rinpoche gently circled the spoon in his tea. The muscles of his face were working so that I thought he might burst out laughing any second. "Not so much fun as bohling," he said, and I had the sense then that he was toying with me, that everything he said on that night was coming from the comic place in him, his leather-handled bag of spiritual tricks.

"There's a bowling alley in the city near where I grew up. I'll take you, if you want."

Rinpoche grinned and nodded, tapping his spoon against the rim of the cup, and then took a long drink.

"All college professors aren't like that, you know," I said. "I taught in college once, met some good people."

"They were good people, the professors at the golf."

"She was nice, but I found him very hard to be around. That kind of humor, that . . . I don't know."

There was a small glass vase between us, three gladioli in a few ounces of water. One of the gladioli had dropped a petal—brushstroke of purple on fine white cloth. Rinpoche drank the last sip of his tea, then set the cup aside, took the petal with his thumb and second finger, placed it on the middle of the saucer in front of him, and turned the cup upside down to cover it.

"I feel a lesson coming on," I said.

He waved his hands around a moment, the way he sometimes did, and his voice changed slightly, as if he were drawing words up from some deep well of confidence. "The flower is the good inside every person," he said. "The cup is like a wall, to protect. Many people have that wall."

"Armor," I said.

He nodded.

"Why?"

"Because to live without the cup means you must feel the world as the world really is. People make the armor from their smartness, or their anger, or their quiet, or their fear, or their being busy, or their being nice. Some people make it from a big show, always talking. Some make it by being very important. Many people do not make it, though, and those people can begin to see the world as it is. You do not make it too much, Otto."

"I'm flattered. It's something Jeannie and I have consciously tried to do with our children—not make ourselves so authoritarian, so far above them, that we cut ourselves off. We've tried to do that with each other, as well. To live unarmored."

"This is why you are a good man," he said, with a twinkle.

"Right. . . . You're coming at me sideways again, I suspect. I have just as many defenses as Matthew, is that it?"

"Not so many, no."

"Good."

"And your sister," he said, "has none. An open soul. Why she is the special person."

"Is she?"

He nodded. "Very much. Very, very much."

At that moment, his rugged face, so pliable and unreadable, sent a particular signal. "You're in love with Cecelia, aren't you," I said. "I just realized that."

Instead of giving me a real answer, he lifted the cup off the petal again and I could see there how delicate and fragile it was, almost silken, finely painted and veined, already drying up in the heat of our harsh world.

• • •

RINPOCHE PAID FOR the meal in cash. We left the Boathouse and strolled back across the parking lot, past the scene of his miniature golf triumph, and along the road that led to our motel. We were moving through the very last of the daylight by then and it was as though, with the disappearance of the sun, a guerrilla army of scents had risen up and laid claim to the air. Lake water, flowers, fish. I even thought I could detect the fragrance of drying wheat from the grain elevators of Duluth somewhere out of sight behind us.

Just as we were about to turn in to our motel, the evening light underwent a subtle change. Rinpoche took hold of the sleeve of my shirt and tugged me at an angle away from the building and toward the shoreline of the inlet. He led me right up onto the bank, and there, beyond the light chop of purple water, we saw just the tip of a full moon break the horizon. We stood there while it rose, enormous and peach colored, the bluish marks like fresh bruises on its surface. It was a magnificent show, really, the incremental appearance of this other sphere 240,000 miles away; the subtle changes in the light and shadows around us. Even the water seemed to resonate in response to the huge lunar eye, whitening now, already starting to grow smaller as it climbed.

We watched until it had gone in size from silver dollar to dime, and then we turned and went toward our rooms.

"If a person could really see it," Rinpoche said to me in a quiet voice, "really see the thing that we just saw as it is truly, without putting a name between his mind and the fact of what you call, in your language, the moon, then that person would have no cup over his good. Do you understand? No armor. That person would not be afraid. That person could love and that person could let another person give him love, and he could feel the ground he walks on like love, and the air he breathes like love."

I said, "I feel the ground I walk on like dirt. So I guess I'm not there yet."

He laughed his happy old laugh. An elderly couple going in the front entrance turned to look at him, at us, and frowned in tandem.

I asked Rinpoche if he'd consider taking a swim with me before his nightly meditation, but he had nothing to swim in, he said, and I said, "*Niente, rien, nichevo,*" and we went along the hallway laughing at that, too, almost like friends.

THIRTY-NINE

In the morning I was glad I'd made the massage appointment. The soreness wasn't as sharp as it had been the day before, but I still felt as if I'd been beaten all over with a two-hundred-dollar putter. We checked out of the motel and drove across the bridge that links Wisconsin and Minnesota. To our right, sunlight glinted and sparkled on the greatest of the Great Lakes—it looked like an ocean from our vantage, and you could just make out the curve of the earth, an almost undetectable bend in the blue landscape.

My father's parents had liked to drive to Duluth once or twice a year—their idea of a big-city holiday—and they'd taken Cecelia and me a few times. Between the downtown area and the shore sprawled a jumble of railroad yards and grain elevators. "That's where your morning cereal comes from," my grandmother had told me, more than once, pointing at the grain elevators, and I remembered struggling to wrap my mind around the idea that the wheat we grew on our land went into trucks, and the semis made the long overland trip to a place like Duluth, and the grain was then sent by ship all over the world. It made Duluth seem, to my child's mind, like the invisible heart of the American way of life, an exotic, bigger, more important place, far from our bland home territory. For a time in my late teens I'd even had a persistent fantasy of living there and writing novels about the men on the docks and on the freighters and the women who worked in the noisy diner my grandparents had liked on West Superior Street.

I'd joined Rinpoche for part of his morning meditation that day—nothing major to report, just a sort of general calming down—and so we got off to a bit of a late start. No time for anything but a quick coffee at the registration desk and then we were crossing the bridge and diving into city traffic. I found the address, just off Main Street, found a place to park, and told Rinpoche I'd meet him back there in an hour and fifteen minutes, and that I'd be a new man. "Why don't you try to find a bathing suit for yourself," I told him. "We're going to be cutting across the top of Minnesota today and it's supposed to be warm and there are lots of pretty lakes. I thought we might take a swim."

"In Skovorodino we swim, you know . . ." he turned his hands in toward his body.

"Naked."

"Yes."

"Well, we do that here sometimes, too, but there are places where it's better to have something on. Get a suit, we'll have some fun."

"Massage good," he said.

"Thanks, I'll try to."

• • •

DUE TO BACK TROUBLES, tennis injuries, and my old football knee, I've had enough therapeutic massages over the years to know almost the instant I feel a pair of hands on my skin whether they are well trained or not. It's like tennis, and writing, and lots of other things: If you've had some experience you can gauge a player's ability almost before he or she actually strikes the ball; you can get a sense for the writer's skill, or lack of it, from the first paragraph. Jane Aleski was the therapist's name, in this case. She ran a small spalike operation on the second floor of a newly refurbished office building in downtown Duluth. From the first touch I knew she was a master. Lying on the table beneath a warm sheet, I gave her, in brief, the story of my yoga adventure, and she laughed in a way that made me comfortable. As she worked—neck, back, legs—I tried to do a kind of meditation, focusing on the idea of the cup over the petal and attempting to let her massage all my armor away. I knew there wasn't much in the way of defenses between me and Jeannie, me and the kids. But I also knew that, at work, and with Cecelia, and with almost all of my friends, and with my parents before they died, there was a way in which I'd hardened myself just slightly. My personality had solidified. I'd learned to react by habit instead of really being present. With my parents, for instance, I'd taken to playing the role of college-educated son, the executive from back East, leaving Cecelia to take on the role of flake.

"Traveling with your family?" Jane asked, because I'd told her about the yoga class, but not about the limber Skovorodinan at the front of the room. By this time she'd turned me onto my back and was sitting at my head, massaging the knotted muscles between shoulder and neck.

"No. . . . I'm accompanying a monk, actually. A sort of spiritual teacher. Volya Rinpoche."

"Volya Rinpoche! How wonderful! I've read all his books, every one of them. Are you, what would the word be . . . a disciple?"

To my complete surprise, I found myself pausing before answering her. And when I did answer, I found myself avoiding the question. "My sister is, I guess. I'm doing it as a favor to her. She couldn't get away from her clients. But I did finish one of his books last night."

"How is he in person?"

"Funny. Odd. Easygoing, except when he's playing one of his tricks. He had me fasting for a whole day yesterday, and I'm not like that, believe me."

"People say he's actually the incarnation of the Buddha. Or some kind of Jesus-Buddha-Moses combination."

"Who says that?"

"I don't know. I subscribe to a Buddhist magazine, just out of curiosity. I have a regular meditation practice, that's all. I'm not really so much of a Buddhist, I guess, just a person looking around for a belief system that makes sense. I probably read it in one of those issues someplace, or heard it at the meditation center. Your trapezius muscles are like granite, you know, and that is not a good thing."

"It was the yoga. He tricked me into doing a yoga class. I've been in agony the last two days."

"We'll fix you up. I'm just curious, though, does it feel like he's the Buddha?"

"He doesn't even call himself a Buddhist."

"Neither did Buddha."

"Right. Jesus wasn't a Christian, and so on. Funny how that works."

"So he doesn't, you know, recite sutras or anything?"

"Not really, no. It's like he takes something from a bunch of different traditions and mixes in some of his own. It's hard to put a finger on exactly what he believes or doesn't believe. I'm a little bit of the smart-ass, skeptical type, but I have to admit I like being around him more and more as time goes by."

"And he's teaching you?"

"He's offered to. I've started to meditate a bit, just to try it out."

"Meditation saved my life."

"Big statement."

"Big but true. If I ever found a meditation teacher I thought was the real thing, I'd drop everything and follow anywhere."

"Well, he's thinking of starting a retreat center of some kind just west of Dickinson, North Dakota, so I suppose you could follow him there if you wanted to. It's our family land, actually."

"Really? Do you know what kind of blessing you'll get for letting him use your land? If he is the Buddha, or some great being like that, I mean? You'll be set for eternity."

Jane laughed when she said it, and I laughed, too. But I have to say I felt a small chill along the sides of my arms. She might have been touching the nerves that ran there, I don't know. But I know I felt a chill, or a sense of . . . I don't know exactly what to call it. Three or four times now in the past few days I'd felt it. Seese would have called it a premonition, or an "energy message." But I did not deal in energy messages, and so it was strange to me, a sort of intermittent knocking at the door of my house of belief.

When Jane had finished and I was paying and thanking

her, she handed me a business card on the back of which was written the name of another therapist, this one in Bismarck. "If you need a massage while you're there, this is the woman to see. An old friend. If you don't mind, I'll call and tell her about the retreat center, okay? She'd be interested. I might be interested, myself. It's not every day you get a chance to sit with the Buddha."

"Or play miniature golf with him," I said.

She gave me a strange look, eyes squinting, little smile.

I thanked her again, and went back out onto Duluth's cobbled main street a new man.

FORTY

Before leaving Duluth, and my pleasant childhood memories of its old-style downtown, Rinpoche and I passed an hour at a breakfast place Jane had recommended, the Chester Creek Café, up on the hill, not far from the university. I thought we might run into Matthew and Eveline Fritton there because it was a college crowd: graduate students and profs, a few moms with young babies in the watery morning light, twelve kinds of coffee, a BRING THE TROOPS HOME sign in the window. Someone had left a copy of *USA Today* on the table, and between spoonfuls of granola and sips of Italian dark roast I took in the news about the terrorist investigation in Great Britain, the new restrictions, the stories from Iraq, all death and trouble on that day. For me, for most Americans, the war stood as merely a dark background to our comfortable everyday lives. American men and women were dying there, and having their arms and legs blown off there, and Iraqis were perishing by the tens of thousands, yet there was a way in which most of us seemed able to keep those facts at arm's length. It was not that we didn't care; of course we cared. But if we'd had a child there it would have been a different kind of caring, more intense, more immediate, more than just ink on a page and sorrowful thoughts in the workday's open spaces. But Jeannie and I didn't have a child there, and would never have a child there as long as the military was composed of volunteers, and there was something about the whole thing that felt dishonest and wrong to me, some kind of national puzzle we were not even close to working out, some kind of perfect balance we were being asked to strike between too little armor, as a nation, and too much. Iraq had been on my mind since the start of the trip—how could it not be with the radio hosts ranting and the newspaper headlines writ large—but I had not broached the subject with Rinpoche even once.

We took the expressway south from Duluth a short ways and then switched to Route 2 West, a classic old American highway that runs across the northern tier of the Lower 48, from Michigan's Upper Peninsula to northern Idaho. Ten minutes outside the city we entered in the Great North Woods, and it was there that I began to feel we were leaving the Midwest behind and rolling out into yet another of America's subcultures. Whereas most of Wisconsin and Illinois had been tame and fertile, we had moved into the great West now, wild and mostly unpeopled (gray wolves still lived here), and I wondered if Rinpoche could feel the difference. The two-lane strip of tar was busy with logging trucks, eighteen-wheelers, and Winnebagos and cut across a landscape of swamp and small ponds, with stunted birch and fir trees standing like lace on a green, ragged wilderness. There was something free about it, untrammeled. It worked a little magic on the eastern soul.

"I'm curious," I said to Rinpoche, after I'd been running the question through my mind for an hour, "what you think about the war, terrorism, September 11, and so on. I finished your book last night, I liked it, I learned from it, but you don't really address specific issues there, so I'm wondering what your stance is on all this."

"All this is the world," he said after a moment. "This has always been the world. I feel this world as a sadness in my own body."

"Right. Me, too. But what I meant was, from your perspective, from a spiritual perspective, what is the right response to something like the terrorist attacks? Is it ever right to go to war? In self-defense? In others' defense?"

Another long moment of silence, and then, "Jesus let people nail him in his hands and feet. He did not fight them."

"Right, okay. But that was Jesus. What if you don't have the courage or spiritual advancement to do that? What if your children are being attacked and you don't think it's right to allow it to happen?"

"You should protect your children."

"All right. So what is the correct moral stance on the war, is what I'm asking."

"There are people," he said, "who are past being hurt, beyond being hurt. You should know this is true. You should try to become one of those people, to make an understanding with yourself that you are not your body, that you are something bigger. That is your work on this earth, do you see? Every experience here is to teach you to do that. Living, dying, every experience."

"And if that's beyond you at this point? I mean, if you are someone who still identifies with his body, then what?"

"You should try not to war."

"And if you try and can't avoid it? If you think it might prevent further killing in the future?"

"You should try not to kill to stop killing. Try. It is very hard. Sometimes I think it is not possible for many people. Only to try is important. Even not to have violence in your thoughts is important."

"Not easy."

He made a one-syllable laugh, something without much humor in it. "This is not a world for easy."

"All right. Have I used up my questions for the day?"

"No."

"Okay then, why are there evil people in the world? Why are there people who rape and kill and abuse and steal from other people and fly jetliners into buildings? Why is it all set up this way?"

He lifted his hands, as I'd seen him do before, and let them fall back to the tops of his thighs. "Every day," he said, "many times every day, you can go one way or the other way. You can go with anger or not go. Go with greed or not go. Go with hate or not go. Go with eating too much or sexing too much, or not go. Two ways."

"The digital universe."

"Sorry?"

"Nothing. I interrupted. Go on."

"These feel like small things, small choices, but every day, across one life, across many, many lives, if you choose the good way, again and again and again, in what you are thinking and what you are doing, if you choose to go away from anger not toward, away from hate, not toward, away from armor, not toward, away from falseness, not toward . . . then you become this person like you—good, not stealing, not hurting. Some people made good choices in their past lives and so, like you, they are given maybe an easy life for this time. Not the perfect life, not the life with no trouble or pain in it at all, but a life where it is easier to turn the mind to the spiritual part. You, my friend, you have work that you like not hate, a wife that you love and live with by peace, children that are good not bad. Is this true?"

"Yes."

"So you have a small quiet space in your mind from that. And that quiet space gives you a chance to see deep, deep into the world if you want to. Another choice, yes? You can take that choice and look deep, or no. But if a person goes the other way, little choice and little choice toward the bad and the selfish, life after life, hour after hour, then this spirit does not have the good incarnation, so does not have the quiet space. Sometimes that person becomes the one who kills, who rapes, who hurts. Other times, in this life, they maybe make a big change to the good. Do you see?"

"But why must the bad hurt the good? Why did you go to prison, for instance? Why did they kill Jesus, and Gandhi, and Martin Luther King, and so on?"

"I don't know the *why*. I know the *is*. This is the world and always the world. Always, since when the Bible was made, since when the ancient stories in all religion were made. Inside the big world that you cannot control, you have the small world of you that you can control. In that small world, if you look, you can see whether to go this way toward good, or the other way toward bad."

"Or remain neutral."

"Yes, but if you see good and don't go, that is not neutral. To me, to my lineage, it is not the case that God is up in the sky looking at you and judging you. It is more easy than that, and more hard. God is God, the Divine Intelligence is the Divine Intelligence, the One With No Name is the One With No Name. But God is just giving out love and giving out love and giving out love, like a . . . like a very nice music always playing. If you hurt people you make yourself deaf to this music, that's all. Not God's fault, your fault. Not God's judgment, your choice, you see? You make yourself no chance to feel God, or the moon going up, or any good love. Life after life you make yourself no chance, and then one life maybe you start to change, and be a little quiet inside, and listen to this music that is always there—for you, for the bad people, always there. Even the most bad people live in their trouble for thousands of lives, and then, one moment," he clapped his hands together hard, "they chose a different way. They go this way and not that way. One choice, another choice. They start to come on the long trip home."

FORTY-ONE

An hour or so into the afternoon we drove into the quiet little metropolis of Grand Rapids, Minnesota—birthplace of Judy Garland—and pulled into a parking space in front of a Chinese restaurant called the Hong Kong Garden. I had been pondering Rinpoche's words for several hours by then, and, when I saw that Ms. Garland had grown up in this humble city, I found myself thinking about Oz, that kingdom of illusion, that place where you came to understand that you'd had everything you needed all along—good witches to call on in an emergency, all the courage, brains, and heart that was necessary in order to manage your way through this life. Oz was that place where the God you were going to for help could not help you, not really. All he could do was turn your eyes to what you already were and ask you to see it differently. Oz was that dreamlike place you returned from and couldn't tell anyone in your old life about, because none of them believed it existed.

And the Hong Kong Garden was that place where you

sought refuge from the ordinariness of northern plains, small-city cuisine.

A decent General Tso's for me. Tea and a little white rice and broccoli for the Good Warlock of the North. A couple of mammoth souls in there for neighbors, taking full advantage of the all-you-can-eat buffet, shoveling the food down as if they'd been fasting all week. I tried calling Jeannie and Natasha—big Judy G. fans—on their respective cell phones, but neither of them answered. I missed my daughter so much that I called back a second time just to hear her recorded voice saying her own name.

Not long after we left Grand Rapids, we turned onto Highway 6 and entered the Chippewa National Forest. There were pine woods on both sides of the road, and I was still thinking about Rinpoche's description of the laws of the world, and I was looking, as we went, for a way to show him another slice of America, to fulfill my half of the deal. During lunch, I had tried to tell him about Judy Garland and the Wizard, what an important part of my childhood—of so many American childhoods—that film had been. But I'd found it difficult to describe the plot adequately and impossible to convey the full impact of the songs and characters. He listened pleasantly enough, blinking, sipping his tea, but it was probably a little bit like him talking to me about the print in the Nepali restaurant in Madison: Some kinds of spiritual lessons just do not move well across cultural boundaries.

Heading southwest now, still on Route 6, I saw a flat concrete bridge ahead of us and a sign by the side of the road: MISSISSIPPI RIVER. "Something you should see," I said, and pulled to a stop in the breakdown lane. We walked along that lane until we were standing at about the midpoint of the bridge. Below us curled the mighty Mississippi, not so mighty at that point, only about seventy yards wide and clean as glass. Stretching east and west from either bank was a buffer of northwoods grassland, greens and yellows shimmering in the hot sun, the water itself as smooth and silvery-blue as a ribbon of polished steel. "This is the most famous American river," I told him. "It starts just north of here and goes for, I don't know, maybe fifteen hundred miles. To New Orleans. To the Gulf of Mexico. All kinds of books have been written about it. There's a lot of symbolic importance to it because it more or less cuts the country in half, east and west, and stretches almost all the way from north to south."

As I was saying this I was standing with one foot on the concrete edge of the bridge, looking down, hands on the guardrail. I saw something—a duck it appeared to be—swimming a little ways below the surface of the water, but there was a particular gracefulness to the way this duck moved. In a moment it surfaced, midriver, maybe thirty yards from us. I could see the intricate black-and-white pattern of its back, and its sharp beak. Soon it was turning this way and that and letting out an unmistakable cry, a quick, high-pitched laughing noise that echoed over the grassland and into the trees beyond. "Look!" I said. "Listen." And I told Rinpoche the bird's name.

The solitary creature went on and on, giving out its trilling, happy cry as if calling to a mate still in the nest. I opened my cell phone and dialed home, and this time Jeannie answered. I said, "Listen, Hon," and held the phone up so she could hear. Rinpoche realized who was on the other end of the line and, after a few seconds, motioned for me to give him the phone. I handed it over.

"Mrs. Otto!" he said excitedly. "Did you hear the fine noise? Yes, yes, the laughing bird. Is very nice! We are here, your good husband and me, and we are hearing this bird! Yes, he is fine, your husband. He misses you. He loves you. I am showing him the meditation wife, does that make you okay? Good! I will show you, too, yes! When are you coming? When are the children coming? I know I will see you, yes? Here is Mr. Otto, my friend. Here is the sound of the wound!"

"Loon, he means," I said, when I'd taken back the phone. "We're standing on a little bridge over the Mississippi. It's seventy yards wide here."

"He sounds like a sweetheart, your traveling companion."

"He is."

"And there's a real live loon?"

"There is. It's incredible. A gift."

"What's this about the meditation wife?"

"Meditation *life*. L. He sometimes has trouble with that letter when he gets excited. Talking to you excited him, apparently, which is something I can relate to. . . . We're fine. We were in Duluth this morning and we should be in North Dakota by tomorrow, maybe even the Bismarck Radisson tonight if I push it. Everything all right there? Kids okay?"

"Anthony made the JV."

"Yes!" I shouted, too loud. The loon splashed a slow takeoff and flapped away. "Tell him his dad is on top of the Mississippi River, rooting for him, scaring birds. And Tash?"

"Two thousand eighty-eight dollars as of last night. She was up before me this morning, if you can believe that. Sitting at the kitchen table, looking at used-car ads in the newspaper."

"Make sure to get her something solid," I said.

"We'll wait for you to get home. Hurry safely."

"I will. Dickinson tomorrow, I hope. I'll call tonight, so I can talk to the kids."

"Bring home a little Dakota soil for me, would you?"

"I will."

All during that afternoon, Rinpoche did not go anywhere near the subject of the meditation wife. I was coming to understand that this was his teaching method: He'd offer a lesson, usually taken from everyday experience, and then allow time for it to sink in, time for the living of ordinary life, which, after all, was the point and purpose of his teaching. It was as though he sensed that I could not absorb too much in the way of new information in any one day without overloading some circuit. And, after my Oz lecture, I sensed the same about him.

Once we put the Mississippi behind us, Route 6 shunted us off onto Route 200, which ran westward past a series of lakes and rivers—Big Sand Lake, Mable Lake, and the Boy River. We stopped at one of them, Leech Lake, because the day was warm and clear and there was a small beach right by the highway where we could see a few people swimming.

Pulled the car in. Got out. Stretched. Went into the woods to change. Rinpoche in a bathing suit was a sight to see, especially since he was wearing some kind of Speedo outfit that really did not leave much to the imagination. I suppose some store clerk in Duluth had been having a good time at his expense, selling the monk a pale blue swimsuit an Olympian might use to minimize aquatic friction but that was really not quite appropriate for a man his size on a Minnesota public beach. For the sake of the sensibilities of the family nearby I tried to hurry him into the water, running in and diving and telling him how wonderful it was—clean, warm, not too deep. All that was true enough, but Rinpoche was a bit timid about his entry and preferred to spend ten minutes doing elaborate yoga poses on the shore, working up a sweat, while the other swimmers could not keep from gawking.

At last he took a clumsy running start, made it in about calf-deep, and went flying forward on his face in a calamitous belly flop. He managed a few furious strokes there in the shallows (I figured it was the way I'd swim, too, if I'd grown up in a place where the river water never got above forty-eight degrees), then flipped over on his back and started laughing. He had a wonderful laugh, as I've said, but it was especially wonderful at that moment, with his toes and brown face sticking up above the calm blue surface and the laughter echoing against the birch trees on the bank as if he were part human and part loon. "Fun! Fun!" he started to sing after a while, still floating. "American fun!" The family moved a ways on down the beach.

We splashed around for half an hour, then came out, dried off, and took turns changing discreetly with a towel and the open car doors blocking the family's view. "Like it?" I asked.

"Kisses. Bohling. Golf. Outside swimming. Now America is my favorite place, and you are my favorite friend. Thank you, Otto!"

"Not a problem."

"Thank you for showing me fun."

"I have the feeling you've had a little fun before you met me."

"Yes, little bit," he said, and he laughed some more, and it occurred to me that the modern spiritual leaders of my tradition were always somber, self-important men, thickly coated in others' idea of who they were supposed to be. Rinpoche seemed free of that. It made me think of a tiny news report I'd read somewhere—browsing the *Times,* probably, with a cup of coffee and a sandwich on the table and a hundred other things on my mind. It had been an article about Pope John Paul, when he was still young, before illness had taken over his life. Apparently, he'd sneaked away from the Vatican for a day or two, in disguise maybe, I don't recall, and taken a couple of runs down a ski slope in the Italian Alps.

ONLY A LITTLE WAYS farther down that same highway, we came upon the Northern Lights Casino, built, more or less, in the shape of an Ojibway lodge. More American fun. I explained to Rinpoche what it was and how it had come to be, and he said he was interested in trying it. We went into the windowless world of ringing bells, flashing lights, and Minnesota retirees sitting dull-faced in front of slot machines, making compensatory payments, a quarter at a time, to the people whose land had been appropriated by their ancestors, so many years ago. It was a treat, I have to say, to sit beside the holy man and watch him watching the spinning dials. He was not a conservative gambler. He would put in four one-dollar tokens—the maximum bet—and push the SPIN button and, when he won, when four or ten or twenty coins clanked down into the bright chrome tray, he'd clap his hands once, fill up his plastic bucket, and start feeding them in again without delay.

"We can cash in our winnings and leave, you know," I told him once, when he'd just made a 7-7-7 score and had a pile of dollar tokens in front of him.

"Not yet, not yet."

After half an hour, Rinpoche was still holding his own, focused on the spinning dial as if the salvation of the troubled modern world depended on it. And then, as so often happens, the machine started to exact its payment for earlier kindnesses. Rinpoche's white plastic bucket went from full, to three-quarters full, to half full, and still he plowed on, feeding and feeding. I'd sworn to myself to keep to a twenty-dollar limit, and had gone through those coins in ten minutes. So I just stood by his shoulder and watched. "It's fixed, you know. Rigged," I said, when I saw that his bucket was now only a quarter full. "Keep playing and eventually you'll lose everything. It's mathematical. Eventually the machine always wins."

But he was a man of faith, not math, and paid me no heed. He had sixteen coins left. Twelve. Eight. He fed the last four in deliberately, as if the problem was that he'd been pushing them into the slot too quickly, not giving the machine enough time to absorb the full measure of his goodness, his earnestness, the blessing of his presence. The wheels spun, the symbols appeared, and they demonstrated convincingly that the machine had no real appreciation for the blessing of his presence. Rinpoche sat there a moment in shock, letting the fact of his losses sink in, and then he was reaching into his robe for his wad of money, already looking around for the place where you changed cash into tokens. I took him firmly by the arm and lifted him out of his seat. "Let's go," I said.

"Not yet, not yet, Otto."

"We're going." I kept hold of his arm and marched him sternly toward the exit, a scene the likes of which I'm sure the security people had encountered once or twice before.

It was always a surprise, going through a casino door and back out into natural light. The casino designers' seemingly innocent, self-contained, artificial playground had cast some kind of magic spell, so much so that, even after only forty-five minutes, it was the bright, relatively quiet and plain outside world that seemed false. And boring. No promise of free money there on the tar streets. No ringing bells when the fates turned their smile upon you.

"I was winning the big prize almost," Rinpoche said, when we were in the parking lot outside the front door.

I led him a safe distance away, toward the car. *It's a fool's gambit,* I started to say, *a trick. I'm surprised you fell for it.* But then I saw his face. The muscles near his mouth were twitching. He was struggling to keep the big smile from breaking through.

"Otto, you saved me," he said, dramatically.

"You could be on stage, you know, Rinpoche. You could be in films."

"Next time I pushed the button," he started to smile, "big prize would be!"

"Right, big prize. You are what we used to call in North Dakota a piece of work."

"Piss of work?"

"Right. Exactly. Get in the car, your highness."

All the way out of the parking lot, and for another mile or two along Route 200, my friend the Rinpoche had his chuckle going. It rose up through his chest, bubbles of joy, and spilled out across the car's leather dash. I was thinking about what the massage therapist in Duluth had said. A reincarnation of the Buddha, or Jesus, or Moses, he was supposed to be, this kooky character. I was thinking that, maybe, if you saw the creatures and objects around you as pieces of a sacred whole, everything temporary, just playing out a role in a dream, then things would be funny a lot of the time, kaleidoscopic, comically absurd.

FORTY-TWO

I had originally planned for us to spend our last night on the road in a place called Detroit Lakes in western Minnesota, about fifty miles from the North Dakota border. But, I don't know, maybe it was hearing Jeannie's voice on the phone, maybe it was the fact that the first two hotels I called in Detroit Lakes said they were booked—some kind of festival going on, Miniature Dollhouse Collectors of America or something—maybe I was just feeling the tug of the old homestead, the reality of my duties there, and didn't want to delay things any longer. Whatever the reason, after I'd made the calls and put a few miles between us and the casino, I asked my companion if he minded stretching out the driving day. "We can probably get all the way to Bismarck," I said. "Then tomorrow we'll have only a short ride."

Rinpoche let it be known that it didn't matter to him in the slightest what our schedule was. He was in no rush, he was never in a rush. He could not remember the last time he'd had such an enjoyable day.

For dinner that night we decided to sample the local specialty and go German. I knew from experience that the phone books in that part of the world could almost have been taken from Berlin or Stuttgart. Five hundred Schmitts, a hundred and fifty Wanners. Many of the Germans had come by way of Russia and Catherine the Great's broken promises. They settled the fertile plains of the upper Midwest, bringing along their farming methods, stern morals, and solid but unimaginative dietary preferences. I remembered that two of the shocks I'd experienced in coming to New York were discovering that Ringling was considered an unusual last name and that most people had never heard of knoephla soup.

We pulled off the highway in a little city called Park Rapids, which had the distinction of offering a two-car-wide parking lane right in the middle of its broad main street. I somehow knew there would be a German eatery there, and after walking less than a block we came upon it, the Schwarzwald Inn restaurant. Inside, it was as I expected, as I'd remembered: pale wood booths, decorative steins lined up by the cash register, wall hangings of Bavarian Fräuleins in lederhosen. And the wonderful smells of frying bratwurst and beer. It was a plain little place, but they had Spaten Premium in bottles (I convinced Rinpoche to take a sip, but did not tell him it had been the first alcohol to pass my lips, fourteen years old, behind the barn at Mickey Schlossen's farm), a meaty menu, and old farm couples in overalls and cotton dresses—for me it was all a snapshot from a childhood album. Rinpoche contented himself with a dish of potato salad and a slice of the brown bread—it arrived already buttered, dense as it was delicious. Yours truly went the bratwurst and mashed route, in tribute to Mom and Pop. I had been thinking about them more and more as we got closer to North Dakota. They'd been a sweet pair, really—unadorned, unself-conscious, hardened by work and weather and girded about by the cool emotional climate into which they'd been born, but decent as the day was long.

I looked up at Rinpoche and told him, "Bratwurst, beer, and bread, my father used to say. No man needs more."

He nodded, swallowed. "I remember also the things my father said to me. He was a kind man, very small for size, very famous where I was as a boy. There were not so many trees there as in America. Hills that went brown color in the summer. You hear the train go by from many miles, and you walk up the hill and see very far, and in the winter there was deep snow, and wind."

"A Siberian North Dakota."

"He used to say the land there made your mind big. Perfect land for meditation."

"No bratwurst and beer though, I bet."

He laughed. There was a spot of butter on his lower lip. "Sausage and beer, almost the same." He paused and took another bite, swallowed, all very deliberate. And then, "He used to say—and sometimes my mother would say—that I, that my when I was born—"

"*That my being born* is how you'd say it in English."

"Thank you, my friend. That my being born made them the happiest of anything."

Here's where our stories part company, I thought, because it was something my parents would never in a million years have told us, even though it might have been true. Kind, yes, but they'd been trained to terseness, and never questioned that. They did not spend a lot of time embracing us, kissing us, telling us what a blessing we were in their lives. Something happened to me then, in the midst of this memory, some small internal tremor. I could not, at first, find any reason for it. Looking at Rinpoche, I felt an unexplained nervousness rising up in me, that's all. And I noticed that I had the urge to fall back on old habits and cover over the nervousness with a cute little remark. I resisted.

Instead of going on, Rinpoche just nodded in a satisfied way, as if cherishing a happy memory. He wiped his lip with one finger.

"You're a reincarnation of some kind, aren't you?" I heard myself say, from out of the center of the nervousness, but there was no mockery in the words. "Is that why it made them happy?"

"Yes. That is why. Also they loved me."

"A reincarnation of who?"

"Just a teacher. In our lineage. No special man."

"No?"

He shook his huge head.

"You sure?"

"Yes, very sure," he said, but for the first time on that trip he wasn't making eye contact when he spoke.

"Are there female reincarnations, too?"

He laughed at this foolish question, seemed to regain his balance. "Of course, Otto. My mother was the incarnation of a great . . . you would call it, I think, a saint."

I had a strong visual memory then, of Rinpoche in South Bend, prostrating himself before the statue of Mary as if he were as Catholic as any Father O'Malley or Sister McFinn. The feeling I had been trying to repress rose up further in me, up into the place between my lungs. I had a mouthful of bratwurst and found I was having difficulty swallow-

ing. I felt as if I were fighting with myself inside myself.
I'm tempted to use the expression "of two minds" except
that I actually *felt* that: There were two distinct minds in
me, old and new, and they were doing battle. I thought of
Rinpoche's recent description of the digital universe, of a
continual decision-making that led the individual soul this
way or that. A or B, A or B. I was remembering, again,
what the massage therapist had said. I was replaying the
things I'd seen and heard between Paterson and here.

"I'm curious about something," I heard myself saying,
when I'd gotten the mouthful of bratwurst down. To calm
myself, I took a sip of the cool, tangy Spaten. "If there are
saints, really, in this life . . . I mean, if they are actual people
and not just a sort of myth we make up after they die, to
give us hope or something . . . I mean . . . I'm not expressing myself very well here." I took another sip of beer, the
Rinpoche watching me now, calm, intent. "What I'm trying
to ask is, if there are actual saints, and maybe even actual
teachers or gods come to earth, I mean Jesus, Buddha, you
know. How does it work? Who sends them? Why are they
sent? What is the mechanism by which a being like that appears in a human womb? . . . I mean . . . does your lineage
have anything to say on the subject?"

"Of course. Yes," he said, smiling a small tight smile as
if he saw right through me. He considered the question for
a moment. "How to tell you?"

I tried to make a wise little remark—*Oh, the usual way,*
I was going to say—but I simply could not get the words
out.

"On this planet, this earth, there is the physical and the
not-physical, yes?" He pronounced the word *fuscal.*

"I suppose."

"You love your wife very much, yes?"

"Yes."

"There is the physical wife that you love—that you can see and touch and listen and smell, yes? And then there is also the not-physical wife that you love that you can't touch, can't see, can't smell. The physical body holds the not-physical, yes, but the not-physical makes go the physical body. Makes go the heart. Makes go the brain, you see?"

"All right."

"On this planet, the physical world is mostly water and stone and air. A few other things but mostly water and stone and air. Those things you can touch, you can smell sometimes, you can see. But what makes go those things?"

"What makes them *run,* you mean. Makes them *work.* Or *exist.*"

He took a drink of water and nodded energetically, as I had seen him do during his talks, but there was something different in the way he was looking at me. His eyes were more intense, the gaze more intimate. He put just the last inch or so of the fingers of both hands on the table to either side of his plate and said, "Love makes them run. That is not my lineage, my *idea.* That is a fact just like when water gets cold it ices. Like that. Some people cannot see this is a fact, but this is. They are blind in different ways but this is a fact: Love makes the atoms go where they go and stick where they stick. Everybody when they see a baby, a small boy or girl, they smile? Why? Because inside themself they know this fact. They know love made this baby, this boy, this girl. They feel this natural rising up of love in themself. Okay, yes? Before, I said to you about God's music that is playing all the time, for everyone. God's music is this love.

And this love that runs our world, sometimes it means that there is help coming from that love, from that . . . *source* you would say, yes? See in your life, in Otto's life, how many times every day you help. Me, you help. Your wife, your children, people you don't know that you see walking by, you help them. And every day maybe somebody helps you. What is this help? It is love. Okay?"

"I'm with you."

"Good. And so, now, bigger idea . . ." He made a large circle with his hands. "Sometimes, many times, the strongness of love in this universe — "

"The strength of love."

"Yes, the strength of love in this universe, it comes very much all at once into some bodies on this planet, the way air comes sometimes very much into a wind. And those bodies, they are a saint, a great teacher, what we call a god. Really it is a piece of God, the way you can have a big wind be a piece of the air on the earth but by itself it is not really separate." He considered this a moment, then went on. "The way you can have light in a line coming through a window," he pointed to his left where a ray of sunlight was angling in and splashing on the pale wood of a table. "*Piece* of the sun, yes, but not the sun really, you see?"

"Okay."

"But what runs the world is that source. Sometimes when a country, when a place on the earth, needs help, or when the whole of the earth needs help, then this love becomes into a human body like a Buddha, a Krishna, a Muhammad, a Mary, a Jesus, a Moses, and so like that. Why at that time, why in that place, that culture, even my father says, 'Don't know.' Why only some of the peoples there see that these saints are pieces of God and others do not see, don't know. But if you look with a clear mind, you know that the world works like this. If you listen very careful to your heart going, if you meditate just on that, you can see that it runs because of this love."

Rinpoche finished and sat back, watching me intently the whole time in much the same way a professor of physics might look at a favored student after chalking a theory onto the board in his office. Do you see? Is it clear? Has the light gone on in you the way it went on in me, years ago?

I must confess then that any urge I had to make a joke had been extinguished. I know I am not conveying this little bratwurst-and-beer encounter with anything like the power it actually had; I'm an editor, not a writer, after all. But at that moment, surrounded by a German-Americana of smells and sights that had been as familiar to me as the quilt on my childhood bed, I felt a physical sensation of another world having been opened up to me. A thick layer peeled away. An obvious truth revealed. Strangely enough, the feeling was vaguely familiar, and after a few seconds' consideration I realized it was a cousin to the feeling I'd known when I had watched my children being born. There was the physical, of course, the blood and mucus, the tissue, the smells and sounds, the cries, the small body making its way out of the larger one. And then, behind or beyond or on top of all that, was something else, some brief glimpse into an enormous, almost an alien truth, momentarily ir-refutable. Some essence of love or generosity was infusing the physical event, it was so obvious. And now here it was again, that same mysterious feeling.

I tried to let that truth sink in, tried to meditate on my heartbeat for a moment, on the heartbeats of the people I loved. I tried, with a bit of success, I must say, to con-

template the source behind the movements of the atoms in
stone and air and water. It was strangely, eerily frightening.
Rinpoche did not seem to feel the need to say anything
more. I excused myself, got up and went to the bathroom,
trying to give myself time to come back to my ordinary
way of thinking about the world. But that way, safe and
familiar and protected by a thick armor of intellectual acu-
ity, seemed almost criminally superficial all of a sudden.
There was the familiar DAMEN and HERREN on the bathroom doors, there was the water coming out of the faucet,
and cells and atoms within that water, and ordinarily that
was as far as I would have gone with it. As if those cells and
atoms had simply materialized one fine day, out of nothing.
As if my children had. As if a college chemistry text was
all the explanation anyone needed for the fact of human
awareness.

Back at the table, a young sister and brother combo—
three and four years old, I guessed—had climbed up into
the booth with Rinpoche. Blond, fine-featured, dressed in
jeans and a NASCAR T-shirt, the boy was sitting on my
friend's knee, and the little girl was standing and leaning
against his shoulder. Their mother looked on uneasily from
the aisle, telling them it was time to leave, that they should
give the man some peace, and so on. I stood a few feet away
and watched. Rinpoche had a hand on the boy's head and
was looking at the girl and making faces, then put a hand on
the girl's head and made faces at the boy. They were squealing, hugging him, and their mother, all apologies, had to
peel them away and shoo them out the door one by one.

I sat and took refuge in the last of my Spaten, in the familiar motions of taking out the wallet, pinching the credit
card, handing it over. But something was turning upside

down inside me; something in the conversation, in the spin of the past few hours, something was making me breathe differently, think differently. I paid for our dinner, but Rinpoche, who was getting the hang of the American way of eating, insisted on adding the tip. He reached into the folds of his robe, brought out half a dozen dollar tokens from the casino up the road, and, with a wonderfully impish expression on his workingman's face, set them in a neat stack on the paper place mat.

FORTY-THREE

It is about 300 miles from Park Rapids to Bismarck. I guessed the trip would take us five hours or so and called the Bismarck Radisson to hold two rooms for late arrival.

By the time we got back to the car and rejoined Route 200, we had, by my calculations, an hour and a half of daylight left. I was glad of that. From other trips, I knew the landscape would change dramatically when we reached the westernmost part of Minnesota and then crossed the border to my home state, and I wanted to point that out to Rinpoche and say, *Look at how flat it gets here. This was all a glacial lake a million years ago. If we turn south we could drive probably five hundred miles — through South Dakota, and then all the way across Nebraska and Kansas and most of Oklahoma — and you'd barely see a hill. It's where most of the wheat is grown in America now, and a lot of the corn, and where most of our beef cattle come from. But 150 years ago these plains were black with buffalo for as far as the eye could see, millions of them grazing together in huge herds. The native people here depended on the buffalo for everything from food to clothing to skins for their tepees. They used to kill them with bows and arrows, if you can imagine that — they'd ride up beside a two-thousand-pound galloping beast and kill it with an arrow. But the U.S. government wanted to settle this land with white people, so they paid men to come out here and slaughter the buffalo because they knew that would make the Indians move away. Sometimes one man would kill as many as 150 in a day, and by about 1900 the buffalo were close to extinction, and the Indians had mostly been chased away, and people like my great-grandparents had been given huge tracts of land — a thousand, two thousand, three thousand acres — on which to build houses and grow crops.*

I'd prepared a whole lecture for him on the history of the Great Plains, the blood and slaughter and hardship and sacrifice lying beneath the placid landscape like karma in a soul—unseen, nearly forgotten, but echoing quietly in every modern minute. It had been a holocaust, some people said. Others claimed it was just the juggernaut of history, the price of progress, the same old story that had been played out all over the globe: the more advanced technology—rifles, ironclad ships, fighter jets, nuclear weapons—always winning out over the tools and rituals of the past.

But shortly after we left Park Rapids, Rinpoche leaned the seat back a few inches and closed his eyes. I was alone with my thoughts and the gradual approach of darkness across flat fields of corn, sunflowers, and soybeans. For a little while I tried to listen to the talk shows. One of the hosts was saying that the solution to the terrorist problem was to drop a nuclear bomb on Mecca. Someone on another station claimed that Christ the Lord was coming soon to cast sinners into eternal fire. Someone else said that all our troubles could be traced to immorality—drugs and drink, abortion, homosexuality (how they loved to talk about homosexuality, these people), high school students coupling without benefit of the blessing of the church or their elders. It was all the fault of the liberals. It was all the fault of the people who insisted on owning guns. It was all a righteous punishment for the bad things someone else had done. Always someone else.

We crossed the North Dakota line just as the very last light of the day disappeared. Tired by then from the long hours of driving, I merged onto Interstate 94, a fast, mostly empty road that slices the state neatly in two: a larger northern piece and a smaller southern piece. Thirty or forty miles west of Fargo I pulled off into a rest area. Rinpoche had not moved. I got out and stretched, still feeling the harsh reminders of my yoga adventure. The moon had not yet risen and the sky was as I remembered it, black, immense, and pocked with points of light, the air sweetened with the fragrance of just-harvested hayfields.

Set beside the mandala of meaning that Rinpoche had laid out for me in the German restaurant, the ideas of the radio talkers seemed like nothing more than the clack and bubble of bickering hens, the oink and push of hogs. I looked at the stars. The world had not changed, not really. With all our impressive technological achievements—the book, the automobile, the airplane, the computer, the looping satellites bouncing TV shows into dry, well-heated homes—we were still the species described in the first parts of the Bible. Some of us murdered and stole and raped; some of us spent our lives chasing money or distraction or the so-called sense pleasures. The family, the village, the tribe, the nation—we still formed ourselves into units in the hope of escaping or softening or denying a kind of ultimate loneliness. And then, conversely, we still seemed to need to divide ourselves into "us" and "them," liberal and conservative, black and white, native and immigrant, man and woman, believer and nonbeliever, Jew and Christian and Muslim and Buddhist and Hindu. We still laughed. We still faced death on a field of interior solitariness.

What if the secret architecture of it all was just as Rinpoche claimed: some cosmic unity there beyond our false identification with the individual body? a love beyond imagining that hid in the molecules of a trillion shapes, causing hearts to beat and rivers to run and lovers to find each other? What if the plain old Protestants had it partly right—that you could have direct access to that breath and pulse of love without the official intervention of the church fathers? More than that, what if, throughout history, there had been people—grand spirits in human form—sent to show us the route out of this mess, a way to embody that love, or merge with it, rather than simply touching it once in a while, with a handful of close souls, in our best moments? What if earth was just a violent stopping place on the highway to some saner, sweeter home, and there were teachers who saw that and had come to help us on the journey? And if there really were such people, what would be the consequence of ignoring them?

Through the open window I heard Rinpoche burp in his sleep.

My cell phone vibrated in my pocket, then rang. When I opened it and said hello, the voice I heard belonged to our daughter, Natasha, named for the Russian-émigré doctor who had guided her so skillfully along the dangerous passage from darkness to light.

"Dad?"

"Hey, honey! It makes me happy to hear your voice."

"Where are you? You sound different."

"Just into North Dakota. Where are you?"

"Home, Dad. It's, like, late. Anthony's passed out on the couch and Mom's right here. She said you were supposed to call and when you didn't we got worried."

"I tried to, right after supper. There was no service where we were."

"How's Aunt Seese?"

"She stayed home, didn't Mom tell you?"

Natasha didn't answer for a moment and I could picture her standing in the kitchen, receiver held against her shoulder in a pose she'd struck from her earliest phone days, her pretty, freckled face turned toward her mother.

"Oh, right, sorry. I, like, spaced. So you're driving with some kind of guru or something, or is Mom making that up? She says you're, like, going to shave your head or something when you get home? She's joking, right?"

"Sure she is. He's a good guy, though, a monk. Volya Rinpoche is his name. Google him and see what you get."

"Okay. . . . Dad?"

"What, honey?"

"Mom says if I come up with the money for the car maybe you guys could cover the insurance, you know, until I get a little older?"

"That's the deal."

"Really?"

"Absolutely. The fine print is you drive during the day at first, decent grades, no fighting with your brother."

A pause. "How about minimal fighting? Reduced fighting? How's that?"

"Agreed."

She squealed her delight into the phone, half child, still, and I felt something go through me. A jolt. A current. A line of electricity that came directly from the Great Spirit itself.

When I heard Jeannie's voice I said, "How did these two creatures come to us?"

"We were good in a past life, must be."

"Exactly my thought."

"I take it you're not in Bismarck yet."

"Just west of Fargo. Another hour and a half, maybe a little more. Rinpoche's asleep. Sorry I couldn't reach you earlier. Yours truly had coffee after his beer and bratwurst, so all is well."

"Good, I'm exhausted. Call us tomorrow, will you? When you get to the farm, call, okay?"

"All right. Sure. Here's my love coming through the phone line."

"I feel it."

"Good, pass a piece of it on to the two troublesome miracles, okay?"

"Okay. Love you."

When I started the car, Rinpoche woke up. I told him we were on the highway in North Dakota, less than two hours from the place where we'd spend the night. Less than four hours from my parents' farm. He grunted, glanced out at the flat blackness, and said a strange thing: "The country of surprise."

I looked at the flat, fertile fields—it was the richest farmland in the state here, and the most expensive—and saw

only a few lights from farmhouse windows, set far back
from the road. There would be a mile or more between
homesteads, the occasional small cluster of buildings at the
crossroads—gas pump, grocery store, grain elevators, train
tracks. Nothing in the least surprising in this piece of the
world, I thought, unless it was a pickup driven by a drunk
running a stop sign in the middle of a February morning.

It was 12:17 a.m. central time when we pulled off the
highway into Bismarck. Not easy to get lost here, just a
straight shot south into the humble downtown, a left on
Broadway Avenue, a right into the hotel lot. Rinpoche and I
carried our bags into the lobby, walked up to the desk, and
found that everything was in order: two standard rooms
on the seventh floor, the plastic key cards in small folders
handed across the counter by a perky young woman with
blond hair and drawn-out vowels. When I thanked her she
said, "Oh-h, almost forgot," and handed me a folded sheet
of the house stationery. My name was on the outside, and
when I opened it I saw this, written in a familiar scrawl:

Brother!
    Surprise! I flew on a plane, I actually did it! I'm in
room 603, asleep probably, I was up all last night worrying about the trip but I made it, no problem! Call me
when you get up, okay? Don't go out to breakfast without me. Can't wait to see you both!
                                        Love,
                                        Your Crazy Sister

FORTY-FOUR

You know how dreams are—the day's thoughts seasoned with hope, fear, and memory, cooked into an illogical stew and served in an upside-down bowl. That night in my sleep I was walking someplace with Natasha, who looked like Cecelia, and then the vice president of the United States was a salesman in a used-car lot where we were shopping for a car and he was handing out free chocolate doughnuts by the dozen. Please, analyze it; I don't care to. I am just reporting what happened. I slept the sleep of the road warrior, had that dream, and woke to the sound of a ringing phone.

"Otto? It's Seese, I didn't wake you up, did I? I'm in Rinpoche's room and we were worried. It's quarter of ten."

"Seese? Quarter to ten?"

"I woke you up, didn't I."

"Sure, but it's all right. Ten o'clock. Oy."

"We're waiting for you so we can have breakfast. Shall I give you a few minutes to shower before I come in and hug you? I'm right next door."

"Yes."

I took my time showering and shaving, not because I didn't want to see my sister, and not really because I wanted to put off the visit to the farm. It was more than that. During the previous six days I had slipped free of my duties as senior editor, husband, father, brother, home owner. I had not paid a bill or washed a dish, not taken the car in for an oil change or Jasper out for a walk, not mediated a dispute between daughter and son, not looked at a manuscript or had lunch with an author or sat in a meeting with marketing department honchos telling us what would sell and what wouldn't. Now, with Seese's voice on the phone line and Dickinson on the docket, I felt as though my real life was standing on the other side of the door, raising a fist to knock. I liked that life, loved it even. But the gravitational field of Volya Rinpoche and the American road had knocked me out of my usual orbit, and I needed to take a breath or two before re-entry.

Clean-shaven, clean-skinned, I hadn't quite gotten my jersey tucked into my chinos when my sister's exuberant *tap tap tap-tap-tap* sounded at the door. Bear hug time. Back massage time. When she at last released me and stepped away to arm's length, I noticed yet again how beautiful she was—the clear eyes, the shining hair and skin, the wonderful smile. She would turn forty in a month, and looked ten years younger. Always a happy, upbeat soul, on that morning she seemed positively euphoric: She had faced her lifelong fear and gotten on an airplane. And, I thought, probably, most likely, she was in love.

"I talked to Tasha and Anthony yesterday," she said, "just before I left, and I told them I was going to surprise you. I hope they didn't spill the beans." Rinpoche was standing behind her and just to the side, another happy face.

I thought back over Natasha's phone call, her small slip. And I said, "These days, teenagers get CIA training at the mall. Not a spilled bean anywhere. When I got your note, I was stunned. Happy and stunned."

"You've changed," she said. "Your, you know . . ."

"You can say it."

"Your aura is lighter. Isn't it, Rinpoche?"

The Rinpoche nodded. It was obvious to all concerned. But I hadn't changed enough to be able to talk about it with my sister.

"Well, your pal here is a good traveling companion, that's all I'll say for now. A good man. And I'm proud of you, by the way, for getting over the flying thing. That's a real accomplishment."

These kind and sincere words resulted in another lengthy embrace. If I hadn't been hungry at the start of the embrace, I was certainly hungry by the time of my release, and I said so.

"I know a place," my sister announced. "Two places, actually. Up for a short walk?"

It worried me, of course—another part that hadn't changed—to turn over the choice of breakfast spots to Cecelia. Why not just sit down here at the hotel, I wanted to say. But I let it go.

We went out the door and along the busier side of Broadway Avenue, headed west, and all during our ten-minute promenade I was the old Otto. I imagined some New Agey emporium, ex-hippies in dreadlocks and tie-dyed T-shirts, serving up seaweed, teeth-breaking organic quinoa wafers, and bark tea. Or, more likely in these parts, a classic Dakotan white-bread-and-chicken-fried-steak Mom and Pop place with limpid coffee and a clientele of good-old-boy ranchers whose idea of conversation was three syllables grunted back and forth across the Formica over the course of half an hour. Was Rinpoche crazy, to think of founding a meditation center here? And not even here, in the relatively cosmopolitan capital, where you might find a soul or two who knew the difference between the peace of Samadhi and a piece of salami, but out where we had been raised, out in dirt-road-and-pickup country, where yoga was for pussies and always would be.

But North Dakota had changed, a bit, while I wasn't looking. The place Seese took us to was an organic bakery that specialized in a sort of cinnamon-roll loaf you could smell from two blocks away. We bought three of the delicious beasts and carried them down to the next surprise—a coffee shop run by a nice fellow named Sia Ranjbar. Ten kinds of coffee, fifty flavors of Italian soda. Computers where you could go online and check your e-mail for a minimal sum. We sat at a table and feasted.

"Rinpoche told me you've been meditating," Cecelia said. "Is that true, Otto?"

"I invoke my Fifth Amendment rights."

"No, really. Have you?"

"Even last night a little before I went to sleep. And I was exhausted."

She was beaming, giving off light. "Isn't it the most wonderful thing ever?"

"After bohling," Rinpoche put in, and we laughed. "After furniture golf."

He had been almost completely silent since our talk in the German restaurant, but I felt that he was watching me, studying me, looking to see if his seven-day tutorial was going to sink into my flesh or be washed off by the tides of everyday life. I was watching him, too. There was almost no physical contact between him and Cecelia, no staring into each other's eyes, hardly an exchange of words, and yet I sensed an intimacy between them, the kind of mind-to-mind or heart-to-heart understanding certain couples exhibit in each other's presence. It's something you can't fake, and can't describe, but clearly they had it. At one point he stood up to get more hot water for his tea, and hers, and when he returned to the table and handed her the refilled cup, his movements had about them a sense . . . I almost want to say a sense of worship, but that would imply something elaborate and staged, what my mother used to call "fussified." *Devotional* is a better word for what I saw. In the religious sense. If his movements could be said to have a tone, then it was the tone of someone laying an offering before the statue of a goddess. I wasn't used to seeing my sister treated that way, and I liked it. I wondered if Rinpoche's famous father had treated his mother that way, if he'd grown up with that as his model for husband-wife relations. And my mind leaped from there to Mom bringing out a tray of hard German biscuits to Pop in the midst of one of his tantrums. And from there to the errand that stood before us on that day.

"We should go," I said. Cecelia and the Rinpoche nodded. We thanked our new friend Sia, went back to the car, and started off for Stark County and all the ghosts that inhabited the landscape there.

FORTY-FIVE

In order to get to the two-thousand-acre Ringling farm, you take I-94 West from Bismarck, ninety-nine miles across sweeping, fertile countryside, and through the small city of Dickinson. From Dickinson, you travel south on State Route 22, then turn onto a gravel road. The gravel road comes to a T, you take a left on another gravel road, and bear right after another few miles, and this smaller road—our driveway, really—goes on for half a mile between gently slanting wheat fields, crosses a small stream (Seese and I always called it "Snake River," but it has another name), and deposits you in front of a white clapboard farmhouse with outbuildings behind and old cottonwoods all around.

There is little, really, to distinguish this property from hundreds of others in central and western North Dakota. Two thousand acres is an average size for the farms there. My parents planted what everyone else planted: soybeans and wheat and sunflowers, a little corn, barley, or canola. Vegetables in the fifty-foot-square plot out the back door.

There are two barns and three galvanized steel grain storage bins on stilts. In order to appreciate the place, you have to get out of your car and walk the fields—say, just after the wheat has been harvested and the hay rolled into bales as tall as a man. You might come upon a prairie rattlesnake under one of those bales (as Seese and I did one August morning), and you might see a scampering cottontail or two, and you'll likely startle a covey of pheasant, partridge, or ruffled grouse in the sagebrush and wild prairie rose near the river. But mostly, if you stand quietly for a time, you'll get a sense of the vastness of the sky and of the land beneath it, a great, rich, untroubled emptiness that feeds a good percentage of the world.

Not much was said as we made the drive. Rinpoche sat up front with me, as he'd done since New Jersey. Cecelia sat in the middle of the back seat and seemed content to take in the countryside, fingers spread out on her belly in some kind of new meditation pose. As we approached the intersection where my parents had been killed (there was no way to avoid it without traveling fifteen miles out of our way) I could feel the tension in her, and in me. She leaned forward and put a hand on the top corner of my seat, then on my shoulder. I slowed as we passed the spot, but did not stop. "This is the place where my parents died," I said, for Rinpoche's benefit, and I could see his beads and lips working, and I hoped—of course I hoped—that the system of helping he'd described was something that extended beyond the grave, that what he called "the not-physical part" of Ronald and Matilda Ringling existed, still, in some other dimension, and that his prayers and ours would give them some small comfort there. Cecelia leaned back and wept quietly for a few minutes, then she stopped and put her hand on my shoulder again. Soon, we were turning onto our road, raising a magnificent plume of dust over what had been our parents' fields.

For all of that morning I'd managed to put out of my thoughts the notion of handing over this property to Rinpoche. On the one hand, it seemed patently absurd for him to start such a venture here, and for my sister to give away the only security that life would ever hand her. On the other, the land did have a certain unmistakable spiritual quality to it; or at least the Catholics seemed to think so: There was a Benedictine monastery not far behind us, in Richardton. For me, the question came down to this: What would my parents have wanted us to do? Farm their acreage, I supposed. But that was not an option. Next on the list would likely have been selling it to someone else who would do the farming, and making sure the proceeds of the sale went to the Ringling children and grandchildren.

"Almost there," Seese said from the back seat, and I rode the last hundred yards through a circus of mostly happy memories—the smell of turned-over earth in spring, the Christmas sleigh rides, the first time Jeannie and I had brought Natasha and then Anthony here.

I pulled into the unpaved circular driveway, turned off the engine, and got out. My sister was crying again. I held her against me for a moment, then turned and went up the three wooden steps, across the front porch, used my key in the door, and opened it to a hot, musty hallway and living room and a set of stairs leading up to the place where I'd slept when I had been a boy. A flood of memories washed over me: all those years, all those meals and conversations and arguments and dreams. Rinpoche took my sister's hand—the first time I'd seen him touch her—and she began leading him through the small downstairs rooms, telling him what they had been used for in those days. We'd had people come in and put everything into boxes, roll up the rugs, pack up the photographs and pots and pans, so the house felt oddly empty and stale to me. Even so, I could almost hear my parents' voices. My mother singing at the piano on a Saturday night. My father standing at the kitchen sink, remarking on the weather, or thanking his wife for a meal, or expressing his irritation about some chore one of his children had forgotten to do in the barn. For so many years it had seemed like nothing would ever change here: The larger picture, the big questions, had been submerged in an ocean of duties and moods and the mundanities of survival.

A sad wash of thoughts hit me then. I stepped out into the back yard, meandered past the unplanted garden, and found myself going along the path that led to Snake River and what I'd called my "secret hiding place" on a big, flat stone, on the bank, in the cottonwoods.

That stone had been one of the places where I'd worked through my own wondering about the pain and purpose of life. As a teenager I'd hated my parents here, at moments, and hated my sister, and myself. On happier days, I'd brought favorite books here to read in the long summer evenings, and a snapshot of my first girlfriend to stare at in privacy, and the thick letter from the University of North Dakota that I found in the mailbox one day after school.

It was a place where I had always been able to step out of my own daily struggles for a clearer view, and I did that now, again. The core of my life was Jeannie and the children, I knew that. Nothing could change that, I thought, at first. And then I realized that, of course, something would change it: Our family love wasn't immune to the subversion of time. Something was changing us with each breath, each second. The delusion of youth was that you believed you'd never reach middle age, and the delusion of middle age made you believe you could go on more or less indefinitely the way things were. Yes, the kids would grow up. Yes, you'd grow old and eventually pass away. But, really, there were so many pleasures to be had between now and then, so many tennis games, so many meals, so many weeks at the Cape and the ski lodge, so tremendously much to do before that other stage of life eventually set in.

My mother's mother, May, had died in one of the upstairs bedrooms of the house that stood only a few hundred feet from my secret hiding place. I was a junior in high school, and on the night she died, I was sitting in the living room with the TV off, a schoolbook in my lap, Seese in her room, and my parents upstairs at the deathbed. "I'm dying! I'm dying!" I heard my grandmother scream, six or eight times, and there was such surprise in her voice, such raw terror. It was an awful thing for a teenager to hear. And yet, at the same time, in my wise-guy, sixteen-year-old, know-everything way, part of me had almost wanted to say, "What did you expect, Grandma? That you'd be exempted?"

What I wanted to take hold of then, sitting on that stone beside the parched streambed, was a dependable method by which a person could lead an ordinary life, cherishing the ordinary comforts and pleasures, fulfilling the ordinary familial and professional duties, and still be able to make the transition from here to who-knew-where when that time came. And make it at peace. I had wanted to find that method, it seemed to me, for many years. In some buried, secret, papered-over place inside myself, from the hour of

Grandma May's death, I had wanted that. And I knew, sitting there, that if I had the courage to reach down beyond all my strategies, my pride, my clever humor, my busyness and wants and penchant for distraction and judgment, my resistance to Cecelia's odd enthusiasms, and arrive at the place where intuition and intellect joined forces—the place where a person came as close as humanly possible to seeing the world as it was—in that place I would have to admit to myself that Volya Rinpoche knew a secret about living and dying in peace and might be able to pass that secret on to me. On our strange trip, I had caught a glimpse of that truth. I could no longer deny it. The only question now was: What did I intend to do about it?

I remembered, at the start of the trip, saying to my sister that I was a Christian, old-fashioned Protestant stock. How strange then that after all my mental and physical travels I returned, not to those rigid doctrines exactly, but to the stories we'd been raised on, the fieldstone foundation of my faith. Precisely reported or altered by church elders, it did not really matter to me at that moment because every one of those stories circled around essentially the same idea: that there was another dimension to this life as surely as the earth turned; that there were people, there had always been people, who sensed that dimension and made some kind of leap of faith to be in harmony with it. And there were others who did not. It was about choosing between A and B, yes and no, and sometimes those choices were petty, and sometimes they were of enormous importance. It was about cruising along in the comfortable vehicle of old habits and ways, old thought patterns, old conceits, or sensing some new truth and setting off on foot. Sure, there were phonies and charlatans claiming to know The Way. But at some point you had to stop closing yourself off because of them. At some point you had to risk the ridicule of the mob, of your own internalized voices, and try to see clearly what had been set in front of you in this life, and try to act on that as bravely and honestly as you could, no matter what kind of rules you'd previously been living by. At some point before the blue pickup ran the stop sign on an ordinary, cold morning, you'd be asked to believe in some possibility that transcended newspaper headlines and TV shows and the opinions and assumptions of your friends. And how you responded to that would have a greater impact on your life than anything else you'd ever decide to do, or refrain from doing. I could see that. Sitting there on my rock, in my few minutes of North Dakota solitude, I believed I could see that very clearly.

In a little while, Spanakopita Cecelia came and found me. She sat beside me on the rock and told me, as I knew she would, that what she wanted to do was to sell off fifteen hundred acres of our land and have all that money—after taxes and commission—go to my children. The house, and the remaining five hundred acres she wanted to give to Rinpoche, to start his first North American meditation center. He could lease the five hundred acres and probably manage to live on the small income from that and from his talks. He could turn the larger barn into a dormitory and meditation hall and live in the house himself. She hesitated a moment, as if afraid of something, and then, still looking at me, said, "And I want to move back here and live with him as his spiritual wife." I watched her say that, one strand of her blond hair moving in a tiny breeze.

I didn't say anything at first. I was studying her. I was thinking about what I had thought about.

She did not take her eyes from my eyes. She said, "Otto, brother, I'd like it if you'd agree to this without having bad feelings. I'd like it if maybe you'd bring Jeannie and Natasha and Anthony out once every year or so, not to meditate or anything but just to be here with us, for Thanksgiving or something. The last thing I'd like, I guess, the most important thing maybe, is for you not to think of me as some kind of nutcake. That would mean more to me than you realize."

I looked at her. The wild hair framing her extraordinarily beautiful face, the floppy, too colorful dress, the sandals that were supposed to massage your acupuncture points and keep you free of illness. I imagined what our father and mother would have said about her plan and her choice of mates, and then I looked at her in a certain way we'd had of looking at each other when we were kids, and I said, "Nutcake is as nutcake does." And after a second or so, she laughed her happy, kid's laugh, and the sound of it went sailing out over the plains.

We stood up then, but before we started back to the house, I said, "Do you have a name for her yet? My niece, I mean."

She watched me for a breath or two, and then I was enveloped in the hug of hugs, my fingers against the muscles of her back, tears soaking through the shoulder of my shirt to my granite-hard, and still a little sore, trapezius muscles. When she at last released me she stood back and there was printed on her features a mix of bashfulness and pride, and something else, too. "Did he tell you?"

"I intuited. I've got kind of a psychic thing going lately."

She slapped me on the arm.

"I'm happy for you. Jeannie and the kids will be ecstatic."

"I'm afraid," she said through a smile.

"Jeannie can talk to you . . . about the delivery and everything, you know. She's great that way. We can give you a couple of hints about the bringing up."

"Okay, thanks, but not that. I didn't mean that. I meant, about . . . who she is supposed to be and everything. I want to do it right, and I'm not sure I'll be able to."

Cecelia had crossed then into the territory of past mockeries, the territory of my unbelief. She—a poor psychic from Paterson—had been chosen to bring a kind of savior or teacher or saint into the world. A special being, a distillation of the Great Love—that was the story. I felt words rise into my mouth, and though I did not say them, I knew she could read my face. Truly psychic or not, she was my sister, after all. I struggled just the smallest bit with my old self, and held off for a few seconds, and at last ended up saying, "You're the perfect person for the job."

And she smiled, watching me, happy as I'd ever seen her.

"Let's go in," I said. "You can call Jeannie and the kids and give them the big news."

But as we were walking back to the house, something happened inside me; one old thing that had been bending and bending finally broke. Sure, there was a bit of a mocking voice squeaking out its familiar song, but all you had to do, really, was just watch it like you'd watch any other thought float past. Watch life do its thing, watch the end of life do its thing, and try to go toward the good side when you could see it. We went in the back door, through the kitchen, and found Rinpoche sitting there in Pop's old leather recliner, as if it were some kind of throne. I went part of the way across the room toward him, and then I stopped and got on my knees and bent down and touched my forehead to the old pine boards in front of him and stayed like that for a while with my sister watching. Because that seemed like the right thing to do.

○—April 17, 2006–May 24, 2007

AUTHOR'S NOTE

THIS IS A WORK OF FICTION, and all the characters are imaginary. But the story is based on an actual road trip I made from Bronxville, New York, to Dickinson, North Dakota, in the summer of 2006. With a few small exceptions (I don't think there is an O'Malley Auditorium at Notre Dame, for example), the inns, hotels, restaurants, buildings, and roads are described with as much accuracy as my notes and memory have allowed, though, in many cases, through the very subjective lens of my own opinions and tastes. Although I did transplant one radio broadcast (about Biblical corporal punishment) in place and time, I made nothing up: the words of the radio programs described here are, again, as accurate as my memory and notes permit. The same is true for billboards, landscapes, locations of crosses by the side of the road, and messages posted in front of churches and homes and at the edges of Ohio fields.

Rinpoche's ideas are drawn from thirty years of reading across the religious, philosophical, and psychological spectrum and meditation retreats at Catholic, Protestant,

Buddhist, and nondenominational retreat centers and monasteries. For those interested in these ideas, here, in no particular order, is a sampling of my readings over those three decades: the Bible; the writings of Thomas Merton, especially *Zen and the Birds of Appetite, The Wisdom of the Desert,* and *Asian Journal; Tao Te Ching* by Lao Tsu; *Cutting Through Spiritual Materialism* and *Shambala* by Chogyam Trungpa; *Psychoanalysis and Religion, The Art of Loving,* and *The Sane Society* by Erich Fromm; *The Road Less Traveled* by Scott Peck; *The Way of Perfection* by Teresa of Avila; *The Real Work* by Gary Snyder; *When Things Fall Apart* and *The Wisdom of No Escape* by Pema Chodron; *The Tibetan Book of Living and Dying* by Sogyal Rinpoche (also his lectures and talks in person and on tape); the retreat talks of Seung Sahn; *Fire Within* by Thomas Dubay; *I and Thou* by Martin Buber; *Saving the Appearances* by Owen Barfield; *Freedom from the Known* by Krishnamurti; *What the Buddha Taught* by Walpola Rahula; *Going to Pieces without Falling Apart* and *Thoughts Without a Thinker* by Mark Epstein; *Ordinary People as Monks and Mystics* by Marsha Sinetar; *Light on Life* by B. K. S. Iyengar; the talks of Father Thomas Keating and the retreat talks of Lama Surya Das; *The Inner Life* by Hazrat Inayat Khan; *The Only Dance There Is, Be Here Now,* and *Grist for the Mill* by Ram Dass; *The Book of Job* in Stephen Mitchell's translation; *The Spiritual Teaching of Ramana Maharshi; The Art of Happiness* and talks by the Dalai Lama; *The Parables of the Kingdom* by C. H. Dodd; *The Essential Mystics,* edited by Andrew Harvey; *The Miracle of Mindfulness* and talks by Thich Nhat Hanh; *Poetic Vision and the Psychedelic Experience* by R. A. Durr; the personal example of my father's mother; the novels of Dostoevsky, Hesse, and Maugham; the stories of Isaac Babel; the poetry of Walt Whitman and Anna Akhmatova; and the nonfiction of Carlo Levi and James Agee—among many other creative works. My gratitude to all these teachers and writers and to those not named here.

A CONVERSATION WITH THE AUTHOR

QUESTIONS AND TOPICS
FOR DISCUSSION

A CONVERSATION WITH THE AUTHOR

One gets the impression in reading your novels, especially those dealing with spiritual matters, that you are probably a deeply spiritual person yourself. Is that an accurate description, and if so, are these novels an expression of your beliefs and in some regard autobiographical?

I guess it's true that I'm a spiritual person, though the word *spiritual* always calls to mind somebody who is not part of the average, ordinary, everyday world, and that is not the case with me. From childhood I have been interested in what I think of as "the big questions": Why are we here? Why do we suffer and die? Why does suffering seem to be spread around unevenly? Why does evil exist? Why does beauty exist? Etc., etc. I was brought up in a very devout Catholic family, but I have traveled away from that—while still holding on to a lot of what I got from it. I practice meditation regularly, and have done so for thirty years. I do yoga, though not much better than Otto does. I have read widely across the religious spectrum, as you can see from the list of books in the back of *Breakfast with Buddha*. I have gone on retreats—Catholic, Christian, nondenominational, Zen, Tibetan Buddhist, Quaker/solitary—but the ideas in the books I write aren't always my ideas or beliefs. Sometimes they are, but often they are just questions that I want to explore via the characters.

A lot of novels that are spiritual in tone and content tend to be either overtly religious or patently sentimental, but you clearly aim at avoiding either path. Why is that?

Well, it is very dangerous territory for a novelist. I mean, look at all the killing that has been done in the name of religion, all the family fights, divorces, arguments! I think the best way to approach it is with a sense of humor and without trying to convince anyone of anything. I don't want to be a preacher, and I don't want my books to seem preachy. I want to entertain, maybe to make people think about things, but I'm not in the enlightenment business. You can spoil a novel very quickly if the reader thinks you have a particular agenda and have built the story around it. I have my ideas and beliefs, but I try to be open to those of others. And I try to find common ground among all the belief systems.

In explaining your belief system, you once made the following statement: "In a mysterious fashion not completely understandable to us, everything moves the individual toward humility." Please elaborate.

If you are young, beautiful, strong, and talented and live long enough, all of that will be taken away from you. If you are tremendously rich, you can't carry your wealth across the threshold of death. Those are facts, not tenets of any religion. For all but the most conceited or desperately insecure, it seems that you get wiser as you age, and that wisdom and humility go hand in hand. I know it isn't that simple, and I know some older people are far from humble. But it seems to me that life is a kind of boot camp, designed to break you down and build you up in a different way—if you let it. So you lose your ability to sprint a hundred yards, but maybe you gain something more important in the process.

Humor, or at least a humorous approach to life, plays a big part in your novels. Do you include humor in an effort to lighten the approach to serious subjects, or do you actually view the world with the same humor that infuses your work?

Both. Certainly, as I mentioned above, I put humor into these novels intentionally. In my earlier books, which were not so overtly spiritual, there wasn't nearly as much humor. I like humor in real life, too, though I can't honestly say I always see the funny side of world events. Some things are sad, or awful, or painful, but in most lives there are these windows of time in which you can laugh, and it seems like a good idea to take advantage of those opportunities when they come along.

It is apparent in this novel, as in your previous one, *Golfing with God,* and your newest, *American Savior,* that you feel that organized religion in America, if it has not become corrupt, has at least lost its way. Why do you feel this way?

I want to qualify that. For a lot of people, millions of people, organized religion is a wonderful thing and an important part of their lives. I understand that and respect it, in part because I grew up among people who felt that religion gave their life a good structure. But I also know a large number of people— good, caring, sensitive, compassionate people—for whom organized religion just does not work. The ideas are stale, the language is stale, the rituals do nothing for them and do not seem connected to their everyday lives. What really bothers me, and what I went after in *American Savior,* is when religion, instead of being something that a person uses to become more loving and considerate, turns into something people use to justify their own hatred or close-mindedness. That tendency has been part of human psychology for thousands of years, but the form it takes here, now, is abhorrent to me.

In this novel, your main characters, Otto Ringling and Volya Rinpoche, both men with strong personalities and distinctly different temperaments, embark on a road trip to Middle America, each undertaking his own journey of discovery. Which did you come up with first, the idea of writing a novel about the clash of beliefs or of writing a story that played out over a road trip?

The road trip. I had always wanted to see North Dakota, always pictured it as this mostly empty, beautiful, stark, striking place that was in some odd way spiritual. I like the idea of adventures, or road trips, voyages, expeditions. I am not capable of climbing Everest, so this seemed like something I could enjoy doing, and that would be a nice canvas on which to paint a story with some ideas in it. I made the first half of the trip alone, then went home, waited for school to get out, and made the second leg—Chicago to North Dakota—with my wife and daughters. I think we were all surprised at how much we liked North Dakota.

One gets the impression at the end of the novel that Otto Ringling has been deeply affected by the things he has learned during his journey back home. Please project a year or so ahead in his life and tell us where he is and just how he has changed.

I might write that story in a sequel some day, who knows? I guess his life would still have its same exterior shape. He is a family man, loves his wife and kids, and likes his job. He is not about to throw all that away and go live on the old farm. I picture him as having a meditation practice, as paying attention to things he used to ignore. I think he'd make two or three trips a year out to spend time with Rinpoche and get his spiritual counseling. He might eat just a bit less, or a bit more thoughtfully. He might be a notch less cynical. He'll be a good uncle to Cecelia and Rinpoche's child.

How do your characters make themselves known to you? Where do you find your inspiration?

I write by the seat of my pants, almost always without an outline. I just start, and that seems like opening the floodgates, or drilling a well. All kinds of stuff comes out, and usually very quickly. (I wrote most of *Breakfast with Buddha* while I was actually making the road trip.) After a few decades of doing this I have the confidence that I can sort out most of the bad stuff and refine most of the good, so I just let things flow at first and then rework it. I think I've written the last few books in a month or six weeks, then spent a year revising.

What's next for you?

In this vein, I honestly don't know. A spiritual memoir, maybe, if I can find a way to make that funny or somehow different. I have a book coming out on golfing and eating in Italy. That was fun to research. I have a thriller coming out at some point next year. Right now I am going to take a little break—it's been a pretty intense pace the past few years—play some golf, spend time with my daughters, maybe meditate a little more, maybe take the time to write a novel longhand, which is the preferred method for me. No retirement in sight, in other words, and I enjoy all of this.

QUESTIONS AND TOPICS FOR DISCUSSION

1. How do the first scenes of Otto with his family set the stage for what happens in the rest of the novel?

2. In what ways does Otto change over the course of the story? What key moments during the trip play a part in his evolution?

3. How would you describe Cecelia? Is she, as Otto says, "as flaky as a good spanakopita crust"? Is there some substance to her?

4. Do you believe Cecelia changes over the course of the story, or do you think it's only Otto's opinion of her that changes? Share specific scenes that support your view.

5. Which events or remarks in the novel convince you that Rinpoche is a legitimate spiritual teacher? Were there situations where you doubted his authenticity?

6. Humor is often employed a way of making us relate to a particular situation. How does the author use humor in this way? Are there particular passages that were especially funny to you? If so, why?

7. The book is partly about "meaning of life" issues, but it also has a lot to say about contemporary American society. What

does Otto see and hear that makes him encouraged or discouraged about the state of American life?

8. Discuss the role landscape plays in the story.

9. Jeannie, Anthony, and Natasha are minor characters in the novel, but how do they serve to round out Otto's character? How do they influence your feelings about Cecelia and Rinpoche?

10. Amish country, the Hershey's factory, a bowling alley, a baseball game, taking an architectural tour of Chicago, playing miniature golf, swimming in a Minnesota lake, why do you suppose the author chose these kinds of activities? Discuss the purpose each activity serves in the story. What would the book have been like had these activities not been included?

11. When Otto comes across the metaphor of the piano-playing boy in Rinpoche's book, he says, "If I had been editing the book, I would have written in the manuscript margins, 'Work this,' meaning that the author should take the general idea and sharpen it, make it clearer to the reader" (page 174). Yet Otto can't get the the plight of the piano-playing man out of his mind. Why do suppose that is? What aspect of the metaphor is unsettling to Otto? Do you find it unsettling? If so, why?

12. How would you characterize what Otto experiences after sitting with Rinpoche for two hours in silence (page 237)? Have you ever experienced the pleasure of a quiet mind? Was it similar or dissimilar to Otto's reaction?

13. Do you believe Rinpoche is changed by the end of the trip with Otto? If so, to what degree is Otto responsible for that change?

14. Do you believe the ending of the novel was the best ending for this story? If the story were to continue, where should it go from here?

On the Road Again . . .

Algonquin's long-awaited follow-up to *Breakfast with Buddha*—one of our best-loved "word of mouth" best-sellers—finds Otto Ringling and Mongolian monk Volya Rinpoche on another unexpected road trip. Rich with humor and wise in its commentary on modern American life, *Dinner with Buddha* takes us along on an exhilarating path of self-discovery with two of the most intriguing men in modern fiction, whose lives seem to be forever entwined.

Dinner with Buddha
a novel by Roland Merullo
ISBN 978-1-56512-928-3
E-BOOK ISBN 978-1-61620-516-4

ROLAND MERULLO is the critically acclaimed author of five books of nonfiction and twelve novels, including the Revere Beach Trilogy, *Golfing with God, American Savoir, Lunch with Buddha,* and *The Vatican Waltz.* His latest novel is *Dinner with Buddha.* He lives with his wife and children in Massachusetts. His website is www.rolandmerullo.com.

Other Algonquin Readers Round Table Novels

Water for Elephants, a novel by Sara Gruen

As a young man, Jacob Jankowski is tossed by fate onto a rickety train, home to the Benzini Brothers Most Spectacular Show on Earth. Amid a world of freaks, grifters, and misfits, Jacob becomes involved with Marlena, the beautiful young equestrian star; her husband, a charismatic but twisted animal trainer; and Rosie, an untrainable elephant who is the great gray hope for this third-rate show. Now in his nineties, Jacob at long last reveals the story of their unlikely yet powerful bonds, ones that nearly shatter them all.

"[An] arresting new novel. . . . With a showman's expert timing, [Gruen] saves a terrific revelation for the final pages, transforming a glimpse of Americana into an enchanting escapist fairy tale." —*The New York Times Book Review*

"Gritty, sensual and charged with dark secrets involving love, murder and a majestic, mute heroine." —*Parade*

AN ALGONQUIN READERS ROUND TABLE EDITION WITH READING GROUP GUIDE AND OTHER SPECIAL FEATURES • FICTION • ISBN-13: 978-1-56512-560-5

An Arsonist's Guide to Writers' Homes in New England, a novel by Brock Clarke

The past catches up to Sam Pulsifer, the hapless hero of this incendiary novel, when after spending ten years in prison for accidentally burning down Emily Dickinson's house, the homes of other famous New England writers go up in smoke. To prove his innocence, he sets out to uncover the identity of this literary-minded arsonist.

"Funny, profound. . . . A seductive book with a payoff on every page." —*People*

"Wildly, unpredicatably funny. . . . As cheerfully oddball as its title."
—*The New York Times*

AN ALGONQUIN READERS ROUND TABLE EDITION WITH READING GROUP GUIDE AND OTHER SPECIAL FEATURES • FICTION • ISBN-13: 978-1-56512-614-5

Saving the World, a novel by Julia Alvarez

While Alma Huebner is researching a new novel, she discovers the true story of Isabel Sendales y Gómez, who embarked on a courageous sea voyage to rescue the New World from smallpox. The author of *How the García Girls Lost Their Accents* and *In the Time of the Butterflies,* Alvarez captures the worlds of two women living two centuries apart but with surprisingly parallel fates.

"Fresh and unusual, and thought-provokingly sensitive." —*The Boston Globe*

"Engrossing, expertly paced." —*People*

AN ALGONQUIN READERS ROUND TABLE EDITION WITH READING GROUP GUIDE AND OTHER SPECIAL FEATURES • FICTION • ISBN-13: 978-1-56512-558-2

Responsible Men, a novel by Edward Schwarzschild

When a divorced man from a family of mostly upstanding salesmen decides to change his less-than-honorable ways, things do not go exactly as planned. This is the story of three generations of men struggling to be good sons and good fathers in a world of big dreams and bigger temptations.

"Marvelous. . . . It's impossible to avoid falling for Max." —*Entertainment Weekly*

"A compassionately and deftly told story."
—William Kennedy, Pulitzer Prize–winning author of *Ironweed* and *Roscoe*

AN ALGONQUIN READERS ROUND TABLE EDITION WITH READING GROUP GUIDE AND OTHER SPECIAL FEATURES • FICTION • ISBN-13: 978-1-56512-543-8

The Ghost at the Table, a novel by Suzanne Berne

When Frances arranges to host Thanksgiving at her idyllic New England farmhouse, she envisions a happy family reunion, one that will include her sister, Cynthia. But tension mounts between them as each struggles with a different version of the mysterious circumstances surrounding their mother's death twenty-five years earlier.

"Wholly engaging, the perfect spark for launching a rich conversation around your own table." —*The Washington Post Book World*

"A crash course in sibling rivalry." —*O: The Oprah Magazine*

AN ALGONQUIN READERS ROUND TABLE EDITION WITH READING GROUP GUIDE AND OTHER SPECIAL FEATURES • FICTION • ISBN-13: 978-1-56512-579-7

Coal Black Horse, a novel by Robert Olmstead

When Robey Childs's mother has a premonition about her husband, who is away fighting in the Civil War, she sends her only son to find him and bring him home. At fourteen, Robey thinks he's off on a great adventure. But it takes the gift of a powerful and noble coal black horse to show him how to undertake the most important journey of his life.

"A remarkable creation." —*Chicago Tribune*

"Exciting. . . . A grueling adventure." —*The New York Times Book Review*

AN ALGONQUIN READERS ROUND TABLE EDITION WITH READING GROUP GUIDE AND OTHER SPECIAL FEATURES • FICTION • ISBN-13: 978-1-56512-601-5